# INCIDENT
# AT
# CRAZY WOMAN CREEK

\* \* \* \* \*

## FREDRICK W. BOLING

ISBN 0-9722808-1-2 (previously 0-7414-0046-4)

Published by:

## BIGHORN PUBLISHING

35 La Canada Way

Hot Springs Village, Arkansas 71909

Printed in the United States of America

# Author's Comment

After Custer's Seventh Cavalry was all but wiped out on a barren knoll east of the Little Big Horn River in 1876, a new era dawned in Wyoming. The U. S. Army, determined to avenge their tarnished image, set out to subjugate or annihilate every Plains Indian tribe in the West. It would only require about ten years for their campaign to be accomplished. All of Wyoming's high plain east of the Bighorn Mountains, once controlled by Brulé and Oglala Sioux, was to become an open-range pasture for great herds of cattle. In 1879, Moreton Frewen, an emigrant from England, bought out the 76 brand from Sweetwater rancher, Tim Foley, and drove his huge herd to the Powder River Basin east of the Bighorns. This event was soon followed with thousands of beef cattle being turned loose by quickly organized cattle companies. Nonresident foreigners owned controlling interests in many of them. Within a few years, migrants began to arrive intent upon staking homestead claims along streams where they would farm and raise a few cattle. The open-range cattle companies hired hundreds of cowboys, many of them from Texas, to manage their herds. This was a mix that was destined to generate major conflicts. Farms and small ranches had to be fenced with barbed wire to protect their grass from foraging herds owned by open-range cattlemen. In turn, the open-range herds became targets of rustlers—a number of them being cowboys that wanted to build their own herds. Many a calf or yearling, which was unbranded or had its brand altered, wound up in their pastures. And some of the homesteaders helped themselves to this wandering source of stock to build their own herds. Thus, open-range cattle barons, homesteaders and rustlers were set upon a collision course that would result in a conflict known as the Johnson County Cattle War of 1892. The culminating battle was fought at the TA ranch compound located in a bend of Crazy Woman Creek.

INCIDENT AT CRAZY WOMAN CREEK is a story based on events leading up to and following the battle at the TA Ranch.

For all of the men and women pioneers who forged the mountains and high plains of Wyoming into what she is today, a land where equality prevails because of their love for justice and the law.

# PART ONE

## LONG ROPES,
## RUNNING IRONS AND CATTLE
## BARONS

*Among a people generally corrupt, liberty cannot long exist.*
*Edmund Burke (1729–97), Irish philosopher, statesman*

# Chapter One

Nate Hamby needed a shave, a bath, and a change of luck. He knuckled his bristled chin and pondered yet another episode of bad luck as he squatted beside his firepit on the banks of the Powder River. While mulling over the last few days of misfortune, he stared at smoldering embers coaxing bubbles from a can of pork and beans and listened to bitter brew gurgling within the blackened belly of his coffee pot. He was losing his fight to bring justice to Wyoming. Nate shivered, buttoned his sheepskin parka, and snugged its fleecy collar high about his neck and chin. An evening wind had suddenly turned cold as it rushed across Wyoming's high plains from the eastern slopes of the Bighorn Mountains.

This land, once the home of buffalo, pronghorn antelope, deer, Chiefs Red Cloud and Dull Knife, was changing. The buffalo and chiefs had disappeared during the previous decade. By now, in 1891, antelope and deer were vying with longhorns and Herefords to graze the Powder Basin's bluestem grass. Ranchers and homesteaders were turning this virgin country, once the hunting grounds claimed by Red Cloud's Sioux and Dull Knife's Cheyenne, into cattle spreads and farms.

Splashing hooves fording the Powder alerted Nate to the three riders approaching his camp. Two were boys, maybe sixteen or eighteen at the most. The third was considerably older. Nate poured coffee into his tin cup and sipped while squatting next to the fire.

"Howdy, pard," the older rider said. "We smelled your java clean down t'the river—mind if we share a cup?"

"Help yourselves."

The three slipped off their horses and pulled tin cups out of their saddlebags. "I'm Jess Bass," the older man said, "and these is my boys. Chip's the towhead and Hank's the skinny one."

Nate eyed the trio and decided not to reveal he was a federal marshal. "Howdy, I'm Nate Hamby. The coffee's ready."

"Thanks, fill my cup, Chip."

"Sure, Pa."

Bass squatted beside the fire. "I see y'only got one can o' them beans."

"Nope, I've got more."

"That right?" Bass said, sipped coffee and stared at the bubbling beans.

Nate got up and pulled two cans out of his saddlebags. "That's all I have. You're welcome to them."

Bass tossed both cans to Hank. "Open 'em up and put 'em on t'cook. Where y'from, Hamby?"

"The Wagon Box."

"That's up near Sheridan?"

"Yeah."

"I've heard o' your spread. Say, we're lookin' t'work. Might you be needin' three good hands?"

Nate did not miss the running irons lashed to each of their bedrolls. *Rustlers and maybe highwaymen to boot*, he thought, glancing at the old .45s with well-worn walnut grips slung low on their hips. "Nope, I've got all the hands I need," he said, massaging the chill from his crooked right arm.

Bass glanced at Nate's withered right hand. "Well, mighty sorry t'hear that."

The towhead cocked his head toward Nate's horse and winked at Jess Bass.

Nate struggled to pull a leather glove onto his left hand and then reached for his can of cooked beans.

Jess Bass nodded at the towhead, pulled a pair of wire-cutting pliers from his hip pocket and offered them to Nate. "Take my pliers. A glove won't keep you from gettin' burned."

Nate picked up the can with the pliers and set it on a flat rock. Wire-cutting pliers in the pocket of a man who was wandering over the high plains of Wyoming wasn't hard to figure. Plenty of grazing land was enclosed by barbed wire as more and more owners of small ranches fenced their land. Some of the finest cattle in the state grazed those pastures and wire-cutting tools could open a fence quicker than a bronco could buck off a pesky rider. Roping and branding mavericks was one thing, but cutting fences to rustle cattle whose ownership was unquestioned was thievery most Wyoming folks felt to be worthy of the rope.

Nate handed the pliers back to Bass. "Thanks—where you fellas from?"

"Buffalo," Bass said as he chewed beans.

Nate knew everybody in Buffalo, most on a first-name basis. *This character is lyin' through his beans,* he thought. "How long you lived there?"

"Aw, maybe two months. Say, you sure got a good lookin' sorrel."

Nate was growing more wary of his uninvited guests. The two shifty-eyed boys grubbing beans from a single can continued to size up his campsite.

Bass tossed his empty can into the fire. "We'd best be ridin'. Thanks for the coffee and beans."

Nate nodded, watched the three drifters mount their horses and wondered when he would meet them again. As the trio rode southeast, they were quickly swallowed by the dim twilight of evening.

He bedded down near the dying fire. The saddle blanket covering him and the saddle beneath his head smelled of stale horse sweat. His Colt .45 lay next to the saddle within an easy grasp of his left hand. He listened to yelping coyotes and watched a glittering display of meteors slashing fiery trails across the heavens. The sorrel, champing on a hat full of oats, added cadence to nature's nocturnal melody. The lullaby was too much. His eyes slowly closed.

The trenches east of Richmond and Petersburg crept from the recesses of his memory. Four years of victories and defeats had leeched the spirit from his beloved Virginia. Out of the darkness, shadows trudged toward the James River Bridge, the last defenders of a defeated Confederacy retreating toward Appomattox. The retreat became a rout. A rider-less horse reared when Nate leaped into its empty saddle. The beast bucked, again and again, in a frenzy of flying hooves, hurling him high into the air. He crashed against a boulder crushing his right shoulder and arm. "Damn, that hurts," he muttered, half awake, half asleep.

Nate's eyes opened as he rubbed the ache from his crippled right arm. The setting moon was balanced on the high peaks of the Bighorns. Nate knew the time was between those hours of darkness and dawn when all of nature, except the human species, settles into silence. His sorrel was stomping restlessly. Man's God-given instincts began to awaken him to the invisible danger crawling through the sage. The sorrel lurched as a strange hand reached for its hackamore. Nate rolled free of his bedding into a low crouch. His left hand, grasping the .45, leaped toward the shadowy figure as it threw itself across the sorrel. In an instant, the Colt recoiled, slamming itself against the palm of Nate's hand.

"Aaaaahee!" the shadow cried. Obeying his new master, the sorrel reared, spun about and charged away through the sage. The Colt roared twice more but the fleeing sorrel and its rider were out of range.

Rage surged through Nate as he stoked the campfire with a stick. He piled more driftwood collected from the riverbank onto the glowing coals, made a pot of coffee and sat on his saddle waiting for sunrise.

"You dumb blockhead. You knew what those sneaky bastards were up to," he muttered, pouring a cup of coffee. "It's humiliating as hell for a U. S. marshal to get his horse stolen from next to his bedroll."

Just as Nate had decided to walk on to the ranch, the crunching noise of wagon wheels came from the ford. A driver's profanity urging his mules out of the river echoed across the dew-covered sage. "Hah. Hah. Git up there you godfersaken knotheads. Pull, you ornery half-jackasses. Ol' Spud ain't got all day."

Nate peered toward the river, stood up and waited while the wagon rumbled toward him. He recognized the bewhiskered old man driving the wagon toward his campfire. It was Spud

Hawkens, an old muleskinner who Nate and his partner, Hap Dugger, had met after coming to Wyoming. They had shared Spud's fare, a rabbit roasted on a spit, one evening during the autumn of 1883 as they traveled up the old Medicine Bow Trail. "Howdy, Spud, hop down and have a cup of coffee."

"Well, I declare, if it ain't Mister Hamby. What you doin' out here on the Powder?"

"I was headin' for home, but someone sneaked up and stole my horse just before dawn."

Spud wrapped his reins around the brake lever and jumped down. "Did you get a shot at him?"

"I hit him but he kept ridin'."

"Why don't you throw your stuff into my wagon and I'll have these knotheads drag y'on home. How far is it?"

"'Bout fifty miles. Hap and I own a ranch up on Little Goose Creek."

"Say, how is ol' Hap? Ain't seen him since meetin' you fellers down on the Medicine Bow Trail back in eighty-three."

"He's fine."

"Still guzzlin' sour mash?"

"Every chance he gets."

Spud champed his cud of tobacco and spat. "Reckon we'd better get goin' soon as I have that coffee. It'll take these knotheads a while t'cover fifty miles."

Three days later, Nate and Hap followed the sorrel's shod tracks across the Powder Basin, southeast from Nate's campsite, toward several towering flat-topped hills called Pumpkin Buttes. Smears of dried blood on the gray-green sage along the trail testified to the rider's wound. The job at hand was simple— pursue until the fleeing horse thief was brought to bay.

Nate and Hap were good trackers with many years of experience. Both had ridden together across the hills of eastern Oklahoma as deputy U. S. marshals. However, their backgrounds were quite different. Nate was a Virginian, a Confederate veteran having served in the Rockbridge Artillery during the entire Civil War. He was educated, a graduate of Washington College at Lexington, Virginia in 1860. The war had left him penniless and with a useless right arm. He was determined to become as proficient with his left hand as he had been with the right. He spent many hours quick-drawing an old Navy Colt .44 from behind his belt buckle. He became quick— quicker than any of his friends with whom he had competed on Sunday afternoons shooting at empty whiskey bottles in the hills west of Lexington. His reputation with a handgun rocketed after he won several high-stakes shooting contests. This led to his first job as a lawman when the Virginia Tennessee Railroad hired him as a detective.

He became bored with riding trains and sleeping in hotels. Newspaper headlines reporting the exploits of the James gang in western Missouri led him to an undercover job with the Pinkerton agency. Using the name of Nate Hardin, he rode into the James brothers' hometown, Kearney, Missouri, posing as a cousin of Texas outlaw John Wesley Hardin. His assignment was to infiltrate the gang and learn the plans for their next robbery. He was to pass that information to an undercover agent who traveled the countryside as a whiskey salesman from St. Joseph, Missouri.

After several weeks, he was successful in being included in the gang, making friends with Cole Younger, a key member of the gang. However, the James brothers were cautious, trusting nobody outside of their circle of friends. One week after the gang met to make plans to rob an Iron Mountain train, Nate saddled his horse on a pretext of riding into Kearney for some poker. Frank followed and watched Nate meet the whiskey salesman who the James brothers knew to be a Pinkerton agent.

With his cover blown, Nate spent several weeks trying to escape revenge vowed by Frank, Jesse, and Cole. A chance meeting with U. S. Marshal Bledsoe at a tavern in Indian Territory led to his being hired as a deputy U. S. marshal for Judge Parker's court in Fort Smith, Arkansas.

He was now in his early forties, tall at six-four and had wavy, red hair streaked with gray. His hat, a black Stockman's Stetson with its band sweat-stained, shaded expressive blue eyes couched beneath bushy brows. He always wore a black leather vest, which he had designed. Being obsessed with his crippled right arm, he had the tailor include long flaps that extended over the hips.  In the right flap was a pocket in which he hid his withered hand, mostly from his own eyes.  Angled across his belly next to his belt buckle, he carried a single action Colt .45 in a left handed double loop holster.  His bearing was erect, square shouldered on the left, but the right shoulder sagged.  His manner was settled, principled in speech, yet an element of shyness occasionally surfaced.

His partner, Hap Dugger, shared Nate's determination to be an independent rancher.  He, Nate, and Tom Albert, all deputy U. S. marshals that had ridden together for seven years in Indian Territory, came to Wyoming in 1883.  They were determined to find the land in the West that they had heard touted by cattle drovers crossing Indian Territory.  They saved their money and vowed to ride to Colorado, Wyoming, or Montana before another year passed.  They dreamed of settling near the Rocky Mountains where the bluegrass is tall enough to brush the belly of a horse.  That day came in the spring of 1883 as the three former lawmen rode toward the high country to build the cattle empire of their dreams.

Unlike Nate, Hap was uneducated, having completed only three years of schooling.  He was a Yankee and a veteran of the Union Army.  He had pursued the Confederates, Nate included, across Virginia until Lee surrendered to Grant in the McLean house at Appomattox.  However, they did not meet until ten years later when their friendship grew as they rode together across the hills of Indian Territory.

Like Nate Hamby, Hap Dugger stood tall.  He wore his hair long with white strands dangling beneath the brim of his old "Sugar Loaf" crowned Stetson.  His long white mustache covering the corners of his mouth joined a white goatee that drooped beneath his chin.  His manner was crude, plain spoken and quick tempered, but steadfast with friends and enemies alike.

"Here's where he joined the other two," Nate said, pointing at the sorrel's shod tracks as they mingled with those of three barefoot ponies about five miles from Nate's campsite.  A cold firepit marked the spot where the trio had spent the night.

Nate stepped out of his stirrup, walked around the camp and kicked at charred sage lying in the firepit.  "I wonder which one of those rustlers walked back to steal my sorrel."

"I reckon we'll find out soon enough," Hap replied. "Their tracks is headin' toward the Belle Fourche River. I bet they's headin' for Tom Waggoner's over at Newcastle."

"Reckon so—they probably don't know Waggoner got strung up for dealin' stolen horses."

"Let's get goin'. They've got a big head start.

*  *  *  *  *

Waggoner was a settler living in a two-room log house on his ranch near Newcastle, a thriving town near the Black Hills in northeastern Wyoming. He was a known dealer in stolen horses, shipping many of them out of Wyoming on the railroad. Upwards of a thousand of them were grazing on his ranch on June 4, 1891, the day he had met his maker.

On the 15th of August, the sheriff of Weston County, Josh Green, weary of not getting convictions in the state court, had requested Nate's assistance in the investigation of Waggoner's demise. Maybe, if a violated federal law could be determined, they could do better in the federal system and deal with WSGA arrogance.

Before returning home and encountering the Basses at the Powder River crossing, Nate had found what he expected at Waggoner's house. Waggoner's common-law wife described the gunmen that came to their door on the fourth day of June. There were three of them, all wearing Wyoming Stock Growers' Association cattle-detective badges. The three had taken Waggoner from his home at gunpoint. Later, his bloated corpse was found hanging from a tree limb in a ravine two miles from his home. The deed, now becoming more frequent, had become the official policy of the Wyoming Stock Growers' Association. They had grown weary of the lax justice practiced by the courts, so they decided to bypass the courts. Their new policy was to catch rustlers and horse thieves and hang them high or give them lead-justice

The hoof prints led to a grove of cottonwoods on the Belle Fourche River about two miles from the headquarters of a sheep ranch owned by Carter Viscontier, an emigrant from Australia. Many horse tracks and charred driftwood in a firepit indicated the riders had spent considerable time next to the river. Bloodstains beneath a lone cottonwood were stark evidence of Nate's bullet continuing to drain life from its victim.

They forded the Belle Fourche and followed the thieves' trail heading southeast. The midday heat sucked moisture from them and their horses as hot winds swept across the high plains from the arid Red Desert beyond South Pass. Gradually, the wiry sage began to be replaced by waving shoots of green bluestem grass. They pressed on until they reached a boundary marker near the high watershed of Lodgepole Creek.

Its message was clear:

Sailing C Ranch

Rustlers Beware

Bearers of Running Irons WILL be hanged.

Signed,

Jack Shetland, owner and member of WSGA.

In 1879, the Wyoming Stock Growers' Association came into being. Its parent organization had begun in 1873 when the cattle industry was limited to the lands along the Union Pacific Railroad crossing southern Wyoming. The rest of Wyoming belonged to the Indians, mostly Sioux. In 1879, three years after Custer's Seventh cavalry was cut to pieces on a bluff overlooking the Little Bighorn, Moreton Frewen came to Wyoming. Frewen, an emigrant from England, turned the first herd of cattle loose along the Powder River to graze bluestem. They would reproduce into the thousands, grow fat and bring him prosperity. Within five years, nearly 200,000 head grazed east of the Bighorn Mountains. He and several other Englishmen would own two-thirds of them. These vast herds required many cowboys to manage them on the high plains, which covered thousands of square miles.

Farmers began to immigrate into the territory to homestead. They brought barbed wire, plows and seeds to plant, all an abomination to the open-range cattlemen. Nearly every cowboy dreamed of owning his own ranch and building a herd of his own. Unbranded maverick calves were fair game to these riders of the range, but not considered so by their employers. Thus, rustling, barbed wire and dirt farmers had to be dealt with. These rich cattlemen, recognizing that their growing empire was threatened, decided to become organized. Greed and power was destined to creep into the Wyoming Stock Growers' Association as these pioneering cattlemen fought for their open-range and the cattle roaming across Wyoming.

Nate pointed at the sign. "I wonder if Bass stopped long enough to read this?"

"Naw, him and his pups probably cain't read. Their tracks are headin' right on into Shetland's ranch."

The tracks took a more southerly course when they reached Lodgepole Creek. A grove of cottonwoods and willows along the creek bank came into view. The dervish blades of a windmill were howling atop a wooden derrick pumping clear well water into a galvanized tank. The scent of fresh water loosened Hap's parched tongue. "Yahoo! There's sweet nectar down there for sure," he yelled, nudging his horse's flanks. "Git up you dried out knothead."

After drinking their fill and watering the horse, they followed the trail left by the one shod and three barefoot horses down the creek bank toward a grove of trees. Abruptly, the trail disappeared into a sea of horse tracks about three hundred yards from the trees. "Whoa," Nate pointed toward a large cottonwood on the creek bank. "What do you make of that?"

"Looks like Jack Shetland meant what his sign said."

While staring at at three men dangling from lariats tied to a large limb, Nate recalled an execution he had observed in Fort Smith, Arkansas. It was a hanging ordered by Judge Isaac Parker and carried out by hangman George Maldron on the town square It had been a warm spring day fifteen years earlier in 1876 when he rode into Fort Smith. Tucked in his vest pocket was a letter from Judge Parker asking him to be in his office at 10:00 A.M. to begin his duties as a deputy U.S. marshal. In the courtyard was a gallows constructed of new oak timbers. A crowd of men, women, and children were watching a cadaverous hangman, attired in black, prepare six men for execution. The silence cloaking the square was suddenly broken when the gallows' flooring fell away with a loud slam and six hemp loops snapped taught.  A sickening thud echoed across the courtyard and then a deafening silence fell over the square as six black-hooded corpses swung to and fro.  Gradually, their gyrations ceased.

"Reckon we'd better ride down there to see if it's Bass and his cubs," Hap said, wiping sweat from his face and neck.

It wasn't easy to be certain of their identity, but Jess Bass and his two boys had been hanged.  Their blackened, bloated faces with tongues protruding had already been visited by flying scavengers.  Sunken sockets where eyes once lusted after another man's horse were glutted with buzzing green flies.  Matted blood stains covered the towhead's shirt and britches from a mortal bullet wound near his left armpit.  Nate's .45 had been cheated by Jack Shetland's lariat.

"Well, sir, don't reckon we can bury these fellas," Hap said.  "Ain't got no shovel."

Nate yanked free a torn piece of paper pinned to Jess Bass's shirt.  He read the note scrawled across it by a nearly illiterate hand and handed it to Hap who read it aloud:  "Them that's livin' by the runnin' iron dies by a rope on the Sailin' C."

"We'll have to come back to bury them," Nate said, stepping into his stirrup.   "These tracks ought to lead us to Jack Shetland's house."

# Chapter Two

They found Nate's sorrel nuzzling a pile of hay in Shetland's corral. His left side bore purple streaks of dried blood belonging no doubt to the towhead. Nate whistled. The big gelding perked up his ears and trotted toward the corral fence. "Hello, old fella," Nate said, stroking his old friend's muzzle.

"I can see he belongs t'ya," an elderly cowboy with craggy features called while walking from the barn.

"He's mine all right. Are you Jack Shetland?"

"That's me. Who might you fellers be?"

"We're U.S. Marshals Hamby and Dugger."

"I reckon you want to get your horse?"

"I do, but first I'd like for you to tell us how he got into your corral."

"You seen them three hangin' up by the crick? Me and my hands strung 'em up several days ago. They brought three runnin' irons onto the Sailin' C."

"Why didn't you hold them for the sheriff?"

Shetland's weathered features grew stern with hawkish eyes glaring at Nate. "That good-for-nuthin' judge over at Newcastle would only turn 'em loose. The sheriff's a good man, but he can't get any convictions. So, we're goin' t'carry out justice our own selves on the Sailin' C."

"Vigilante hangin' doesn't have any place in a civilized country."

Shetland guffawed. "Civilized you say, Marshal? They ain't nothin' civilized way out here. Everybody ridin' loose in these parts is either a thief or plannin' to be one. You ought'a know. How'd that boy come by your horse? Reckon you didn't loan it to him."

"No, he stole it, all right. Did you or your hands notice the towhead had been shot?"

Shetland nodded. "Yeah, we did. Did you shoot him?"

Nate swung a leg over his horse, stepped to the ground and

faced Jack Shetland. "I shot him as he jumped on my sorrel. I intended to kill him. That's plain enough. But, I wouldn't have hanged him without a trial."

Shetland didn't blink or look away from Nate's intense glare. "Get your horse out of my corral, Marshal, then get off the Sailin' C."

"We will and if you'll loan us a couple of shovels we'll bury those fellas."

Shetland wagged his head. "No, leave them be. I want them t'remind rustlers what awaits them on the Sailin' C or any other ranch owned by a member of the Wyoming Stock Growers' Association. Let the buzzards take care of 'em."

"You didn't understand Marshal Hamby's request," Hap bellowed. "He ast you for a couple of shovels."

"They're in the barn. You can leave 'em by the stock tank."

\* \* \* \* \*

Nate's right arm dangled stiffly from his shoulder. The muscles and nerves were wasted. However, his left biceps, grown full and dominant, easily guided the shovel's sharp blade into the rocky bank of Lodgepole Creek.

Hap, resting under the tree whose arcing limb had given up the three rustlers, reached for the shovel. "I'll finish that hole."

While Hap finished digging the last grave for the three corpses, Nate pondered the range war that was in the making between the Wyoming Stock Growers' Association and homesteaders running smaller ranches and farms. It was common knowledge that WSGA members disliked all of the courts outside of Cheyenne. According to them, the judges were too lenient and too many juries winked at rustling and rustlers. A blatant example of that vigilante policy now lay on the ground waiting to be buried. The rotting corpses of Jess Bass and his two boys had been tried, convicted and hanged after being judged by a vigilante cattleman and his jury of cowhands.

Nate was Wyoming Territory's last U. S. marshal. His appointment was continued for the new state when President Harrison signed a bill admitting Wyoming to the Union at 5:30 P. M. on July 10, 1890.

Becoming a lawman in Wyoming was something Nate had

wished to avoid. He hadn't considered such a possibility until May 15,1888 when he called on Judge Micah Saufley in Cheyenne. Wyoming Territory had three justices appointed by the President and confirmed by the Senate for four-year terms. They served as individual district judges and together as the Territorial Supreme Court. Thus, they had jurisdiction over cases arising under both federal and territorial law. Any appeal went from the Territorial Supreme Court directly to the United States Supreme Court. These three justices met annually as the Territorial Supreme Court at Cheyenne. They individually traveled to each county seat within three judicial districts. They tried to hold two terms of court at each of these towns, but vast distances to cover these districts would lead to long and costly delays in litigation. This system continued until October 11, 1890, when the new state judicial system went into effect.

The rawboned Judge Saufley was a Baptist, a Democrat and a Confederate veteran, having served as a member of "Morgan's guerrillas." He was reading a document when Nate walked into his chambers in the Laramie County courthouse. Saufley's mouth was obscured by a flowing black mustache, which was joined at the sides by a thick goatee streaked with gray. He sat tall and rigid as a starched shirt. A black frock coat, too large for his lean frame, sagged from his shoulders. On his desk, a Blackstone law book laid next to a loaded pearl-handled Colt .45.

"Good mornin', Judge. I'm Nate Hamby."

The judge studied Nate for a moment. "Ah, yes, Sheriff Angus up at Buffalo wrote that you were coming to see me. Pull up a chair."

Nate pulled an envelope from his pocket and handed it to Saufley. "Sheriff Angus asked me to bring this to you while I was here on business."

The judge slit open the envelope with his pocketknife, studied the penciled letter and removed his pinch-nose spectacles. "Well, Mister Hamby, do you know the contents of this letter?"

"No, Judge, I don't."

"He says you are a former deputy U. S. marshal."

Surprised by the judge's statement, Nate nodded and stammered, "Why.... uh.... yes.... uh.... I am."

"Where abouts?"

"Uh.... Judge Parker's court at Fort Smith from '76 till '83."

"I see. Why did you quit marshaling?"

Nate pondered the question while combing the fingers of his left hand through graying, sandy hair. "After the war, I decided to come west. I lost everything durin' the war. The Yankees stole our land. All three of my brothers died at Shiloh. A useless right arm crippled me. I never saw my parents again after I went to war. Both had died before the war was over. So, I had to get out of there and start a new career. I became a railroad detective and then worked for the Pinkerton agency for a while before hiring on with Judge Parker as a deputy U. S. marshal. Judge Parker didn't allow his deputies to collect rewards in Indian Territory until several of us threatened to quit. That's how Hap Dugger, Tom Albert and I saved enough durin' seven years to start up ranchin' out here.

"I reckon you heard that Marshal Tomlin was killed up at Rawlins last month?"

"Yeah, I did."

"President Cleveland wants me to recommend someone to take his place. Sheriff Angus thinks you'd be a good one."

"I got no time for bein' a lawman. My partner and I are buildin' a ranch on Little Goose Creek up near Sheridan."

"Have you considered that you could lose your ranch if the WSGA has its way?"

Nate slammed his fist against the arm of his chair. "That ranch is ours! Nobody is goin' to steal one acre from me again."

"They control Wyomin' Territory and are plannin' on ownin' Wyomin' when we become a state. President Cleveland wants a U. S. marshal with enough guts to stop them."

"I don't know...."

Interrupting Nate's recollection, Hap climbed out of the last hole, tossed aside his shovel and walked toward the remains of Jess Bass. "These pits are deep enough. Let's cover up these stinking corpses."

* * * * *

While riding along the Bozeman trail toward home after burying the Basses, Nate pondered the disregard for the law by the WSGA. He detested being a lawman, loved the land, blooded horses, the lowing of cattle grazing on bluestem, the eerie bugle call of a bull elk on a crisp autumn day and gaggles of smoky Canada honkers filling Wyoming skies at the end and beginning of winter. He loved a hundred other amenities bequeathed by a land once shared only by the Sioux and Cheyenne. He found them all in Wyoming on the Wagon Box. Now it could be lost. Judge Saufley's warning kept repeating itself. "Somehow, we've got to stop them."

"Who?"

"The Wyoming Stock Growers' Association."

"That means Tom Albert."

"I reckon it does, but it was him who decided to pitch in with Wolcott and the WSGA."

"Yeah," Hap said, "Tom sure got his nose out o' joint when we didn't settle down there in Colorado."

During the summer of 1883, the three former deputy federal marshals had traveled from Fort Smith across Indian Territory and Kansas into Colorado where they hoped to discover a place to build their ranch. They found a ranch already established near Fort Morgan along the Platte River. Nellie Chambers, recently widowed when her husband was gored to death by one of his longhorn bulls, owned it. The ranch was covered by stunted bluestem, the victim of a harsh drought. The cattle were gone, sold at a loss by Nellie Chambers rather than let them starve. Tom mistakenly surmised that she was desperate and made her an offer to buy several thousand acres along the river, but she refused. It was all or none. Access to the Platte River had to be maintained for the entire ranch. She would not divide her vast land holdings. With the price beyond what they could pay or borrow, the three men rode toward Cheyenne.

"If we had, I reckon he'd still be with us."

Hap chomped his chaw, spat, and wiped brown spittle from his goatee. "Aw, naw he wouldn't. Tom turned bad 'cause he always wanted to be the head bull."

Nate gazed at Cloud Peak, its snowcap shrunken by the

summer sun. "I suppose he did. He and Major Wolcott took to each other like whiskey and good times when we met him back in '83 at the Cheyenne Hotel."

A lot had happened to them since that fateful meeting on September 15, 1883. Meeting Major Frank Wolcott had brought an end and a new beginning for Nate, Hap and Tom. They met a fork in the road that day in Cheyenne.

As they sat in the Cheyenne Hotel bar, Major Frank Wolcott overheard them discussing where they should go in search of their dream. He was seated at another table, contemplating a shot glass filled with Scotch whiskey, when Hap raised his glass to propose a toast. "Here's to ridin' an easy-gaited horse, sleepin' in a dry bed and drinkin' good whiskey ever' day."

"Hear! Hear!" Wolcott said, raising his glass. "I'll certainly drink to that."

Several more toasts brought Wolcott to their table. The conversation, which followed, would bring change for Nate Hamby, Hap Dugger and Tom Albert. "Custer's blunder on the Little Bighorn was a great boon to Wyoming cattlemen," Major Frank Wolcott said, waving his cigar like a maestro's baton. "The Army doesn't turn tail and run after a whipping like that. The Sioux and Northern Cheyenne found that out. It's been seven years, and they're all dead or stuck in an encampment outside some fort. All of their hunting ground north of the Platte is up for grabs." He grabbed a handful of cigars out of a humidor, crushing them in his fist. "We're going to grab it up. Just like this!"

*At ten cents a cigar, that's an expensive gesture*, Nate thought as Wolcott tossed the crushed stogies into a wastebasket.

From the beginning of their conversation, Wolcott extolled the glorious virtues of his past and the power he wielded within the Wyoming Stock Growers' Association. In Nate's opinion, Wolcott's claim to military genius while serving the Union during the Civil War and bragging about his rise within the ranks of the cattle baron's caste in Wyoming were so much self-serving hogwash. "I gather you're concerned about somebody beatin' you to the grab?"

"Homesteaders! They're rumbling out of Nebraska in their

broken-down wagons loaded up with plows and brats. We've got to stop them."

"How do you plan on gettin' that done?" Tom Albert asked.

"By any means," Wolcott snarled.

*The man sure has a vicious streak*, Nate thought as he observed Wolcott's twitching face and violent gestures. "If cattlemen want that land for grazin', they'll have to homestead it first."

"That's impossible. You can't homestead range land, but you're right about our getting it first."

"Sounds like you need some range detectives," Tom said.

Wolcott turned to face Tom. "You've got a real fine idea there. What did you say your name was?"

"Tom Albert."

Wolcott picked up a decanter of whiskey and refilled Tom's glass. "I've nearly given up on county and federal lawmen helping us. We've got a big problem with rustlers. They're taking a big chunk out of our profits. We've got to stop them."

"What about the homesteaders?" Tom said, reaching for his glass.

"Why can't we do both?"

Tom glanced at Nate. "We might be able to help. All three of us are ex-lawmen."

"Where did you men ply your trade?"

"For Judge Parker in Indian Territory."

"I'm done with all that," Nate said. "We came out here to raise cattle and that's what I'm goin' to do."

"We can do both."

"Na-a-aw, Tom," Hap drawled, "Nate's right."

Wolcott scowled and turned toward Tom. "Well, let's you and me do it. How about it?"

"I'll think on it."

"Sure! You do that. Say, I'd like for you men to meet a couple of my friends."

"Who are they?"

"Hubert Teschemacher and Fred deBillier."

"When?"

"How about supper tonight?"

Nate wanted no part of Wolcott. *I've seen enough of this rooster*, he thought. *He's wearing trouble like a suit of armor.* "We came out here to start up a ranch. Remember, Tom?" Nate said and stood up. "Let's ride on up and look over this Powder Basin Wolcott's been talkin' about."

Tom turned toward Hap. "How about you, Hap?"

Hap tended to speak his mind and had little regard for tact. "Nate's right! Ain't got no call to go runnin' after this little strutter and his dandified friends. Let's ride on out o' here."

Wolcott became livid and bounced out of his chair. Hap stood up, his six-four frame towering over Wolcott. Wolcott shook his fist, yelling, "This Territory belongs to the WSGA. That's my friends and me. You had better get out of Wyoming while you can."

"Mister Wool—cott," Hap drawled. "You'd best tuck that fat fist of yours back in your pocket before I shove it in your ugly face."

Like a fighting cock, Wolcott began to prance around. Losing control, he screeched profanity at each one of them.

Tom glared at Hap. An opportunity was melting away. His ambition to become rich and powerful was not going to be denied. He rightly figured Teschemacher and DeBillier had to be powerful members of the WSGA. His decision to spare Major Wolcott from any more of Hap's rudeness came swiftly. He stepped between them. "Your dumb mouth is out of control, Hap Dugger. You owe the major an apology."

"Naw, I don't. We ain't what he called us."

"You can all go to hades," Wolcott yelled, barging out of the room.

"You're a hollow-headed bumpkin," Tom chastened. "What do you mean, insulting him like that?"

"Hap was wrong," Nate said, "but you know that's just the way he talks."

"Well, I've got my belly full of his crap. Both of you can ride on out, if that's what you want. I intend to make amends if I can."

* * * * *

After a ten-day ride, Nate and Hap reached Buffalo, a new

town near Fort McKinney on Clear Creek. Several log houses had been built along Main Street. Three log buildings with clapboard fronts and a livery stable made up the commercial section of town. Robert Foote operated a trading center that took up a fourth of a block on the west side of the street. A sign over his store boasted: "Foote's Trading Center. You Need It? We Got It".

South of Foote's store was the office of Dr. William T. "Spoon" Spoonhour. "Doc Spoon", as everyone called him, had supposedly studied medicine abroad. At least, that was the rumor promoted by Doc. He had a diploma hanging on his parlor wall written in Latin that nobody could read, not even Doc. The space where "William T. Spoonhour" had been penned in fancy script was ruffed up. Most believed the name of its original honoree had been erased. Some said Doc won the thing in a poker game at Cheyenne and decided to begin practicing medicine. These questions really didn't matter since Doc Spoon could dig out bullets and count pills as well as most frontier physicians.

Next door to Doc Spoon's office was Buffalo's most frequented bar and bawdyhouse. Katie's Saloon and Entertainment Emporium was the tallest building in Buffalo and Katie reigned over her establishment like a ship's master. Her girls called Katie's quarters on the third floor "the penthouse." The second floor housed seven young women who solicited clients downstairs in Katie's saloon, which occupied the entire length of the building. Nightly entertainment was presented on the stage at its farther end and a long mahogany bar filled the north wall. Ten tables for poker players, two crap tables, a faro table and a roulette wheel completed the furnishings. When the bar was open for business, "Fingers" Slocum's loud piano could be heard above the din of rowdy customers.

Another rumor in town was that Doc Spoon enjoyed special privileges in Katie's establishment. Granted by her for his certifying that her "girls" had no diseases.

Next to Katie's was Buffalo's social center, the two-storied Occidental Hotel. Its proprietor, Charles E. Buell, had just completed his new building with six bedrooms on the upper floor, each with a dormer window. A long porch sheltered the hotel entrance. On the first floor were the lobby, a bar, other guest rooms, a kitchen and a dining room where the chef, Dutch Jake, served up plain dishes.

Nate and Hap left their mounts and pack horses at the livery stable and walked up the street to the hotel. All Nate could think about was a hot sudsy bath followed by a big juicy steak. "I'm goin' to the bathhouse," he said, unlocking their door.

Hap tossed his saddlebags onto the dresser. "Me too."

Chung Hoi Lee was proprietor of Chung's bath, tonsorial parlor and laundry next door to the hotel. Chung's black hair was plastered down with perfumed pomade. He wore black snakeskin boots, gray pin-striped britches and a white shirt with a black shoestring tied into a bow against the collar. A white oilcloth apron protected this attire. Chung went from tub to tub providing hot water, bath powders, soap and a constant flow of Chinese-accented conversation. Nate and Hap sat in large copper tubs filled to their waists. Repeatedly, Chung poured hot water and sprinkled bath powders into their tubs. His comments were: "Ah, this very good." "You want smell good?" "Make skin feel good." "You like more hot water?" "Here, have cigar, I light for you." "When you finish, I rinse off soap with mineral water. It make you healthy. Only four-bit more—Okay?"

Nate interrupted Chung's steady prattle. "Hey, Chung, bring us a jug of Jack Daniels."

"Oh, Mist' Hamby, Chung no have whiskey. Need go get next door. Okay?"

"Sure thing. How much do I owe?"

"You pay later, so?" Chung replied, apparently hoping to get a much better price for his services after they had consumed enough spirits to dull their wits.

Upon returning with a jug of Jack Daniels, Chung kept their glasses filled and tubs steaming. His downfall was Hap's tolerance for whiskey derived from drinking booze every day. Hap also prized his haggling ability. "Now, Choong," Hap said, "your sign says six-bits for a bath. How come you're chargin' us two and a half bucks?"

"Oh, Mist' Hap, you too dirty six-bit. You pay more."

Hap pulled on his boots. "Your sign says seventy-five cents and that's all you're gettin'."

"Okay, bath cost six-bit. Mineral water cost four-bit. Extra hot water cost six-bit. You pay two buck. Okay, Mist' Hap?"

"Well now, Choong, how do I know you rinsed us off with mineral water? Felt like plain ol' branch water t'me."

Rage darkened Chung's eyes. Nate was aggravated at Hap for trying to out haggle Chung. Before Chung could respond, Nate yelled at Hap, "Oh, pay the man his two-fifty. We're goin' to need another bath before spring. You want him to scald you next time?"

"Now Nate...."

"Here, Chung, is my two-fifty," Nate said. "How much for the whiskey?"

"Chung thank Mist Hamby. I charge whiskey at hotel. You go pay Mist' Buell."

Hap handed Chung two-fifty. "Damn it, Nate, I had him down to two bucks."

The following morning they walked up the street to Aunt Deana's place, the only boarding house in Buffalo. Spending the coming winter in the Occidental would cost too much, so Aunt Deana's would have to do.

"That smells like fresh bread bakin'," Hap said as they climbed the porch steps.

Nate rapped on the front door. As it opened, a rotund lady with black hair and ruddy features smiled and wiped flour from her hands on a stained apron. "Good morning, gents—what might I be doin' for you, pray tell?"

"We need room and board for the winter," Nate replied.

"Why am I keepin' you standin' on the porch? Come in—come in—welcome. I'm Aunt Deana Murphy. What might be your names?"

"I'm Nate Hamby."

"And I'm Hap Dugger, Aunt Deana."

"I've one room left. It's upstairs in the back over the sun porch. Would you be wantin' to see it?"

Nate realized room and board would be hard to come by in Buffalo. "Yes, but we'll take it."

"I charge by the week," Aunt Deana said as they climbed the stairs. "Five dollars each it will be. I serve three meals every day, except I don't cook supper on Sunday. Breakfast is at seven, dinner's at noon and supper's at six. The privy's out back. You can do your bathin' up at Chung's."

Nate hadn't heard a word that Aunt Deana said. His attention was riveted on a young woman who was following them up the stairway. Before Nate could muster the courage to speak to her, Hap doffed his hat and bowed like a victorious matador as she passed by. "Howdy, ma'am, reckon we're goin' t'be your new neighbors."

She smiled at Hap's pompous gesture. "That's nice," she said and hurried down the hallway.

# Chapter Three

Hap's bent for drink and poker was to make the three-block walk to Katie's place an everyday stroll. Nate lost his interest in drinking and gambling with Hap after he met *the girl on the stairs* at breakfast the next morning. He had just spooned a large helping of scrambled eggs onto his plate when she walked in and took a seat. He found her to be quite pretty, no more than thirty-five and too young to be living in a frontier village like Buffalo. His eyes scanned her brown hair fastened tightly into a bun on the back of her head, leaving only a few wisps spiraling in front of her ears. Her limpid green eyes glanced at him as he reached for a bowl of scrambled eggs, causing him to nearly upset his coffee mug. "Mornin', ma'am," he said, fumbling with the bowl. "Would you be carin' for eggs?"

Her lips tilted into a smile as she reached for the bowl. "Thank you, sir."

"You're welcome, ma'am," he said, and reached past Hap for a platter of sausage. "Would you be likin' some sausage, too, ma'am?"

Nate's eagerness brought a scattering of snickers from the boarders as she shyly blinked. "Thank you, sir."

Hap, suddenly aware of Nate's awkwardness, glanced at him and the young woman. "I can pass stuff to the lady, too. You don't need to drag your sleeve across my plate doin' it."

"Oh, I do beg your pardon." Nate then checked his sleeve and raised his arm for all to see, making eye contact with several of the boarders. "See—my sleeve doesn't have a particle on it."

Along with the other boarders, the young woman began to laugh.

Hap pointed at little clumps of eggs that had been scattered by his own fork. "Look beside my plate where your sleeve shoved all my eggs."

"You have my apology," Nate said, glancing at the young woman. "Have some more."

A tiny brown mole just above the corner of her mouth moved slightly upward as she winked at him. Nate was ecstatic.

At that moment, Aunt Deana walked in carrying a large coffee pot. "Well now, let's make Mister Dugger and Mister Hamby feel welcome. Come along now, introduce yourselves while your coffee I'm pourin'."

The young woman dabbed her lips with a napkin and smiled at Nate. "Mister Hamby, Mister Dugger, my name is Beth Todd. I'm Buffalo's only school teacher."

Beth Todd was born in Kentucky, a niece of Mary Todd Lincoln.    Her father had served as an agent under Allan Pinkerton during the war, but his true vocation was spying for the Confederacy.    His superiors never found out his dual role until several years after the war's end.    Some of his letters to Confederate General John Winder, the provost marshal of Richmond, were discovered in files that had not been destroyed. By this time, Beth and her parents had moved from Washington, D. C. to Independence, Missouri. Amnesty by President Johnson had saved her father from prosecution.

During the war, Beth had visited her aunt and uncle a number of times. She and her cousin, Tad, had enjoyed romping about the halls and rooms of the White House while playing hide and seek. She found Tad's favorite hiding place to be under Lincoln's desk. When she came into Lincoln's study looking for Tad, Lincoln would grin, wink at Beth and point at his feet where she would find Tad curled up between his boots.

Beth graduated from Smith College in Northampton, Massachusetts in 1875. While a student, she had become a devoted proponent of the rights of women to vote and to be equal with men. She was determined to be independent, to choose where she would live and to teach children in some remote region in the West. That place turned out to be Buffalo, Wyoming Territory when she answered an advertisement placed in the *Kansas City Star* by Charles Buell soliciting a schoolteacher.

Beth was petite, just over five feet in height. Her eyes were like two emeralds that flashed when she spoke. Her walk was brisk, always seeming to be in a hurry. A smile, which came easily to her full lips, often erupted into laughter. She enjoyed life, people and especially teaching children.

"Pleased to make your acquaintance, Mizz Todd," Hap said.

"Me…. Uh...me too," Nate said, hesitated, and searched for words, any words that would impress this pretty schoolteacher. Several boarders snickered. A man sitting next to Nate, his hair white as the clerical collar he was wearing, chuckled and offered his hand to Nate. "I'm Father Cleetus Turnbill, the rector of St. James Episcopal Church."

Nate hardly heard him. Hap grinned and pointed his fork at the rector's outstretched hand. "We're both mighty proud t'meetcha, sir. Whenever ol' Nate wakes up, he'll shake your hand."

"Pardon me, Father," Nate said, "I didn't catch your name."

"Turnbull—Cleetus Turnbull."

Nate was completely smitten by Beth. His eyes moved to take in each boarder as they introduced themselves. His mind, however, was aware only of Beth Todd.

Hap wiped his mustache and goatee with his napkin and slid back his chair. He stood up and walked around the table shaking hands with each boarder. To each of the men, he said, "Mighty proud t'meetcha, sir."

There was only one other woman besides Beth. She always sat at the head of the table, having bestowed upon herself the unofficial position of table master. She always called upon Father Turnbill to say grace before allowing anyone to begin eating. She would close the mealtime by saying, "Now everyone take your plates and utensils out to the kitchen and put your napkins in the hamper beside the door."

"Howdy, ma'am," Hap said, holding out his hand. "Mighty proud t'meetcha, ma'am."

Patience Smythe was shocked, withdrawing from his outstretched hand. "Yes, Mister Dugger," she said with regal shyness. "I'm quite pleased to meet you, too. I'm Patience Smythe."

After hesitating for a moment, Hap realized his hand was not going to be touched by Patience Smythe. "Yes, ma'am," he said and walked on to meet the other boarders.

Patience Smythe's eyes followed Hap until he returned to his chair. His long white hair, sweeping mustache and goatee had impressed her immensely. The corners of her mouth curved into a fleeting smile as Hap seated himself. "Mister Dugger and Mister Hamby," she said, her eyelids fluttering like a flirting young maiden. "Welcome to our little family. We would like to invite you both to our family hour we spend together after supper each evening. We play checkers and chess and we like to gather around the piano to sing our favorite songs."

"Well, Mizz Patience, that sounds like a ripsnorter," Hap lied, intending to spend each evening at Katie's place. "I reckon we might just jine you one evenin'."

"Yes, we sure will," Nate said. "Hap and I sing all the time out on the trail. Don't we, Hap?"

"Like a couple o' bayin' coonhounds."

Hap's response brought chuckles from the boarders, but Patience ignored his crude reference. "We will be looking forward to your singing with us this evening,"

Hap, wishing to avoid any further contact with Patience Smythe, left soon after breakfast. "Nate, it's plain to me that Smythe woman is settin' her bonnet for my car—cass. I ain't about to gather with her after supper or no other time nuther. I'm goin' to see Doc Spoon."

"Doc Spoon? What for?"

"So's I can tell that woman I ain't feelin' up to no checkers or no singin'. Y'see, I'm gettin' a touch o' the 'tizum comin' back on my hipbones."

"Why are you scared of some old maid?"

"You dumb corn-federate, I ain't afraid o' her. She's not only plain like ugly, but she thinks she's some kind of big boss. Her givin' everybody orders all the time. That woman's got the longest and skinniest neck I've seen and her eyes is so close together, I swear her eyelashes done got tangled while she was battin' 'em at me."

"Aw, Hap, she's not that bad. Her neck is a bit long, but you're exaggeratin' about her eyes. They just look close because her face is a tad long and she isn't so bossy. I'll bet she could be real comfortin' to any man she took a likin' to."

"Well, then, you gather with her, but I ain't goin' to," Hap said as he left for Doc Spoon's.

Doc's office smelled of chloroform. Hap sat down in a rickety chair beside a dented brass spittoon, tarnished green from many years of use. The waiting room was vacant, the hour being so early. He noticed a piece of paper hanging on a nail driven into the door to Doc's office. He squinted to see what was written on it. "Please knock and be seated," he read aloud. Not wanting to get up, he stomped on the floor and waited for Doc Spoon to appear.

"Who's making all that racket?" Doc asked, opening the door. He was wearing an old red bathrobe that was frayed along the bottom. His gray hair was disheveled; eyes bloodshot and gray stubble covered his face.

"I'm Hap Dugger, Doc. I need t'talk with ya."

"What is so all fired important that you had to wake me up? It's the middle of the night."

"Naw, it ain't." Hap flipped open the metal cover of his pocket watch. "See here, it's half-past seven in the mornin'."

Doc squinted at Hap's watch. "Well, come on in, then."

Hap followed Doc Spoon through his office and into his kitchen. "Put some coffee on to boil while I get dressed," Doc said and disappeared through the door into his bedroom.

Hap finally managed to get a fire built in the stove. "Hey, Doc, where do you keep your pot and coffee?" he yelled out of frustration with the clutter in Doc's kitchen.

The door to Doc's bedroom opened and a very pretty woman with auburn hair walked in wearing a filmy white robe. Hap couldn't pry his gaze away from her trim figure.

"Never mind, I'll make the coffee. Doc's not the best housekeeper in Buffalo is he?"

" 'Scuse me, ma'am," Hap said, recovering from the surprise of her appearance. "I'm real sorry I disturbed ya. I didn't know Doc was married."

She pulled a blackened coffee pot out of the cupboard and dipped water from a bucket into the pot. "Oh, Doc and I are just good friends. I don't believe I've seen you around Buffalo before. I'm Katie Hall. I own the saloon and emporium next door."

Hap wondered, *why is a pretty woman like Katie sleepin' with an old sawbones like Doc Spoon?* "No, ma'am, we ain't met. I'm Hap Dugger. Me and my partner is winterin' down at Aunt Deana's place."

"Well, now, why don't you and your partner come on up to my place this evening for a little entertainment?" Katie asked as she cranked Doc's coffee grinder. "It's the only place in town that caters to handsome fellows like yourself."

She laughed at Hap as he swallowed hard. "Yes'm."

"Then you are coming up to see me this evening, aren't you?"

"Yes'm, I sure am."

"Call me Katie, you handsome devil."

"Aw'-right—Katie."

Doc Spoon walked into the kitchen, rubbing bay rum on his face. "Ain't you two got that coffee made yet?" Doc said without expecting a reply. "You been to breakfast, Hap?"

"Sure have, but I could handle some more coffee."

"Well, let's go into my office while Katie brews some up. What kind of problem you got that needs my help?"

Ten minutes later, Doc had Hap leaning across his examining table with Hap's pants down to his knees. Doc was probing Hap's rectum with his finger. "You say your hips has got the 'tizum? How about your pissing? Your prostate gland is a mite big. Making water okay?"

"What's my pissin' got to do with my poop-chute? It's my hips that hurts."

Doc finished his examination, ripped off his rubber glove and plopped it into a basin of soapy water. "Just what is it that's giving you trouble?"

"Well, I reckon it's that I'm scared of gettin' chased by the ugliest woman in Buffalo, maybe in the whole territory of Wyomin'."

Doc began to chuckle. "Patience Smythe?"

"Yeah, didn't take much ponderin' to figger that out."

"Well, there's no other woman uglier than her in Buffalo, but I don't understand. Do you want me to poison her?"

"Aw, no, I just want you to write out somethin' about my 'tizum so I'll have a good excuse t'not gather with that skinny-necked witch. Kin you do that for me, Doc?"

"I suppose I can."

Doc scribbled on a sheet of paper and handed it to Hap. "That should keep you from gatherin' with Patience."

Hap held the note out at arms length and read it aloud. "'To whom-ever it might con-cern. This is to certify that Hap Dugger is ailin' with relapsin' ague. When he's feelin' poorly, leave him be. Signed, Doc Spoonhour.' Reckon that'll do me real fine, Doc. I'm obliged. How much I owe?"

"Oh, four-bits will do," Doc replied, pouring some white pills into an envelope. "Leave these quinine pills and my note on your dresser. Aunt Deana's the nosiest woman in town. She'll tell Patience what you're taking and what my note says. You can count on that for sure. Now, let's go see if Katie's got that coffee made."

Katie had returned to her quarters, but the freshly brewed coffee awaited Hap and Doc. After he'd finished drinking a mug-full, Hap handed Doc a silver half-dollar. "Thanks a lot. My thirst has turned to somethin' more warmin' than coffee. I believe I'll just slap-foot on over to Katie's place."

"I'd go with you, but I've got some sick folks to see."

Hap's ruse got off to a sputtering start that evening. As he sopped the last traces of gravy from his plate with a slice of Aunt Deana's light bread, Hap groaned and grabbed at his back. "Oh, you dear man," Patience said. "Are you in pain?"

"Yeah, Mizz Patience, my ol' car-cass is a bit on the poorly side. Doc Spoon said my ague is comin' back. I ain't up to gatherin' with you folks this evenin'."

"Oh, of course you aren't, Mister Dugger. Now, you shouldn't be coming down to the dining room when you are feeling so badly. From now on, you just say so and I'll bring your meal up to your room. Oh, you poor man, you do look a mite peaked."

"Yes'm, but that won't need be. I ain't no in-val-ud."

"Nonsense! Men are all the same. Now, you go on to your room and I'll bring your pie and coffee up to you right away."

Patience's sudden urge to mother Hap was a turn he had not considered. Nate wasn't helping any either. While trying to stifle an outburst, laughter spewed between his fingers. Patience's deep concern for Hap turned into livid anger toward Nate. "Mister Hamby, you should be ashamed of yourself. Mr. Dugger is ill and your behavior is intolerable. Where is your compassion?"

"I'm right sorry, Hap," Nate said, trying to keep from laughing."

"Aw, that's awright," Hap said and washed down the last bite of pie with several gulps of coffee. "Let's mosey on down t'Katie's for a little outin'. It'll ease my ague."

What you fella's having tonight?" the bartender asked, sweeping a filthy towel through a puddle of whiskey.

Nate plucked several free cigars from a drinking glass on the bar. "Make it a jug of Tennessee sour mash."

Katie's Saloon and Emporium was thick with blue cigar smoke. Clicking sounds clattered from the roulette wheel and dice bouncing across crap tables. Bedlam seemed to rule. Loud voices blended with the staccato of clanking glasses and bottles. Profanity was on every gambler's tongue as losses depleted their table stakes, but an occasional gleeful shout encouraged the losers to keep on betting. Whiskey was being poured freely and Fingers Slocum pounded his piano keys without letup. Nate and Hap found an empty table beside the stairway to the second floor where Katie's gals plied their trade.

"This place sure is rollin'," Hap said while filling their glasses.

Nate handed Hap one of the free cigars. "Sure is."

Just as Hap took the stogie, Katie, wearing a lavender gown highlighted by sparkling sequins, walked onto the balcony above their table. Her presence shut the room down as if a deity had appeared. She flipped her handkerchief at Fingers who smiled, flashed a gold tooth, tipped his black bowler hat and began to play, *I'll Take You Home Again, Kathleen*. His fingers flashed up and down the keyboard filling the simple melody with rollicking chords. As she slowly descended the stairs, Katie began to sing and wave her silk handkerchief at each customer until she reached Hap. He blushed like a teenager as he looked up into her flashing blue eyes. Finishing the last note, she drew her handkerchief across his head mussing his neatly combed hair and winked. "You are coming up to see me tonight aren't you, honey?"

"You bet, Katie. I sure am."

"See you later, then."

She climbed a short flight of steps onto the stage. The seven girls from upstairs joined with her in the evening performance. All were dressed in short pleated skirts showing plenty of leg. Tight, low-cut bodices hoisted and exposed most of their bosoms to the leering men. Their songs and dances were aimed at bringing in plenty of customers upstairs after the show. A ploy that always worked, a little too well at times, causing arguments and fist fights to break out over which girl belonged to which lusting gambler.

The crowd of men stood up, clapped, whistled and yah-hooed after the last song. The applause went on until the last girl disappeared into Katie's Emporium. Katie stood on the balcony, waving her handkerchief and bowing to the crowd, then she raised her hand for silence.

"Now fellas, my girls are ready to entertain you inside the Emporium. If any of you aren't acquainted with the house rule, I'm going to say it again. You've got to get your name on the list of the girl of your choice." She pointed to a swarthy man climbing the stairs. "Mike will be at this door with the appointment book. He takes care of everything. You got a question, ask him. You all have fun now." She looked down at Hap, winked, left the balcony and went into the Emporium.

Hap was ready to go upstairs that moment, but so were most of the others. Their enthusiastic response to Katie's invitation jammed the stairway from bottom to top. Hap's downing one more belt of whiskey earned him last place on the bottom step. Finally, he blew up after several fruitless tries to move through the crowd. He leaned back and yelled, "If you mongers don't let me by so's I can go see Katie, I'm goin' t'stomp every one of ya."

A burly hulk halfway up the stairs turned and picked up

Hap's challenge. "Yeah, you and what others goin' t'help ya?"

Hap pointed at Nat. "Me and my friend sittin' over there. He'll be more than I need, I figger."

Nate held up his left hand. "No, Hap, I'm not fightin' so you can get first place at a whorehouse." To Nate's regret, his reference to Katie's Entertainment Emporium as a whorehouse emptied the stairway. Her irate customers scrambled down the steps, some jumping over the railing to challenge him. As brawls often go, there weren't any fighters for or against Nate's point of view once the first blows hit his jaw. A good fight was too much fun to waste in beating up only one man. Hap took advantage of the situation by scrambling up the stairs. He yelled at Mike, "Open that door and lock them sons o' perdition out behind me."

Several minutes of furious battle vented the brawlers' entire bent for violence. Nate lay on his back behind the bar, tossed there by the burly hulk. His jaw throbbed and ears rang as he stared toward the ceiling. Rubbing his jaw, he said to nobody in particular, "You'd think I insulted their mothers."

Hap knocked on Katie's door. The sounds of the fight down in the bar were barely audible since her private quarters were on the third floor. "Katie, it's me, ol' Hap comin' t'call."

The door opened. Katie, holding a half-filled champagne glass, smiled at him. "Come on in you handsome devil."

Hap walked in and closed the door. "Howdy, Katie. You sure look purty t'night."

"Well, thank you, honey. They are fighting again downstairs?"

"Yeah, ol' Nate done insulted your customers by callin' your place a whorehouse. He's a wild Rebel with only one good arm, but I figger he's able to take care o' hisself, so I came on up t'see ya."

"I'm glad you did. How about some champagne?"

"I hear tell that stuff'll give ya calico fever in the worst way, y'know, sorta like turnin' a geldin' into a hard blowin' stud."

Katie laughed. "That's right, come on into my bedroom and I'll pour you some."

The four glasses of champagne he downed stirred Hap's lust

into a carnal itch, begging to be scratched. Everything about Katie had begun to seduce him: The fragrance of her perfume, the cleavage of her bosoms accented by the bedroom lamp, her flirtatious glances while sipping from her glass as he scanned her from her purple slippers to the spiraling auburn ringlets framing her face. All fanned the flames of his imagination.

Finally, their unspoken ardor kindled more desire than Hap could handle. "Katie, you do know how t'heat a feller up. I declare."

"It is a bit warm in here, isn't it." She stood up and walked behind a screen painted with Chinese characters and birds of paradise. "I'll get into something cooler. French champagne does get one's blood to flowing doesn't it, honey?"

"Sure does."

When Katie came out from behind the screen, Hap could only gape at her flawless skin and lushly rounded breasts tipped with light brown nipples. All she had on was a green garter belt and black lace hose. "Whoopie, Katie, if y'ain't the purtiest women ever I've laid eyes on."

She beckoned him to her with a curling finger. As she lay down on the bed, Hap fumbled with the buttons on his pants. "Come here you handsome devil. I'll help you with those buttons."

# Chapter Four

Katie struck a match and lit Tom's cigar. "Hello there, I see you smoke real Havana cheroots."

Tom Albert blew smoke across the table. "Yeah—Thanks for the light," he said between puffs, "this your place?"

"All mine," Katie said, pulled back a chair and flashed a seductive smile. "Mind if I join you?"

"Sure. Let me buy you a drink."

"Bring me a bourbon, Homer," Katie called to the bartender. "I see you're wearing a badge. Are you some kind of lawman?"

Tom glanced down at the silver shield pinned to his vest. "I'm chief inspector for the Wyoming Stock Growers' Association."

Katie liked what she saw—a handsome fellow in his mid thirties with silvered black hair and a mustache that drooped below the corners of his mouth.

The corners of his winsome blue eyes crinkled as he smiled back at her. "What's your name, pretty lady?"

"Katie Hall. What's yours, handsome stranger?"

"Tom Albert."

"Where you from, Tom Albert?"

"Oh, I reckon you could say I'm from Cheyenne, but after meeting you I'm stayin' right here in Buffalo."

She knew that Tom's talk was pure blarney, but Katie was flattered and showed it as her cheeks flushed. "I like that. Where are you staying?"

"Where do you recommend?"

"The Occidental. If you tell Charley Buell that Katie sent you, you'll get his best room."

Tom finished his whiskey and slid the glass onto the table. "Thanks, Katie, I've got some pressing business, so I'd better go do that right now but I'll be back. You can count on that, pretty lady."

"I'll be here, handsome stranger."

Tom pushed back his chair to leave, hesitated, and then asked, "Nate Hamby and Hap Dugger wouldn't be around?"

Katie's eyebrows arched upward. "They friends of yours?"

"Sort of. You know where I can find them?"

"Aunt Deana's boarding house. It's the two-storied white house next to the school."

"Thanks, pretty lady," Tom said, tossing a silver dollar onto the table.

* * * * *

Nate was standing at the Occidental's bar sipping whiskey he had just poured from a jug of Jack Daniels when trouble sauntered up beside him in Tom Albert's boots. "Slide me a glass, bartender," Tom yelled as he draped an arm across Nate's shoulders.

Nate's back stiffened at the sound of Tom's voice, which echoed through the whiskey-fog numbing his brain. He weaved a bit, turned and tried to focus his eyes on the silver badge pinned to Tom's vest. "I see you, uh, made up with, uh, that rooozter, Wolcott."

"Yeah, I did," Tom bragged, reaching for Nate's jug, "and now I'm chief inspector for the WSGA."

Nate grabbed Tom's wrist. "That's the trouble with you, Tom. You see somethin' you want, you take it. No askin'. Just take it."

Tom pushed him aside and laughed as Nate staggered and tumbled over a faro table. His six-four frame sprawled across the floor. Silence fell over the saloon with all eyes staring at him. Ignoring Nate's floundering, Tom poured himself a glassful from Nate's jug and gulped it down in one swallow.

Nate struggled to his feet and slammed the toe of his boot squarely into Tom's rear. "I'm goin' to ssstomp your butt," he yelled just before Tom's left fist slammed into his belly. "Uuuuh!" erupted between Nate's lips. He staggered backward, trying to get air into his lungs. Tom lunged toward him with his head lowered like a Mexican bull. His head plowed into Nate's belly. Another "Uuuuh!" burst from Nate's mouth as he slumped to the floor. Whiskey had sheared his strength much the way Delilah had subdued Samson with a haircut.

Nate awoke with Doc Spoon moving an open bottle of aromatic spirits of ammonia beneath his nose. Sizzling noises echoed in his head and nausea gripped his stomach as he struggled to sit up. "Damn, I'm sick."

Nate spent the night in agony while nurturing a growing dislike for Tom Albert. By morning he had vowed to even things up, no matter how long it might take.

\* \* \* \* \*

Nate and Hap soon discovered Henry Cardin, Buffalo's historian in residence. Every town in the West had someone like Henry who could enlighten any stranger about the goings-on of the area since its creation. Truth and fiction got confused in Henry's mind as he entertained strangers with his tall stories. Hap listened to the old trapper telling colorful tales while sitting on a bench next to the forge in Tettleton's Blacksmith Shop just off the main street.

"Ol' Runs-With-Limp were plum dead," Henry Cardin said to Hap. "I could tell from his gazin' up at me where he were layin' down at the bottom of Scutter's Rav-een. That's just t'other side of Powder River Pass, y'know. One leg were folded together like a closed-up pocket knife. His Sharps lay t'one side with its stock busted clean off. He were dead all right. No doubt about that."

"What kilt him?"

"Well, it 'peared like he was throw'd into that rav-een. I figger a mountain cat jumped him up on the cliff above Scutter's Rav-een. His back were all clawed up but nuthin' had et on him."

"Don't reckon a grizzly kilt him?"

Henry Cardin, dressed in filthy buckskins, leaned toward the forge and spat. "Aw, no, weren't no grizz'. A grizz' would have buried him until he got rank, then he'd dig him up and et him. Nope. Weren't no grizz'."

"Well, I declare, was Ol' Runs-With-Limp some kind o' chief of them Cheyenne?"

"Med'cine man. He were a med'cine man. He weren't no ordinary Cheyenne, neither. I 'member the first time he limped into my camp up in the Bitter Root Mountains. Night were comin' on. A mountain flurry had just started. Them flakes big as saucers fallin' into my fire sizzled like bacon fryin'. This here Indun dressed up in winter skins came skippin' along givin' out a real sickly soundin' chant, 'Eee—Yaa—Hee—Yaa—Nee.' Right off, I could tell he were tetched. Afore he'd eat any of the grizz' I had a roastin' on the fire, he pulled a deerskin pouch out o' his satchel. He dumped what was in it out onto the ground and sat there stirrin' them things with his finger. All of a sudden he jumped up and danced around that fire yellin' somethin' fierce."

"What things were in the pouch?"

"They were med'cine. Y'understand? They was things like bear claws, elk teeth, eagle talons and stuff tied into a furry ball. Don't ast me how they do it, but med'cine men can purdict most anythin' just lookin' at that stuff."

"Well, Henry, I've got t'get on down t'Lawyer Cobb's. He's got some maps for me and Nate t'look over."

"Awright, better watch ol' Cobb. He's good at gettin' to folks."

\* \* \* \* \*

"Come on in Mister Dugger," Frank Cobb said when Hap opened the door to Cobb's office. "I was just showing Mister Hamby some of these maps."

Cobb was sitting behind his big oak desk that was covered by a maze of papers strewn across it. Red suspenders stretched across the lawyer's bulging belly. An Indian skull, a quart of whiskey and a chewing tobacco humidor sat on a shelf behind his high-backed leather chair. An old tarnished brass spittoon, surrounded by stains from near misses, sat next to his chair. Cobb's bloodshot eyes blinked while he peered through steel-rimmed pinch spectacles perched near the end of his bulbous nose, blushed red from too much whiskey.

"Yeah, come over here and look at this map," Nate said to Hap.

"Ol' Henry Cardin says the Cheyennes won't let us graze any of the high meadows."

"Ol' Henry is a spinner of tall tales," Cobb chortled. "You can't believe most of what he says. The Army has cleaned out most all of the hostiles."

Cobb walked around his desk, leaned over and looked at the map. "I've ridden over a lot of this country," he said, moving his finger over the map. "I believe this area up on Little Goose Creek is where you men need to build your spread. There are some good high meadows above there in the mountains. Most of that area will be available for open range grazing in the summer. If you take advantage of those meadows, your ranch on Little Goose Creek will have better grass for wintering your herd."

"Sounds good to me," Nate said. "Can you get all the legal descriptions ready to make our claims and applications to buy land up there?"

"Yes, I've hired Dewitt Jones down at Cheyenne to come up and do the surveying."

"When can we ride up to Little Goose Creek?"

"Whenever you want. How about tomorrow morning?"

Next day, the three men rode between the white-crowned Bighorn peaks and a lake named after Father Pierre Jean de Smet, an early missionary to the Flathead Indians in the Bitter Root Valley of Montana. "Ain't seen nothin' that blue afore," Hap said, pointing toward the cobalt-blue water cradled in the reddish-brown sandy valley below.

The farther north they rode, the more spectacular the green phalanxes of conifers became as they spread over the foothills. Herds of mule deer, spooked from their bedding grounds by the riders, bounded up the rocky hillsides like leaping kangaroos.

The polished gravel on the bottom of Little Goose Creek shimmered as clear water cascaded along its meandering course. Grassy hills from the eastern horizon to the snow-capped Bighorns had taken on varying hues of green. Melting snow covering the watershed was at the peak of the spring runoff. Cobb, Nate, and Hap were silenced by the view as they sat their horses on the mountainside.

Hap finally stepped off his gelding, knelt down, dug his fingers into the soft earth and plucked out a handful. He held it beneath his nose and sniffed its awakening fragrance. "Nate, I mean t'tell ya, ol' Cobb has found us one piece o' God's earth."

Cobb stood in his stirrups and swept his hand in a wide arc

from north to southeast. "You're going to own all this. Little Goose Creek will be right in the center of your ranch from here to well past the Bozeman Trail. About a mile down there on the north bank of the creek is a grove of pine, box elder and cottonwoods. That would be a good place for your main buildings."

Nate thumped Cobb on the shoulder. "This is goin' to be one fine place to live. Soon as Jones gets the surveyin' done why don't you ride back to Cheyenne with him and take care of all the legal work?"

"That's what I plan to do."

* * * * *

They named their ranch the Wagon Box. Dewitt Jones discovered the old Wagon Box battle site to be on their land. The battle got its name in 1867 when soldiers from nearby Fort Phil Kearny successfully fought off an Indian attack from an improvised fort of wagon boxes.

Nate and Hap spent the summer and autumn of 1884 building a house and pole-shed on Little Goose Creek. Nate ordered supplies from Cheyenne, but they were slow in arriving. They had to be freighted from Rock Creek Station on the Union Pacific Railroad by John Hunton's ox-drawn wagons up the Medicine Bow Trail to Fort Fetterman. Then Gus Trabing's bullwhacker's hauled the supplies up the Bozeman Trail to the Wagon Box. During the summer, nine wagonloads of supplies arrived. The days were filled with sawing and hammering as the pair hurried to complete the house and a pole-shed before winter.

When the buildings were completed in November, they rode to the 76 Ranch to purchase a hundred and fifty head of cattle from Moreton Frewen. He was a wealthy Englishman who had come to Wyoming in 1879, establishing his ranch at the junction of Powder River's three forks. Frewen built a large two-storied log house whose grandeur was unequaled at the time. The locals called it "Frewen's Castle."

"Welcome to the 76 Ranch, gentlemen," Frewen said as he shook hands with them. "My foreman says you are starting a ranch up on Little Goose Creek."

"Yes, sir, we are," Nate replied. "We are interested in

buyin' some stock.  Col. Peabody over at Fort McKinney tells me you might be able to help us."

"I might, Mr. Hamby, but before we talk about that, I'd like to say something about your enterprise."

"What's on your mind?"

"You are settling on my land.  My cattle range into that area and it's an unwritten law out here that whoever uses the land has first claim to it.  Do you follow me, sir?"

Nate sensed the need for tactful diplomacy.  This Englishman seemed straightforward and he was a powerful open range cattleman.  Nate nodded.  "Yes, I believe I do."

"Ah, yes, then won't you gentlemen have a seat.  Would you care for a cigar?"

"No, thanks," Nate said.

"Some whiskey, perhaps?" Frewen asked as they sat down in chairs upholstered in buffalo hide.

"No, thank you," Nate said before Hap could respond.

"Well, now, gentlemen, I'd like to hear your response to what I said about the land you're settling on."

"I appreciate your claim to that land, Mister Frewen, but we have legal possession of it."

"Maybe so, but you know as well as I that claims and purchases from the government take three to five years to finalize.  I've plenty of time, as you Yankees say, to toss a rattler into your bed."

Nate's ire swelled at being called a Yankee.  "Mister Frewen, I'm not a Yankee.  I'm a loyal son of Virginia.  I defended my home against the Yankees."

Moreton Frewen was startled by Nate's response.  "I apologize.  I meant no insult.  I must confess my ignorance in such matters.  Please forgive me, sir."

Hap picked dried mud from the heel of his boot as he sat with his bowed legs crossed.  "Well sir, Mister Frewen, me and Nate fought that war on opposite sides.  He was a Reb and I were a Yank.  We've settled that between us.  Reckon we're all Yanks, now?"

Hap's comments quieted Nate.  The war *was* over.  "Yes, Hap, I s'pose we are.  I apologize, Mister Frewen."

"Very well, but you must not take lightly my claim to that land. How do you propose we can resolve our dispute?"

Nate pondered the question. Regardless of what Moreton Frewen claimed, they had established legal possession of their land. Cobb had taken care of that. "Well, I don't believe there is anythin' to resolve. It did belong to the government; now it belongs to us. I might add, your grazin' area covers many times more land than we have claimed."

"You have a point, sir, however, you gentlemen had better be prepared to deal with me and my lawyers in this dispute. Enough of that, you expressed an interest in purchasing cattle from me?"

"Yes, that's why we're here," Nate replied. "Are you interested in sellin' us a hundred and fifty head of your prime stock?"

"Yes, I am. I have over six thousand on my north range that we will be gathering during spring roundup. If you join us we will cut them out for you."

"What's your askin' price?" Nate inquired.

"Ten dollars for longhorn yearlings and calves—fifteen for cows and steers—twenty for bulls."

"Longhorns all you got?" Hap asked.

"No, I have a fair number of Herefords, but I prefer Texas longhorns. They do better on arid range land."

"We don't want longhorns. A lot o' the Wagon Box range is covered with good bluestem grass."

"That's right," Nate added, "and there's plenty of water in all the creeks. Herefords will do just fine."

"They will cost you two-dollars a head more."

"Make it a dollar."

"That's provided you let us pick out the stock we want," Hap added.

"Done," Frewen said as they shook hands on the deal. "I'll send you word when to meet my men."

Riding back to the Wagon Box, Nate pondered Frewen's threat. He and Hap had worked too many years to give up their ranch. They would fight Frewen or anyone else if necessary.

"Reckon old Frewen will toss a rattler at us?" Hap said as

they rode toward the ranch house next to Little Goose Creek.

"I reckon he might."

* * * * *

The following month, on the 28th of December, Cobb pulled a flask from his hip pocket. "You want a drink?"

"No, thanks," Nate said.

"Well, I do hate to drink alone," Cobb wheezed and filled a tumbler with booze..

Nate handed Cobb a letter he had received from the Cheyenne Land Office. "I want your legal opinion about this

Cobb nodded, slipped on his spectacles and unfolded the letter. "When did you get this?"

"This mornin'."

"I see," he said, and began to read the letter aloud. "Please be informed that a formal protest to your homesteading and land acquisition purchases on Little Goose Creek has been filed with this office. Secretary Thomas Adams, acting on behalf of the Wyoming Stock Growers Association, has requested that your patents and titles be declared invalid on the grounds that you bore arms against the U. S. Government during the Civil War. Our office requests that you file your reply within thirty days. Sincerely, Clayton Babcock."

"What do you think?"

"Don't worry about Adams's protest. It doesn't amount to anything. Congress settled this question with the Amnesty Act in seventy-two."

"Does that law apply to homesteading?"

"Yeah, it applies. Adams's protest is a bluff. Forget it."

"It may be a bluff, but Frewen has vowed to toss a rattler into my bed."

"Oh, you believe Frewen is behind this?"

"Who else? He's the WSGA in these parts."

"Yeah, I suppose so," Cobb said, folding up the letter. "Frewen and his cronies sure don't want anybody homesteading anywhere in Wyoming."

"I wonder why he agreed to sell cattle to Hap and me."

Cobb chuckled and slurped a long draft from his tumbler. "Frewen may be a pompous Englishman, but he ain't against turning a profit. I wager he did all right on his deal with you."

"No doubt about that. It didn't cost him a penny to market those beeves."

Cobb emptied the tumbler with several sips and belched as he looked over his spectacles at Nate. "Well, you let me handle this. By the way, did you know Tom Albert is hanging around Buffalo a lot these days?"

"No... any idea why?"

"Oh, yes, he's got his eye on our pretty little schoolmarm."

Nate pondered the enmity that had replaced his friendship with Tom. Tom was overly ambitious, impatient, aggressive, determined and had a way with women. All of these traits made him a formidable adversary, no matter in what area of endeavor. Nate was angrier with himself than Tom. The ranch had become his sole interest, leaving little time for anything else. He picked up the letter and stuffed it into his vest pocket without saying a word.

Cobb frowned as Nate stood up to leave. "There's a dance out at the fort Saturday night. Why don't you ask Beth to go with you?"

"I'll think on it."

"What's there to think about?"

Nate massaged his useless right arm as he pondered Cobb's challenge. He hadn't danced since before the war. The quadrille and Virginia reel, which were the only dances that he knew, required two good arms and hands; something that he didn't possess anymore. "Well, Let me know anything you find out about Babcock's letter. I've got to get some supplies over at Foote's,"

"If I was twenty years younger, I'd go ask her for myself," Cobb called as Nate left.

After leaving Cobb's office, Nate and Robert Foote began loading Nate's wagon with supplies in front of Foote's store. One question continued to bother Nate. If Cobb was right, why did Adams protest to the land department?

Johnson County Sheriff Frank Canton ambled up to Nate's matched team of dapple-gray draft horses and began to look them over.

Frank M. Canton, whose real name was Joseph Horner, was sheriff of Johnson County from 1882 to 1886 when he would lose the race for re-election to W. G. "Red" Angus. He was born in 1849 in Virginia, and had spent most of his youth in Texas where he got into trouble with the Texas Rangers. He finally left Texas following several shooting scrapes. He was also accused of bank robbery, rustling and assault with intent to kill. Joseph Horner had arrived in Ogallala, Nebraska in 1878 as Frank Canton, bossing a trail herd of twenty-five hundred head of cattle. From Ogallala, his trek into the West carried him to the new settlement of Buffalo on the eastern slopes of Wyoming's Bighorn Mountains. He was ironfisted, arrogant and determined to have his way. He was liked by some but feared by many. He was a diligent sheriff for Johnson County, excelling in keeping the peace. Outlaws avoided him because of his reputation. Following his loss to Red Angus, Canton would wear a range detective badge for the Wyoming Stock Growers' Association.

"These horses belong to you, Mr. Hamby?" he asked, rubbing one horse on the shoulder.

Nate slid a sack of potatoes into the back of the wagon. "Yes, they do."

"They are a handsome team. What breed are they?"

"Percheron."

"Where'd you get them if you don't mind telling?"

"From a neighbor."

"You work cattle with them?

Nate laughed. "Hardly."

"Yes, I'd say you're farming the Wagon Box. That right, Mr. Hamby?"

"Some, along Little Goose Creek."

Canton nodded. "Then, you've been building fences?"

"You can't harvest hay on grassland bein' grazed."

"I suppose not. The WSGA isn't going to look kindly on barbwire fences."

Nate climbed onto the wagon seat. "You're right about that. Who sent you over here, your crony, Tom Albert?"

Canton said nothing.

Nate snapped the reins. "Get up hosses."

As he reined his team northward toward home, Nate eyed a gray mare hitched to a new surrey with patent leather fenders parked in front of the schoolhouse. "Whoa," he called, tied his reins to the brake lever, jumped to the ground and walked around the rig, admiring its elaborate leather seats and brass trim. *This looks like something Tom Albert would own*, Nate thought, running his hand over the sleek black fender. *Well, he's just who I want to see.*

"Hello," Beth said as Nate walked in.

Nate smiled. "Hello!"

Tom, sitting in one of the student seats, blew cigar smoke toward Nate. "Howdy." He chewed on his cigar and sneered. "I'm sure glad to see you."

Nate glared at him. "I just talked with Sheriff Canton. Why don't you make threats for the WSGA yourself?"

Tom continued to gnaw on his cigar. His reply through clenched teeth was garbled. "Better listen to him."

Nate handed Babcock's letter to him. "You got anythin' to do with this?"

Tom read the letter and handed it back. "No."

"I don't believe you."

"Well, no matter, looks like you got trouble."

"Cobb says it's a bluff."

"Hah—maybe so—maybe not."

Anger and jealousy coursed through Nate as he stared at Tom. The WSGA was determined to steal his and Hap's land. Now their chief enforcer was determined to come between him and Beth. Cobb was right. He had to do something. "There's goin' to be a dance out at Fort McKinney Saturday night," he said, turning toward Beth. "Would you like to go?"

Beth blushed and glanced at Tom. "I'm sorry. Tom just asked me to go with him."

A smirk spread across Tom's face as he blew smoke toward the ceiling. "I hear Patience Smythe is a real whiz at the quadrillion. Why don't y'ask her?"

Nate's left hand hovered over the grip of his .45. Rage raced through the sinews of his hand, but Beth's presence stayed that final move to draw down on the smirking face of Tom Albert.

# Chapter Five

The 1885 spring roundup on the 76 Ranch lasted nearly two weeks. Frewen, true to his word, sold them 150 head of prime Herefords, each of them selected by Nate or Hap. Several of the 76 Ranch hands helped drive the herd to Wagon Box grasslands along Little Goose Creek where the cattle grew fat and reproduced with a good calf crop during the summer. The ensuing winter of 1885-86 was unseasonably mild for Wyoming. The herd wintered well, but the spring of 1886 would bring change to the Wagon Box.

Cobb hitched up his buggy and drove out to the Wagon Box. The reason for Adams' protest lay inside his valise. It was a letter from the U.S. land office in Washington, D.C.

"I should have known Adams was shooting dice with that protest," Cobb said. While Nate read the letter, Cobb continued. "You can see that amnesty by President Johnson in sixty-nine and congress in seventy-two clears you on that count."

"Yeah, but what's this about Dewitt Jones's survey bein' wrong?"

"Well, that's the rub. Jones screwed up somehow in filing his survey. He's got six months to get it corrected."

Nate wadded up the letter and slammed it on the ground. "Damn Tom Albert and the WSGA."

As Cobb pulled a whiskey flask from his pocket, he peered over his spectacles at Nate. "We don't have any choice but to comply."

"Yeah, I reckon so."

Cobb uncorked his flask, swallowed several gulps of whiskey and offered it to Nate.

Nate shook his head, pushing the flask away. "Go ahead— see when Jones can get it straightened out."

The summer of 1886 parched the high plains of Wyoming. Cloudless skies brought a drought, a harbinger of worse to come. Nate, Hap, and four cowhands rode up the eastern slopes of the

Bighorns to round up their cattle from summer range. The sights and aromas of fall were in the air. The pine, fir and spruce-covered mountainsides were spattered with patches of gold, the kiss of frost having yellowed the groves of quaking aspen. The horses' hooves crunched across steep inclines covered with tinder-dry pine needles. After riding fifteen miles into the mountains, they made camp at Twin Lakes.

Gathering the cattle required two days of hard riding. At dawn of the third day, they broke camp, packed their gear and headed down-country toward the Wagon Box. The herd stretched out into a long red and white stream of bellowing critters. Cowboys yelped, gathered strays and drove the beeves along the banks of Little Goose Creek. Several hundred hooves slashed the drought-hardened ground into powder and sent a thick cloud of dust into the sky above the herd. Nate coughed, spat muddy spittle and tied his kerchief below his eyes to keep from breathing the stifling grit.

The sooty cloud began to clear as quickening winds howled across the mountains. Nate looked at the summits. Dark clouds were tumbling over them, ushering in the severest winter Wyoming would experience for decades. Nate waved at Hap on the other side of the herd. "Hey, Hap!" he yelled, pointing toward the coming storm. "Push 'em hard. There's a blizzard comin'."

Hap pulled a jacket from behind his saddle and waved it over his head. "Hah! Hah!"

Everyone began to shout. The red and white phalanx of bellowing critters erupted into a frenzy. Boiling dust and white flakes mingled above the herd as they raced toward the Wagon Box boundary fence nearly a mile away.

As the last steer trotted through the gate, Nate pulled down his kerchief and wiped grime from his face. "We've got a real blue-norther' abrewin'."

"Yep, that's for certain," Hap said, slipping on his sheepskin parka.

The wind suddenly turned Arctic, pelting their faces with biting flakes as they rode into the corral. By the time the horses were fed, blowing snow obscured the ranch house. The frigid grip of the blizzard was beginning to squeeze life from Wyoming.

Icy winds swirling over Wyoming sculpted long drifts across the high plains and turned all of the creeks into silver ribbons of ice. The sounds of picks and axes chopping holes through the ice were constant. Bellowing beasts crowded around these sources of water, but the plummeting temperature quickly closed them. Keeping them open turned into an unending and exhausting task.

All over Wyoming, within a week, snow and ice entombed all of the stunted grass. If any cattle were to survive, they would have to be fed hay forked from wagons. All too soon, the stacks of hay were gone and cattle strayed in search of anything to eat. The knell of howling winter winds continued. Not till the ides of March brought gaggles of geese winging northward did the winds cease. Warm Chinook winds would soon reveal how devastating the winter of eighty-six had been.

The melting drifts and ice-bound rivers during March and April of 1887 revealed gruesome evidence of the slaughter. Carcasses of frozen cattle filled ravines, cluttered the plains and tumbled along with chunks of ice in cascading rivers. As the days grew warmer, large winged visitors soared overhead. The season of vultures dawned upon the high plains as these great birds vacated warmer climes to feed upon the dead dreams of Wyoming's cattlemen. Packs of hoary timber wolves, grown fat from feeding on ice-entrapped cattle, continued to prey upon the nearly starved survivors.

There were other scavengers beside vultures and wolves that preyed upon Wyoming cattlemen during the year of 1887. Over ninety percent of their herds perished between winter's first snow and the spring thaw. Receivership and bankruptcy touched many of the big and small cattle companies. Their misfortune provided welcome opportunities for scavengers that could raise enough capital to buy them out. One of those opportunists was Tom Albert. It was for a pittance of its value that he bought the M-W Stock Company, which covered over 100,000 acres along the Montana-Wyoming border.

Nate, Hap, and their hands took to the saddle as soon as they could ride out to search for the remnants of their herd. Their foreman, Bill Maner, divided the hands into pairs and assigned each a portion of the Wagon Box to cover.

Maner was a true Texican cowboy. He had ridden up from Texas in 1882 to the Whitehall Ranch in Montana. He worked as a wrangler and then as their foreman for two years before hiring on as the Wagon Box foreman. Bill was a quiet man. When he spoke, it amounted to something. In his opinion, casual conversation was a waste of time. He was tall and skinny and Hap claimed that his legs were bowed wide enough for a full-grown hog to shinny between.

It proved to be a dismal affair. A rotten stench greeted them as Nate and Hap neared a deep coulee nearly five miles from the ranch headquarters. They sat their horses on the coulee's edge and peered into its depths. Dozens of bloated and decaying Hereford carcasses covered the bottom of the ravine.

"Well, Nate, there's a lot o' dead-eyes down there."

"Yeah, all of them ours." Nate reined about and spurred his sorrel into a gallop.

They rode all day and didn't find a single survivor. Every dry-gulch and valley was littered with carcasses of cattle that had sought refuge only to find death. They rode into a grove of willow and box elder trees late in the evening. The bark had been stripped and all of the small branches eaten as high as an animal could reach. Hap pointed at bare tree trunks. "Look what them poor devils done."

"We've lost our herd."

"Yeah, I reckon we might as well head back in the mornin'."

Upon their returning, Bill Maner walked from the corral but he couldn't face Nate or Hap. Instead, he turned and gazed at the poor critters that he and the other hands had brought back. "Well, fellers," Bill said, "them forty-one skin and bone white-face is all we found. The rest are swolled up in coulees all over the Wagon Box."

"Rotting carcasses were *all* we found," Nate said.

"They even ate bark off of trees tryin' t'stay alive," Hap added, stepping out of his stirrup. He ambled over to the corral and leaned on the top rail. "You bags o' bones," he yelled, venting his anger at the survivors. "There ain't enough meat on all o' ya t'fill a coyote's belly."

Without speaking, Nate dismounted and led his sorrel toward the barn.

Nate stared at flames dancing about the fireplace while pondering how they could keep from losing the Wagon Box. Hap pulled out a pouch of chewing tobacco, stuffed a wad into his mouth and offered the pouch to Nate. "Want a chew?"

"No, thanks," Nate said, reaching for a jug of Jack Daniels

After several swaps of the jug, Hap said, "How we goin' to rebuild? Ain't got enough money left t'buy stock."

"I reckon it comes down to borrowin' or stealin'.'"

Hap chomped on his chaw and spat into the fireplace. "Well sir, I reckon there ain't no fit critters left in Wyomin'.'"

"There may be some longhorns. Like Frewen said, they're better at stayin' alive."

Hap guffawed. "Just think we could've bought longhorns. Ain't that a pity?"

"I'll ride into Buffalo in the mornin' and see if Cobb can help us get a loan," Nate said, shoving the whiskey jug aside. "I'm turnin' in so I can get an early start."

Nate rode across the Clear Creek Bridge, down Main Street past the Occidental Hotel and Foote's store. There wasn't a horse, wagon or buggy in sight. The usual loiterers that chewed, spit and whittled were nowhere to be seen.

Cobb was napping beneath an old buffalo robe. An empty whiskey bottle lay on the floor. He was unshaved, reeked of whiskey and did not rouse when Nate called to him. "Cobb! Wake up! I need to talk with you." Cobb continued to snore. Nate gently slapped his face. "It's me, Nate Hamby. Wake up."

Cobb's eyes eased open. "What are you doing here?"

"We'll lose the Wagon Box if we don't get a loan."

Cobb blinked, smacked his lips and reached for the bottle. "This is empty," he said, tossing it onto the floor. "If you don't mind, hand me that jug of sour mash setting in the bookshelf."

Nate uncorked the jug and handed it to Cobb. "Do you think Mister Buell would make us a loan?"

"Buell?" Cobb sat up, eased the jug to his lips and sipped a couple of mouthfuls. "He just holds folk's money in his safe. He ain't in the lending business."

"You got any ideas?"

"Well, let's see." Cobb offered the jug to Nate. "Have some."

"No, thanks, still got a thumpin' head from last night."

"Money's scarce. The blizzard bankrupted most everybody."

"We've got good collateral."

"Not till we get cleared on the survey question."

"When is Jones going to fix the survey?"

"Don't rightly know. Maybe P. C. Slack would make you a loan."

"Slack?"

"Yeah, I've written up notes on a couple of loans he's made."

"Slack's cozy with Canton and the WSGA. He does a lot of business with them."

Cobb nodded and sipped from his jug. "I reckon, ain't anybody else in Buffalo to ask."

"Well, I'll go ask him," Nate said and left for Slack's Livery.

P. C. Slack was a curmudgeon. Stringy white hair flopped over his eyes like the bangs of a sheep dog. His mood was surly which had won him few friends and a growing cadre of enemies. He continued to punch rivet holes in leather harness with an awl as Nate closed the tack-shed door.

"Howdy, Mister Slack," Nate said, walking toward Slack's workbench.

Slack grunted, "Hmmph," without looking up.

"Sorry to bother you—I need to talk business."

Slack grimaced, probably surmising Nate wanted to borrow money. He appeared reluctant, but had never turned down an opportunity to make a profit. "How much you need?" he asked, continuing to punch holes.

"Four-thousand to restock."

"A thousand is all I can loan."

"Only one thousand?"

"Yeah, provided you put up your ranch as collateral."

"The Wagon Box?" Nate said, realizing that Slack was dickering for a cheap buyout if the debt was defaulted. "Our spread is worth close to twenty thousand."

"Well, you can take it or leave it."

"Reckon I'll have t'leave it."

Nate rode the Bozeman Trail toward home, determined to survive with or without a loan.

As Nate crossed Piney Creek while returning from Buffalo, a bullet slammed against a boulder beside the trail. Nate yanked his Colt from its holster and leaped to the ground. His gelding bucked into a frenzied gallop and disappeared over a sage-covered hill.

Nate crouched, scanning the rolling grassland. Several minutes went by with not a thing moving except tall bluestem swaying in the wind. Then he heard the sound of hooves in full gallop. A sorrel with its rider leaning low dashed out of a gully less than fifty yards away. Nate drew a bead ahead of the rider with his long-barreled Colt. The forty-five roared. The rider reeled, his hat flying from his head, but he did not fall as the sorrel galloped away carrying its hatless rider toward Buffalo.

Nate found the nearly new black Stetson with two holes where his bullet had pierced the crown. Inside were several strands of black hair and a few flecks of blood. Nate poked his fingers through the holes while pondering who the hat's owner might be.

The sun had nearly settled behind the Bighorn peaks when Nate finally caught his horse. It was too late for chasing after the gunman, but he was determined to find the hat's owner.

With each mile, Nate's anger mounted. It had been a trying day. Nearly getting shot by a gunman and an hour spent in running down his spooked horse had been infuriating.

The sorrel gelding charged through the corral gate with Nate's spurs feathering its flanks. The horse champed his bit and swished his tail, cantering toward the shed. Nate yanked on the reins and jumped out of his stirrup.

"That ain't no way t'treat a good hoss," Hap yelled, walking from the house.

Nate untied the shooter's hat from behind the cantle of his

saddle. "Yeah, you're right, but this blockhead is a poor excuse for a horse."

Hap spat and wiped his mouth with his glove. "Where'd y'get that hat?"

"Shot it off the back-shooter that tried to drygulch me."

"Somebody took a shot at ya?"

"Sure did."

"Who were it?"

"Don't know," Nate said, pulled his saddle off the gelding and carried it toward the tack shed.

"Where'd he take his shot?"

"Down at the Piney Creek crossin'."

"Y'got any idee who this hat belongs ta?" Hap asked after Nate handed him the Stetson.

"Well, whoever it is has got a sore head. You can see his hair and blood next to the holes made by my bullet."

Whoever owned the black Stetson had to be somebody living in Buffalo, Nate surmised. He was equally convinced that Tom knew who the owner was. He intended to ask him.

"Over behind that clay bank is where the back-shooter waited for me," Nate said, riding over the Piney Creek crossing.

"That ain't very far," Hap said. "He's gotta be a mighty poor shot missin' ya from there."

"Well, no matter, I'm goin' to find him."

They rode into Buffalo just before noon. Tom's surrey and horse were tied to the hitching rail in front of Cobb's office. Johnson County Sheriff Red Angus walked out of the Occidental and called out his greeting. "Howdy, fellas, what brings you back to town, Nate?"

W. G. "Red" Angus, new to being a lawman, had spent his life tending bar in saloons, the latest being Katie's place. A rancher and newspaper reporter, Jack Flagg, had talked Red into running for sheriff against Frank Canton in the election of 1886. Angus, in contrast to Canton, came across as being "common", "salt o' the earth" and a friend you could trust. Flagg's influence was significant in the election. That influence bore fruit since he was one of the many farmers and small ranch owners in Johnson County. The outnumbered WSGA cattlemen did not have enough votes to re-elect Canton.

Nobody in Buffalo was certain just where Red came from. He just showed up one day, riding alone into town. He worked bar for Charlie Buell for several months before being hired by Katie. Her bar was long, needing two tenders, so she hired Red to work with Homer. Cowboys, farmers, soldiers from Fort McKinney and even most of the WSGA cattlemen liked Red. Like many other immigrants to this new frontier straddled by towering mountains, Red probably had left some other place he had wanted to, or maybe had to leave. Nobody seemed to know; none really cared. Red was one of them.

Red Angus was built like a wrestler. His round face, crowned by sandy hair, sported a sweeping mustache of the same hue. His gait was determined and swift. He was pleasant natured and tolerant which was probably acquired from years of handling men grown mean or frisky from too much whiskey.

"Come here," Nate said. "I'll show you."

They dismounted and tied their horses to Cobb's hitching rail. Nate handed the Stetson to Red. "You know who this belongs to?"

Sheriff Angus examined it. "You put these holes in here?"

"Sure did. He tried to dry-gulch me out at Piney Creek crossing. I shot off this bonnet and from the blood and hair inside, I'd say he's got a fair headache today."

Red pulled out the sweatband. "Yes, I'd say so—it looks nearly new; no stains around the brim."

"You can see by the hair stuck in the hat that he's dark headed."

"I can see that." Red replaced the sweatband. "Let's walk over to the store and see if our man bought this from Mr. Foote."

Robert Foote took the hat from Sheriff Angus. "You recognize this Stetson?" Red asked.

Foote pushed his fingers through the bullet holes and turned the hat over to look inside. "Well, can't say, but I did sell a Stetson like this to Frank Canton 'bout a month ago.

"Canton, you say?"

"Yes, he came in wearing his old fur cap, saying he needed a new hat before riding down to Cheyenne on business."

Nate grabbed the hat. "I'm goin' to see Tom."

"I'm going with you," Angus said.

Hap and Angus followed Nate into Cobb's office. Nate handed the Stetson to Tom. "You know whose hat this is?"

Tom raised his eyebrows. "Why do you think I might know that? The country is full of black hats."

"Have you seen Frank Canton lately?"

Tom turned the Stetson over and stared at the bloodstains. "What's he got to do with this hat?"

"I think you know the answer to that. The back-shooter wearin' that hat tried to dry-gulch me yesterday. My money says it was Frank Canton."

"Hey, wait a minute. Are you sayin' I'm responsible? Canton's job is run by Secretary Adams, not me."

"I don't buy that."

Tom shoved back his chair and stood up. "Nate, we've been friends a long time. Why would I order Canton to murder you?"

Nate's voice quivered. "Friends? I've questioned that since you sold your soul to the WSGA. You don't care about Hap and me anymore. Now, are you goin' to tell me where Canton is?"

Tom glanced at Hap. "I can't believe what you're sayin'. You're dead wrong. Sure, I work for the WSGA. Most of our members are good men. We want to keep the grasslands open range, but we don't go around bushwhackin'. Secretary Adams wouldn't stand for that. As for Frank Canton, I have no idea where he is."

Nate clenched his teeth and grabbed the Stetson. "I don't believe you. I'm goin' to give you one more chance to tell me where Canton's hidin'. If he doesn't have a bullet crease in his scalp, I'll take back everythin'."

Tom shook his head. "I wish I could help you, but I don't know where he is."

"Nate's got ever' right t'be sore as a cut yearlin'," Hap said. "It 'pears Canton took a shot at 'im. Like Nate says, if he don't got no .45 track on his noggin, he ain't guilty. Y'ain't knowin' where we might check his hair?"

"That sounds reasonable, Tom," Sheriff Angus said.

Tom pulled out a cheroot, rolled the cigar between his

fingers and pondered Nate's request.     "If Canton tried to drygulch you, he's turned into a loose arrow. I just don't know where he is. I'll tell you what I'll do.  Give me twenty-four hours and I'll bring him in myself."

Sheriff Angus looked at Nate. "That's fair.  We'd all like the truth about Canton."

"All right," Nate said. "You've got your twenty-four hours. If you fail, I want you to understand right now that I'll go after him myself.  If he does have a creased scalp, he's goin' to tell me who gave him the order to dry-gulch me.  Whoever that is, I'm goin' to settle with him.  Personally!"

# Chapter Six

Tom found a big sorrel with a white blaze and white stockings halfway to the hocks of both hind legs in the 76 Ranch corral. These were the markings of Frank Canton's horse, Old Fred.

Tom stepped out of his stirrup and climbed over the corral fence to look over the sorrel. He found the horse to be sound with the exception of a distinct limp favoring his right hind leg. A closer examination revealed that the pastern was swollen from the fetlock to the hoof. Such an injury made the horse too lame to be ridden.

Jim Fulgrim, the 76 foreman, walked with a plodding gait from the bunkhouse toward the corral. Jim was skinny as a pine sapling, bowlegged, and had a grin filled with tobacco-stained teeth.

"Howdy, Tom," he said around a Bull Durham cigarette dangling from his lips.

Tom stroked the sorrel's withers and glanced at Jim. "Howdy, Jim."

"What drags your sorry butt out here?" Jim said, opening the corral gate.

"I'm lookin' for Frank Canton. Is this his sorrel?"

"Yep, that's Old Fred."

"Frank inside?"

"Nope, took one o' our horses and shagged out last night after supper."

"He say where he was headed?"

Jim flipped ashes from his cigarette. "Nope, just said he'd be back t'get Old Fred."

"When?"

"Didn't say."

"Was he wearin' a black Stetson?"

"Nope, had on that ol' fur cap."

"Did he complain about a headache or a bump on the head?"

"Nope—what's this all about?"

"Hamby thinks Frank took a shot at him."

Jim blew smoke past his cigarette and gave Tom a toothy grin. "Well, hell, I wouldn't put it past him, but if he did, I don't think Hamby would be able to bitch none."

"Did you see which direction Frank headed?"

"Southwest."

"Thanks," Tom said, heading for the gate. "When Frank gets back, tell him I need to talk. It's important."

Tom's search for Canton took him southwest to the KC Ranch. Frank hadn't been there, according to 'Cookie Bill', one of the KC cooks. The only other place Tom could think of that he might have sought refuge was the old Bar C Ranch on the Middle Fork of Crazy Woman Creek. There was an abandoned shack in a blind canyon called the *Hole In The Wall* just south of the creek. Only one known trail led into the canyon, making it an ideal hideout. Tom rode northeast. He was running out of time.

The full moon flooded Hall's cabin down in the bowels of the oval canyon. In the future, it would be the hideout of Butch Cassidy, The Sundance Kid and other members of the *Hole in the Wall* gang. The canyon was less than a half-mile in length, cut off on the north side by trees and brush growing thickly below the rim of the canyon. Sheer red-sandstone walls enclosed the remainder of the canyon.

Tom sat his gelding on the canyon rim. In the depths, he could see the abandoned log shack that on occasion was occupied by outlaws and rustlers. Part of the sod roof was washed away exposing its rotting rafters. A thin column of smoke spiraled from the chimney and a hobbled bay grazed behind the shack. He wondered whether the bay had the 76 brand burned into its shoulder; if so, it would be the horse Frank Canton had borrowed from Jim Fulgrim. He had to get closer, just close enough to check the brand.

He stepped out of his stirrup, left his horse ground-hitched and walked down the trail into the shadows of the canyon. Twilight began to brush the red-sandstone walls with strokes of purple and indigo as darkness crept down the mountain's inclines. On the far side of the canyon, thousands of smoky bats were spewing like puffs of smoke from dark crevices etched deeply between palisades of sandstone. In the growing darkness, he could see lamplight coming through a lone window in the shack. He was confident that whoever was inside wouldn't see him.

He made his way around to the backside of the shack to get a closer look at the bay's brand. The grazing bay suddenly raised its head as Tom crept from the shelter of some scrub pines behind the shack. He stopped and stood still, hoping the wary horse would return to savoring the succulent grass, but it was a wish that wouldn't happen. The bay lifted its head and neighed, sending a warning echoing up and down the canyon.

A voice called from the evening shadows on the other side of the meadow, "Plant your boots. Who are you?"

"It's me," Tom yelled, recognizing Frank Canton's voice. "Tom Albert."

"What are you doin' out here?"

"Lookin' for you."

"You alone?"

"Yeah, I'm alone."

Canton stepped out of the shadows holding his Winchester by his side. His handlebar mustache cast a dark shadow over his chin as light from the rising moon bleached his face. "All the same, shuck that hog leg and toss it aside and then walk on over here."

Tom pulled his .45 from his holster and dropped it. He stood unarmed facing a man that could easily kill him with one bullet from his carbine. Nobody would be the wiser since the canyon was miles from the nearest ranch house. He knew Frank Canton wouldn't hesitate to drop him where he stood if he had the slightest doubt about Tom's visit.

Frank took a couple of steps toward Tom and brought the carbine to the ready. "Now kick that .45 away. If you're lyin', I'll plant your butt in this canyon."

Tom slowly raised his hands. He hoped Canton wouldn't shoot an unarmed man, but a chill crept into his chest as Canton brought the carbine to his shoulder. He stared at the Winchester's blue-steel barrel glinting in the moonlight and wondered when the last thing he'd see would be fire spurting from the muzzle. "Damn it," Tom said, his voice quivering like a willow in the wind. "I came out here to warn you about Nate and Angus."

Without lowering the carbine, Frank called another warning. "Spit out what y'got to say."

"Did you take a shot at Nate Hamby up at the Piney Creek crossin' day before yesterday?"

"Who says I did?"

"Nate's got a black Stetson he shot off whoever ambushed him. He and Sheriff Angus believe it's your hat."

"Who says I own a black Stetson?"

"Robert Foote says he sold you one about a month ago."

"Well, I reckon he did."

"You mind my lookin' at it?"

"It got stolen while I was down at Cheyenne a couple weeks ago."

"Well, if that's true, you're out of trouble," Tom said. "Unless, you have a bullet crease in your scalp?"

Frank continued to aim the Winchester without wavering or saying a word. Tom glanced about, hoping to see something that might afford him a chance to save himself. There was nothing except a rotting tree stump that jutted about two feet above the baked red-clay canyon floor. The stump was at least ten feet away, a long way to dive for cover and his .45 was a good five or six feet in the opposite direction. A double-shot Derringer nestled in its holster inside the top of his right boot, but it would be useless at the distance where Frank stood with his carbine. There was no other way to escape certain death if Canton chose to pull the trigger. He had to decide whether to dive for the stump or stand and face whatever Frank intended.

Frank suddenly yelled, "I ain't got no crease."

"Fine, then you won't mind ridin' back to Buffalo?" Tom said, pushing his luck to its limit. Such a suggestion was bound to set hard with the trigger finger of Frank Canton, the official WSGA enforcer. Tom was Frank's superior in the WSGA detective organization, but Frank seldom consulted him about his activities. He was loyal to whoever paid for his services. Once, that had been the good people of Johnson County, paying him to be their sheriff. Now, he was a hired gun for the powerful WSGA or anyone else with the price to pay for his talents. Tom disliked the man and was uneasy with his cunning nature.

Canton guffawed. "I ain't goin' to Buffalo with you or nobody else. Red Angus would throw me in jail."

"If you didn't ambush Nate, Angus can't do anything. I'll make certain of that."

Canton roared, "I ain't goin' back to Buffalo."

"You don't have much time left. I promised to have you in Buffalo within twenty-four hours."

"That's one damned promise you ain't keepin'. Get ready t'shake hands with Saint Peter."

"Before you pull that trigger," Tom said, struggling to speak with a tongue dry as a desert lakebed. "Hamby and Angus know I'm lookin' for ya. They'll be comin' if I don't return before their deadline."

Much to Tom's surprise, Frank's attitude suddenly changed. He lowered the carbine to the ready and began to walk toward Tom who wondered what move the cunning gunman was planning next. Frank stopped about ten paces closer and stood staring at Tom. "Well, Tom, you do have a point. I ain't hankerin' t'face a murder charge. Holster your .45 and let's palaver in the shack."

Tom stooped to enter the one-room log shack, the ridge beam to the floor being only six-feet. Frank lit a coal-oil lantern, and then he bolted into Tom, pinning him on the bunk. He yanked Tom's six-gun out of its holster and slammed it against Tom's head.

When Tom awakened, his wrists were tied, and Frank was dipping water from a bucket into a blackened coffee pot. "Sorry I had to do that," Frank said and placed the pot on glowing coals in the fireplace. "I told you I wasn't goin' back."

Tom struggled to sit up. His head throbbed and blood was trickling down the side of his face. He blinked, trying to focus on Frank. "What now?"

Frank opened the cupboard and pulled out a slab of bacon. "We're stayin' here for the time bein'," he said, as he carved several slices and laid them in a cast-iron skillet. "How about a little grub?"

"Maybe later—I'll take some of that coffee, though."

Frank filled two cups and handed one to Tom. Tom sipped from his and then stared at Frank. "I'd like to know one thing."

"What's that?"

"You've got a crease haven't you?"

"Yep."

"Why did you try to dry-gulch Nate?"

Frank flipped over each sizzling strip with a fork. "Well, the decision to take Nate Hamby down was made before Adams got the WSGA's secretary job. Six members of the WSGA made a list they wanted eliminated. Hamby and Dugger are on that list."

Tom gazed at Frank in disbelief. "You mean to say your people formed a vigilante committee without tellin' me?"

Frank piled bacon onto a tin plate, sliced several stale biscuits and placed them in the pan. "Fried biscuits go down real good. We didn't tell you since your former partners were on the list."

"Does Secretary Adams know about the vigilante list?"

"Ain't nobody been told."

"How come Hamby and Dugger are on that list?"

"They stole their ranch from Frewen's 76."

Tom frowned; knowing Nate and Hap had acquired their land legally. "Not true—they homesteaded and bought every acre."

"The 76 don't look at it that way."

"Who are the six vigilantes?"

"Ain't sayin'."

"Who else is on that list?"

Frank placed a plate of bacon and biscuits on Tom's lap. "Ain't sayin'."

Tom wagged his head in disbelief, believing there wasn't any need for vigilantes in Wyoming, not yet anyway. "Is Nate at the top of their list?"

"Yep," Frank replied, dipping a biscuit into his coffee.

Tom stared at the thong tied around his wrists. "Now what?"

"Ain't decided, that sort o' depends on you.   You with us....or not?"

Tom realized his reply could determine whether he lived or wound up buried in the red dirt of Hall's Canyon.   "Well, I'm not opposed to takin' out rustlers, but killin' Hamby and Dugger is a different matter."

Frank finished his meal in silence.

Tom slid his untouched plate onto the bunk.   "How about some more coffee?"

"Ain't you goin' to eat?"

"I'm not hungry."

Frank picked up Tom's plate.   "That's a shame."

* * * * *

At first light, Frank awakened, retied Tom's wrists behind his back and secured his ankles with several strands of rawhide. His mood was surly as he made another pot of coffee, which he drank himself without offering any to Tom.   After finishing his coffee, he jammed Tom's Colt behind his belt, and picked up his Winchester.   "I'm goin' t'ride up where the trail enters the canyon," he said, glaring at Tom.   "I figger Hamby and Angus will show up today."

Frank's comment did not require a response, so Tom gave none.

"Don't try gettin' away.   Y'ain't got no horse, 'sides there's only one way out and I'll be watchin'."

Tom had little doubt what Canton would do when he returned.   If he succeeded in drygulching Nate and Angus, a .45 slug would erase any witnesses.   *Got to get out o'here*, he thought, looking about the shack.   The gray smoke rising up the chimney from smoldering coals in the fireplace just might be the answer.   He rolled off the bunk, scooted closer to the fireplace, and held his feet over the red-hot coals.   Pain seared his heels as the heat parched his boots.   After pulling his feet from the fireplace and returning them several times, the rawhide caught fire.   A couple of yanks broke it loose.

He managed to cut through the thong binding his wrists after retrieving the knife Frank used to cut bacon and had carelessly left in a pan beside the fireplace.   He placed the knife between his ankles, bent backward and cut through the thong. He opened the door and peered outside. The shear red-sandstone walls rising on all sides of the canyon glistened in the morning sunshine. With Frank Canton watching the southern trail, he knew his only hope was to find another way out. He headed toward the thick growth of pine and spruce obscuring the northern end of the box canyon. Among the trees, he discovered a narrow game trail that switched back and forth toward the canyon rim. He wondered if it would lead him away from Canton's carbine only to face the left-handed fast draw of Nate Hamby. Probably, but there was no other choice.

* * * * *

The sun was high and the day hot as Nate and Red Angus stepped into their stirrups and reined toward the southeast. Twenty-four hours had passed and Tom had failed to return as promised with Frank Canton. They were certain that Canton would seek refuge at the closest WSGA member ranch if he were in trouble with the law in Johnson County. That ranch would be the 76 compound near the Powder River southeast of Buffalo.

After they found Old Fred in the 76 corral, Jim Fulgrim told them about his chat with Tom, and about Frank Canton borrowing one of the 76's horses. He also denied Canton had told him anything as to where he had been or where he was going. When asked which way Tom headed when he left the 76, Jim didn't hesitate to say, "Southwest, toward the KC."

They headed southwest at an easy canter. The afternoon sun was intense, the sky cloudless, and heat waves were shimmering above the high plains. The horses began to blow from the heat, but the heat of the day didn't compare to the furnace of anger burning inside of Nate. He was certain Frank Canton had tried to drygulch him, and he was equally certain that Tom was involved, even the one who ordered it to be carried out. It had been a mistake to allow Tom twenty-four hours to bring in Frank Canton. That was plenty of time for him to warn Frank to get out of Johnson County and take refuge at a more remote WSGA ranch. There were plenty of those, especially along the Sweetwater River in southwestern Wyoming.

"We need t'rest the horses," Red said, motioning for Nate to halt.

Nat pulled out his binoculars. "It isn't very far to the Middle Fork River. "We'd better water them, too."

Nate scanned westward along the Bighorns through his binoculars. He doubted that Canton had headed for the KC Ranch. It was too close to the frequently traveled road that ran from Buffalo to a bridge crossing the North Platte River at Fort Casper. It was more likely that Canton would head for a hideout well known by drifters and outlaws alike, such as the Hall cabin on the Middle Fork River. It would be ideal, being isolated in a box canyon with only one known trail into it.

"Are you thinkin' what I am?" Red asked, watching Nate scan the mountains.

"The Hall cabin?"

"Yep, there or a cave about a mile over Powder Pass in Scutter's Ravine."

Nate gulped from his canteen. "A cave?"

"The Indians used it off an' on in the past."

"Why don't we ride up to the Hall cabin first."

"I agree," Red said, wiping frothy sweat from his horse's withers. "Let's water the horses at the river."

There were only a couple of inches of water in the Middle Fork, barely enough for their horses and canteens. Red pulled out a map of the Bighorns, spread it on the ground, and placed a finger on the map. "Here's the Bar C Ranch house and up the creek a ways is a sandstone canyon. That's the *Hole In The Wall* where the Hall cabin is located."

Nate had heard about the *Hole In The Wall*. For a number of years, it had been a favorite hideout of rustlers who would drive their stolen cattle into the canyon where they would alter brands with running irons without fear of being pursued by lawmen or ranchers. All the rustlers had to do was post one or more riflemen where the trail entered the canyon. Anyone crazy enough to ride down that trail could be easily shot out of the saddle. Like the rustler guards, Canton would be ready for anyone entering the *Hole In The Wall*. It would be especially true if Tom and he were holed up together.

"Canton's goin' to be lookin' for anyone ridin' down that trail." Nate said.

Red folded up his map. "If we go in after dark, we'll have a better chance."

They followed the Middle Fork River as it meandered up the eastern slopes of the Bighorns. Nate continued to ponder the rift that was developing between himself and Tom. It seemed to be deepening into a chasm that was bound to become a pitfall for one or both of them. Whatever was to happen in Hall's canyon, he was determined to have a showdown with Tom and Frank Canton.

After an hour, they reached a bog whose springs were overgrown with marsh grass and scrub conifers. Suddenly, a swarm of hornets filled the air like a swirling whirlwind and slammed their stingers into riders and horses alike. "We gotta get out o' here," Nate yelled, trying to control his unstrung gelding. Finally, mud flew as they spurred their horses out of the marsh onto solid ground. They managed to rein them down, after galloping like two Arabians racing for the finishing pole of a six-furlong race.

Dismounting close to a grove of pines, they tried to ease the pain of their hornet stings with several gulps of whiskey. Red's eyes immediately began to swell. The sites where the hornets sank their stingers and venom into his face and neck were ballooning into red bulging masses. Fortunately, Nate's stings provoked a lesser reaction, but they were still very painful. Red began to sweat and nausea retched his belly until bitter vomit spewed from his mouth.

Red tried to peer between puffy lids. "My eyes are swollen near shut."

"Yeah, you won't be able to see at all before long."

"Damn it! What stinkin' luck."

Nate pulled out his watch. It was almost Six o'clock P.M. If he were to get to Hall's Canyon before dark, there would be little time to tarry before riding on. But Red wouldn't be able to ride anywhere, let alone help arrest Frank Canton or deal with Tom.

Nate unbuckled his saddlebags and pulled out two sandwiches that Dutch Jake had made for them. Red was too sick to eat anything.

"How far is it to the Hall cabin?" Nate said, unwrapping his sandwich.

"I figger about a two-hour ride."

Nate looked at the shadows. A dilemma about what to do stalked him, now that Red was incapacitated. How could he leave Red alone until he could get back after having a showdown with Canton and maybe Tom, too? If he did ride on, he'd have to leave with enough daylight left for him to make it to and from Hall's Canyon before dark. That would mean riding into the hideout when he could be easily seen and bushwhacked by Canton. Also, the country was new to him, having never ridden this far up the Middle Fork before. Yet, if he didn't go on, Canton wouldn't hang around very long before hightailing it for another hideout. He figured Tom could have warned Canton and would be back in Buffalo, claiming that he couldn't find him.

While Nate was pondering what to do, Red spoke up. "You'd better get ridin'. I ain't no use to you now."

"Damn, Red, I can't leave you here in this shape."

"Yes you can. If you don't, Canton will get away."

What Red said was a fact, but Nate didn't feel that he could do it. Red's eyes had become two slits of bulging flesh.

Nate had started to eat when he noticed movement a half-mile up the creek in an aspen grove. He glassed the grove with his binoculars. "There's somebody walkin' this way."

"Can y'tell who it is?"

"Yeah! It's Tom Albert."

# Chapter Seven

While wolfing down Red's sandwich, Tom talked about his encounter with Frank and how he managed to escape. Nate believed that his story was a concoction of self-serving crap. He had ridden with Tom across Indian Territory chasing outlaws for seven years. He'd never pull such a stupid stunt as to get himself into that kind of a mess and the escape was just too far-fetched since there wasn't but one known way into the *Hole In The Wall*.

"Well, Red," Nate said, "what do you think about this? It could be a trap."

Red wagged his head. "Don't know. Is it a trap, Tom?"

"No, it isn't."

"No matter," Nate said, drawing his .45. "You're stayin' here with Red until I get back."

Tom eyed the .45 while wagging his head. "You goin' t'take on Canton by yourself?"

"You're damned right I am. You're going to hug a tree trunk till I get back."

Hugging a tree trunk was a tactic that Nate, Hap, and Tom had used while marshaling in Indian Territory. They found a tree to be just as good as a jail cell for restraining a prisoner during the night while they slept. After hugging the trunk of a tree, they tied his wrists together with rope, leather thong, or rawhide. Of course, the manacled prisoner got little sleep during the night, but he was still there at the first light of dawn the following morning.

After securing Tom to a stout pine and getting directions from Red, Nate reined his sorrel toward the late afternoon sun, the *Hole In The Wall* and a showdown with Frank Canton. The orange rim of the rising moon had begun to cast an eerie glow over the Bighorns by the time Nate reached the rim of the canyon. He tied his sorrel to sandstone outcropping, unsheathed his Winchester and glassed the canyon with his binoculars. Two horses, one a bay and the other a black, were grazing in a meadow beyond the shack with lamplight spilling through a single window and smoke spiraling above the chimney. Canton was probably in the cabin cooking supper, but Nate couldn't be certain. He might be waiting somewhere in the shadows ready to bushwhack anyone walking into the *Hole In The Wall*.

With caution and long learned strategy, Nate crept into the shadows along the trail and headed for the cabin. It was nearly dark by the time he reached the canyon floor and a grove of willows. There, he hid and waited for the lighted window to go dark. As he waited, colder air sank into the canyon. He shivered and stared at the lighted window for at least two hours before it finally went dark. *Got to give him time to get asleep*, he thought, easing a round into his Winchester.

He tarried for another half-hour. The difference between success and failure would be surprise; enough time for Canton to get to sleep and unaware when Nate kicked in the door.

Finally, Nate decided it was time to go. His boot slammed through the door, splintering it into pieces. He leapt into the shack and found Canton's neck. "Aaaaahh!" screeched beneath his thumb as it sank between sinew and larynx. A hand, out of the darkness, grasped Nate's throat. Legs slammed against clay-chinked walls, fingers squeezed and Nate's head felt as if it would explode. He sank into an abyss, its black depths filled with flashing lights. Gradually, his senses returned as the strangling grip about his neck loosened.

Tom left a smear of Canton's blood and hair on his britches as he wiped the barrel of Red's .45 across his hip. He shoved the gun into his holster and struck a match, its yellow flame lighting up the room. Nate coughed and wheezed as he stared at Tom. "How the hell did you get loose?"

"Red untied me after I promised I'd back you up."

"You left him alone?"

"Nope, he's now able t'see well enough for holdin' the horses up on the rim."

"Well, I'll be damned," Nate said, getting up. He offered his hand to Tom. "Reckon I owe both you and Red"

Tom accepted Nate's handshake. "Reckon you do."

Canton groaned and tried to get up. "Stay where you are," Tom said, "or I'll crack your skull again."

After they tied Frank's wrists behind his back, Nate found the crease in Frank's scalp caused by his .45.

The ride back to Buffalo gave Nate time to consider his dilemma. Tom *had* been telling the truth about being cold-cocked and tied up by Canton. He'd also kept the promise given to Red and he had cracked Canton's noggin just in time. However, Tom was the chief WSGA enforcer who could very well want to get rid of Canton and quiet Nate's anger at the same time.

One by one, as they rode into Buffalo, a crowd gathered behind Frank Canton and his captors. Nate shoved Canton into the courthouse jail that Canton had built while he was sheriff. He cut the bonds from Canton's wrists, pushed him into a cell and locked the door. "Make yourself t'home. We'll have Doc Spoon come look at your head."

Frank rubbed his finger over the bump left by Tom's borrowed .45. "No need."

"We insist," Red said. "He'll need to testify about that crease Nate's bullet grooved into your scalp."

"Ain't nobody goin' t'look at my scalp till I talk to my lawyer."

"I already did after Tom cold-cocked you last night," Nate said. "Who's your lawyer?"

"Bertrum K. Smith."

"Smith's a Cheyenne lawyer," Red said. "You don't expect us to wait for him? How about Cobb?"

"No! I'll wait for Smith."

"I'll go get Doc Spoon," Nate said to Red. "We can all hold Canton while Doc takes a look,"

"That's a good idea. Go get Doc."

It required Nate, Tom, and Red to subdue Frank long enough for Doc Spoon to examine his scalp. Doc soon discovered the crease. "Here it is. Your bullet took out a strip of skin that's going to leave a deep scar."

Two weeks passed before Bertrum K. Smith arrived on the three o'clock stage from Casper. He was one of the WSGA lawyers Secretary Adams had hired. He was well known in Cheyenne as being the kind of lawyer you needed to keep you out of prison. When Smith stepped from the stage, Red Angus thought Bat Masterson might have come to town. Smith was dressed in an immaculate black suit with a gold watch chain dangling across his chest. He wore a black bowler and carried a gold-crowned walking stick. "You Bertrum K. Smith?" Red asked, walking toward Smith.

Smith replied with a distinct British accent. "I am and you are Sheriff Angus?"

"Yeah, your client's been lookin' for ya. He's complainin' 'bout our bed and grub."

Smith turned and called to the driver, "Sir, would you have someone take my luggage into the hotel?"

"Sure thing, Mister Smith, I'll take it over there myself."

Smith talked with Canton in his cell for over an hour and then climbed the stairs to Justice of the Peace Carroll H. Parmelee's office.

That afternoon Smith walked into Red's office, handed him a bail bond and requested the release of his client.

Seeing that the affidavit was proper, Red released Canton. Canton and Smith left, stayed overnight at the Occidental and departed the following morning on the stage for Cheyenne. Red saw them off. "You're goin' t'have Canton back for trial aren't ya, Mister Smith?"

"I expect my motion for a change of venue will be granted," Smith bragged. "I'm confident Mister Canton's trial will be in Cheyenne, if he's tried, that is. Good bye, sir."

Red spat, watched the stage roll down Main Street, and cursed Bertrum K. Smith. "You foppish lizard. What a sorry excuse for a lawyer."

\* \* \* \* \*

A week after Canton left for Cheyenne, Red Angus and his deputy, Jack Donahue, tracked two gunslingers heading northwest up Rock Creek. The two gunslingers had entered Foote's store and asked directions to the CD cow-camp and the Wagon Box Ranch. Robert Foote, suspicious of the duo, told Angus about them, describing them as being mean mannered and pushy. One was short, dark-skinned and about five-six with stringy black hair. The other one was big and ugly as a gorilla with a black beard nearly covering his face. Their .45s were tied low like hired killers, but they were wearing WSGA inspector badges. If they were cattle detectives, Red wondered why they hadn't come by the sheriff's office. That caused him to follow them to see what they were up to.

The CD camp was isolated among the foothills east of the Bighorns. The log bunkhouse, barn and corral were nestled in an alder grove on the banks of Piney Creek and were surrounded by grass-covered knolls. The location made its defense a formidable one, one where two well-armed men could stand off a prolonged attack. Red quickly determined that he needed more guns, so he sent Donahue on to the Wagon Box.

Jack Donahue returned with Nate, Hap and Bill Maner, a couple of hours before sundown. "Jack says you're after a couple of slingers," Nate said, stepping from his sorrel.

Red handed his binoculars to Nate. "Yeah, they're in the CD bunkhouse."

Nate crawled up a rocky ridge to get a clearer view of the bunkhouse. "I figure we got two choices, Red."

"What are they?"

"We can ride in and ask what they're up to, or we can flush 'em out."

"They might be who they claim," Jack Donahue offered, "and we ain't got no warrants."

Red buttoned the collar of his parka against the evening chill. "I reckon you're right. But if they ain't who they claim t'be, they can shoot us out o' the saddle. Nate, why don't you fellers circle around back and hide in the barn, then Jack and I'll ride on in?"

Nate, Hap, and Bill stayed out of sight while circling the cow camp until they reached the barn where they waited. A half hour, seeming much longer, passed. Finally, Red called, "Hello, the bunkhouse. This is Sheriff Angus."

There was no reply. The big black-bearded brute, carrying a Winchester, slipped out the back door, crouched beside the well house and took aim at Red and Jack.

"There's a rifle barrel stickin' out the front door," Hap said, looking through a broken window of the barn.

Crouching beside Hap, Bill said, "Yeah, I see it. Red an' Jack's got trouble."

"What now?" Hap whispered to Nate.

Without answering, Nate pushed the barn door open with his foot and aimed his Colt at the brute. "Drop that rifle or you're a dead man."

The startled brute stared at Nate's crippled arm, and then laid his rifle on the ground. "Don't pull that trigger, Hamby."

"Kick that rifle out of the way and get your hands up."

While Nate was disarming the cowering brute, Hap slipped through the back door of the bunkhouse. The dark-skinned gunman spun around. Hap stepped aside as the gunman fired his rifle from the hip. His bullet ripped through the doorjamb. Hap dove to the floor, firing his .45 as he fell. Bill Maner's Winchester bellowed. Both bullets tore into the gunman's chest, slamming him backward through the bunkhouse door onto the porch.

Nate recognized the brute he had captured. Twice, he and Hap had pursued the hulking giant across Indian Territory, but failed to catch him. His name was Booger Schott, an outlaw from Kansas that robbed, raped, and murdered across the central plains.

Nate jammed the barrel of his Colt into Booger's back and shoved him toward the house. "Get along, I want Hap to see your mangy face."

Hap was getting to his feet as Nate pushed Booger through the doorway. "Look who we caught."

Hap stared at Schott. "Well, I declare, if it ain't ol' Booger."

"It's him. Did y'all get his partner?"

"We got him," Red said. "He's dead on the porch."

"Where did you get that range-detective badge?" Hap asked, ripping the shield from Schott's shirt.

"Vigilante Al."

"Who's Vigilante Al?"

"Ain't sayin'."

"How did you come to meet him?"

"Ain't goin' t'say."

"Who's that dead man out on the porch."

Schott glanced at Nate. "Ain't sayin'."

Rage overtook Nate. He grasped a handful of Schott's shirt, shoved him backward and slammed him against the wall. "Who paid you scum to come after Hap and me?"

"Vigilante Al."

Red slapped steel handcuffs around Booger's wrists. "Me and Jack'll take this one back to Buffalo."

"Okay," Nate said, "we'll bury his partner."

Schott remained silent and uncooperative, only admitting to having been hired as a range detective for the WSGA by a Wyoming cattleman who called himself Vigilante Al. Without any evidence to the contrary, Schott was released to the U. S. marshal from Kansas where he would later stand trial and be hanged.

* * * * *

Several days later, Hap scraped manure from his boot on the lower corral fence rail while gazing at several whiteface whose hides were draped over bony frames. They struggled to regurgitate cuds from bloated bellies and were too weak to bellow. Most of the '86 blizzard survivors had grown fat on last summer's bluestem, but these had not thrived.

Bill Maner chomped his chaw of tobacco and leaned on the fence next to Hap. "I wouldn't give a nickel for any o' them rack o' bones."

Hap tongued his chaw and spat. "Reckon they ain't much."

Bill kicked at the fence rail and wiped brown spittle from the corners of his mouth. "Dammit, when are we goin' t'get some more stock?"

"Well, we cain't borrow no money. The WSGA controls them that's got any cash t'loan."

"There's got to be some mavericks for the takin' out on the plains. We could round some up."

"I reckon so, but that ain't legal, 'less we pay $7.50 a head to the WSGA, and they ain't about to sell us any."

"Well, sir, pay or no-pay, they's as much ours as anyone's."

Bill had a point. The WSGA-authorized April 1888 roundup

was not an option. The Wagon Box wasn't invited to participate, because any ranch with barbed-wire fences was blackballed. If you weren't included in the roundup, buying mavericks wasn't allowed. So, if they wanted to round up any, it would have to be done before the official roundup. Hap's impulsive nature leaned toward a quick decision. "I reckon so," he said. "Tell the men we'll ride out at first light."

Rounding up mavericks wasn't easy. There were very few unbranded whiteface or longhorns to be found. Hap, Bill and the Wagon Box hands covered mile after mile gathering only a few skinny yearlings. After a week of lassoing and branding, they drove their newly branded mavericks onto the Wagon Box. Nate sat his sorrel next to the Piney Creek crossing waiting for Hap. "Those critters are nearly all longhorns," Nate said, looking them over.

"Reckon they are. Where you headin'?"

"Buffalo."

"What for?"

"Dewitt Jones got our survey approved in Washington, so Cobb's redoin' some of the papers for us to sign."

\* \* \* \* \*

Nate traveled by stage to Cheyenne to file Cobb's affidavits with the land office on May 15, 1888. During his stay in Cheyenne, he visited newly appointed Judge Micah C. Saufley. The purpose of his visit was to deliver the letter in which Sheriff Angus had recommended Nate for the U. S. marshal appointment. He returned home troubled by the events that were unfolding in Wyoming. Two weeks later, a letter from Judge Saufley arrived summoning him back to Cheyenne.

Judge Saufley was reading a telegram when Nate walked into his office. "Good mornin', Judge Saufley."

The judge lowered the telegram to his desk. "Ah, yes, Mister Hamby, pull up a chair."

"Thanks, Judge."

"I appreciate your quick response to my letter," Saufley said, reaching across his desk to shake Nate's hand. "There're two reasons for my request."

"How can I help?"

"Bertrum Smith is pushin' his motion for change of venue of the Canton trial from Johnson to Laramie County. Maybe you can help me."

"I'm happy to, if I can."

"Do you believe Canton can get a fair trial in Johnson County?"

"Yes, I do."

Judge Saufley nodded, said nothing, and handed the telegram to Nate. "I sent a letter requestin' your appointment to the U. S. marshal's post after our conversation last month. I received this telegram from Washin'ton this mornin'. Please read it."

JUDGE MICAH C. SAUFLEY (STOP) ASSOCIATE JUSTICE SUPREME TERRITORIAL COURT (STOP) CHEYENNE (STOP) WYOMING TERRITORY (STOP) YOUR REQUEST FOR THE APPOINTMENT OF FORMER DEPUTY U S MARSHAL NATHANIEL HAMBY AS THE U S MARSHAL FOR WYOMING TERRITORY IS GRANTED PENDING SENATE CONFIRMATION (STOP) BRADFORD P. COLLINS FOR PRESIDENT GROVER CLEVELAND (STOP)

Nate chewed his lip and folded the telegram. "I wish this had not come my way. There are alliances growin' between good and evil men on both sides of the open range issue. It stands to split Wyomin' apart before it's over."

"I know," Judge Saufley said, stroking his beard. "That's why I need you. Will you accept the President's appointment?"

Wearing a U. S. marshal badge held little appeal for Nate. Surviving seven years in Indian Territory hadn't been easy. Turning one's back toward everyday danger required a certain amount of blind resignation to whatever fate wanted to deal. Your silhouette, whether framed by moonlight or noonday sun, was always a target for guns aimed by evil eyes. It had always been an end to having a cattle spread under the wide-open Rocky Mountain skies. Fate was not dealing much of a hand for Nate. Their herd had been nearly wiped out and then replenished with only the few longhorn mavericks rounded up by Hap.

Borrowing money was nonexistent. A U. S. marshal's salary could buy more stock. It also could open the way for defeating the WSGA, and putting men like Tom Albert, Frank Canton and Major Wolcott out of power. Pondering these facts, Nate made his decision.

"How many deputies will I be allowed?"

"How many do you want?"

"Just one for the time bein'."

"Then you will accept?"

"Yeah, I reckon it's time to buck the WSGA."

After swearing him in, Saufley handed Nate his badge. "Now, Marshal Hamby, is there anything else I can do for you?"

"There is a conspiracy underway by six men to commit a number of murders. Frank Canton revealed that to Tom Albert last summer. Then, two gunmen were hired by some Wyomin' rancher who calls himself Vigilante Al to dry-gulch Hap and me. I was goin' to request a special investigation; however, now that I'm marshal for the territory, I want six John Doe warrants."

Nate arrived back in Buffalo two days later. He walked into Sheriff Angus's office and handed Red the warrants. "Judge Saufley issued these warrants. Any idea who the six conspirators are?"

"Any member of the WSGA could be. The Judge issued these to you?"

"He did."

"Then he must have got ya appointed U.S. Marshal."

"Yeah, he did."

Red held out his hand. "That's great news, Nate, congratulations."

After meeting with Red Angus, Nate walked over to the livery, paid the feed and stable fees and rode out of Buffalo toward the Wagon Box. Upon reaching the Piney Creek crossing, his eyes scanned the hills. No danger could be seen. The country was wide open, high and treeless. The ever-present wind cascading down the Bighorn slopes rolled the tall grass into waves like a restless sea.

Nate reined his gelding into the long driveway leading toward the Wagon Box Ranch house. An eternal cap of snow crowning Cloud Peak glistened in the afternoon sun. It was too high for its whiteness to be erased, even in midsummer. Its majestic beauty reminded Nate of the loneliness he felt. How he longed to share the beauty of the Wagon Box with Beth Todd. But, that wasn't going to happen. His jealousy and hatred of Tom had alienated him from Beth. Tom had diligently courted Beth who saw him as a handsome, charming, intelligent and honest man. She was going to marry him, soon. At least that was what Frank Cobb had told him.

Hap met Nate at the corral gate. "Well, I see ya didn't get shot goin' down t'Cheyenne."

"No, everythin' went smooth."

"Did the Judge say they'd find out who Canton's six connivers is?"

Nate slipped off of the gelding. "Well, sort of, he gave me these warrants."

Hap unfolded the warrants, read the first one and glanced at the other five. "These are all John Doe warrants. What y'doin' with warrants? Y'ain't no lawman no more."

Nate pulled the U.S. marshal badge from his vest pocket and handed it to Hap. "Y'done let 'em talk ya into marshalin' again. Why did y'go and do that for?"

"Raise your right hand."

"I thought we was done with that stuff for good."

"Do you swear to uphold the law?"

"Yeah, I do."

Nate handed him a deputy badge. "Good, pin this on."

"Whose goin' t'look after the ranch?".

"Bill Maner told me he'd do it. I also told him that the ranch was his if the WSGA strung us up."

"Yeah," Hap said, massaging his neck. "They just might do that."

# Chapter Eight

A cowboy galloped his horse along the newly laid track of the Fremont, Elkhorn and Missouri Valley Railroad. "She's a comin'!" he yelled. "She's a comin'!"

A crowd of a hundred or so residents of Casper's "Old Town," along with nearly as many cowboys, began to cheer wildly. Far down the track, a cloud of black smoke puffed upward from the funnel of a small diamond-staked locomotive. Over and over, the engineer of the first passenger train to arrive at the railroad's terminus pulled the whistle cord. The crowd responded by ringing bells, firing guns into the air and shouting loud hurrahs. June 15, 1888 was a day of jubilation as Casper's "Old Town," barely a month old, received the breath of life from the Fremont, Elkhorn and Missouri Valley Railroad.

John Merritt, the founder of Casper, shook hands with Major Frank Wolcott and Tom Albert as they and several other dignitaries stepped down from the passenger coach. Wolcott, whose ranch was near Glenrock, twenty-five miles east of Casper, had been instrumental in bringing the railroad to Casper. Tom and Wolcott climbed onto a crudely constructed platform to address the celebrating throng. Nate and Hap stood in the crowd listening to them proclaim Casper to be the new shipping center for the region's cattlemen.

They met Tom as he stepped off the speaker's platform. "Well, Tom, that was a mighty interestin' speech you gave," Nate said. "I guess Canton wasn't able to get you kicked out of the WSGA."

Tom frowned, ignoring Nate's reference to Frank Canton. "Wolcott wants to meet with you and Hap soon as he's done talkin' with John Merritt."

"All right, we'll be waitin' over at Demorest's Restaurant."

Wolcott and Tom finally walked into the restaurant. "Sorry to keep you men waiting," Wolcott said without a hint of animosity in his voice.

"That's okay," Nate replied, "I reckon y'all had some politickin' to do."

"Tom's going to be the next secretary of the WSGA," Wolcott said, slapping Tom on the shoulder.

Hap was surprised by Wolcott's brag. "Well I'll be damned, you're aimin' a might high right outen the chute ain't ya?"

"Not at all, no sir, not at all," Wolcott said. "He'll be elected. Enough about politics, you want to talk about Canton's conspirators?"

"We just want to know who they are," Nate replied.

Wolcott reached into his jacket, pulled out a small black notebook, laid it on the table and tapped the cover with his finger. "Their names are in this book," he taunted, picked up the book and slipped it back into his pocket.

"Where did you get that book?" Nate asked.

"It used to be in Canton's pocket."

"Used to be?" Nate said, leaning toward Wolcott.

"I suppose you want to know how I came to have it?"

"That's right."

"I got it after Tom Adams took over following Secretary Sturgis's resignation."

"Who gave it to you?"

"I'm not saying. You'd like to see what's in it?"

"That's right."

"It'll cost you."

"How much?"

"Not money."

"What, then?"

Wolcott took a deep breath and slowly exhaled. "Since Canton took a shot at you, he has done his best to turn Secretary Adams against Tom and myself. I'm willing to trade you this book for your indicting only Canton and his six cronies. Leave the WSGA out of it. That's my deal."

"You agree with this, Tom?"

"It's reasonable."

Nate shook his head. "Reasonable? Only, if there isn't anythin' in it incriminatin' the WSGA or other individuals. I can't make that kind of deal."

"Well, I didn't think you would," Wolcott said, tore a blank page from the book, and scribbled something with a pencil. He folded the sheet and handed it to Nate. "The name written there is the only one you're going to get from me. Maybe he will tell you who the vigilantes are, but I sort of doubt it."

Nate unfolded the paper and read the name: Dick Drury. Drury owned one of the biggest cattle outfits west of the Bighorn Range in the Bighorn Basin. Cattle with a Lazy D brand burned over their ribs roamed over thousands of acres of open range. His ranch headquarters was literally a fortified bastion near the Bighorn River. It was difficult to get near Dick Drury.

"How can I be sure about this name?" Nate asked Wolcott.

Wolcott stood up to leave. "You can't. There's one more thing you men need to know. Tom has come a long way since coming to Wyoming. He's chief inspector for the WSGA and he owns over a hundred thousand-acre ranch. He's accumulated more wealth in five years than both of you will obtain in your lifetimes. He's done it by cooperating with the WSGA. You'd better give that some deep consideration. Good day, gentlemen."

Tom stood up to leave, but waited until Wolcott walked out the door. "Adams and Wolcott want to distance themselves from Canton and his conspirators," Tom said. "He'll cooperate if you'll agree to his terms."

"Damn, Tom," Hap said, "you've got a memory short as Tom Thumb. Have ya forgot Adams and Wolcott hired Canton in the first place? Do ya believe Wolcott ain't in cahoots with Canton? Neither one o' them roosters can be trusted."

"Things change," Tom said. "Adams, Wolcott and the WSGA don't want this situation to interfere with statehood for Wyomin'."

"Canton works for the WSGA," Nate said. "You, Adams and Wolcott, are responsible for him and his so-called cronies. You'd better think hard about that."

*  *  *  *  *

Dick Drury, like a few other ranchers who built cattle empires in Wyoming Territory, was tough, tempered by hard work and hard living. In 1874, he drove a beginning herd of beef stock to the Bighorn Basin from Oregon by way of

Montana. He was a big man, all muscle and bone held together by unwavering determination. His face had a handsomeness that only age mysteriously carves out of youthful homeliness. White hair and a long drooping mustache framed a piercing blue left eye and a black leather patch covered his blind right eye. He had lost the eye while branding calves during roundup in 1880 when a rebellious yearling slashed a sharp hoof across his face.

Dick Drury, stiffened by arthritis, waded into the steaming springs of hot mineral water where Shoshone Indians had soaked away their pains for many years. His three sons and several cowboys sat next to the pool with Winchesters cradled across their arms. The day was quite cool for June in Wyoming. Drury let out a pained sigh as he eased his butt into the crystal-clear waters. At the far end of the pool, several Shoshone men with only their shoulders above the water's surface laughed at Drury as he cautiously sank deeper. "By golly, boys," Drury yelled, "this'll scald your hind end. Them Induns must have leather butts."

Drury's oldest son, Jack, yelled back, "Your butt ought'a be saddle toughened to where you could sit on hell's door itself."

Jack Drury was more than a "chip off the old block." He was like a clone. Only the changes of age and two good eyes separated them. "Shut your damned mouth," Dick yelled at Jack. "I can out-ride, out-shoot, out-fight and out-cuss any of you cubs. That includes sittin' in a boilin' pot like this."

Jack, never one to shun a challenge, shucked his boots, pants and shirt. He waded into the painfully hot springs toward Dick. "Oh, yeah?" he yelled. "Move over. I'll be sittin' in here a-laughin' after you're cooked plumb red, old man."

"Well, sit yourself deep and we'll see who's here the longest."

Meanwhile, Nate and Hap tied their horses next to the Drurys' mounts. Nate walked over to a big buckskin stud with a "Cheyenne roll" saddle covered with black steer hide. He lifted the leather skirt extending back of the cantle. Burned into the underside was: "Built for Dick Drury by Frank Meanea. Cheyenne-1877."

Nate patted the buckskin's rump. "This saddle belongs to Dick Drury all right."

"Drury and seven other men must be up in one of those hot springs," Hap said, counting the horses.

"Well, Hap," Nate said as he walked toward the path ascending to the crystallized hot springs basins. "The closer we get, the better chance we've got to talk with Drury."

When they reached the uppermost rim, Nate called down to the men beside the steaming springs. "Which one of you is Dick Drury?"

Nate and Hap stood silhouetted against the blue sky as every head turned upward to see who had called on Dick Drury. Dick shaded his left eye from the bright sun with his hand. Their silver badges identified the intruders as lawmen. "I'm Dick Drury. Who are you?"

"I'm U.S. Marshal Nate Hamby. I'd like to have a little talk with you, Mister Drury."

Dick gazed at Nate while considering his reply. He whispered to Jack, "Ease over there by the boys and tell 'em to stay ready, but let me handle this."

"Aw'right, Pa." Jack shoved himself toward his brothers, Luke and Ramsay.

"Well, Marshal Hamby, as you can plainly see, I'm soakin' my bones. If you want'a talk, come on in and sit a spell."

Hap leaned toward Nate. "Y'take off your duds and wade out there, those fellas with them Winchesters can fill your carrcass full of lead right quick."

Nate nodded agreement. "I'll be right down, Mister Drury," he said, then whispered to Hap, "Stay here and keep your rifle ready. If anythin' happens, shoot Drury."

Nate walked down to the pool, stripped to the skin and waded into the hot springs. Again, the Shoshone men laughed as he winced from the hot water climbing up his legs with each step. "Damn, this water's hot," he said as he reached Dick Drury.

"It sure is. Looks like your right arm can use some hot soakin'."

Nate lowered himself deeper into the pool. "You're right about that. It's takin' some of the ache out of it already."

"I see you told your deputy to keep his Winchester pointed in my direction."

"Your men start anythin', you're a dead man, Mister Drury."

"I figgered as much. If I die, so do you."

"Then, I'd say we're both safe."

Drury laughed. "Reckon so. What y'wantin' to talk about?"

"Do you know Frank Canton?"

"Yeah, I know Canton."

"Major Wolcott?"

"Yeah, why y'askin'?"

"Wolcott says Canton and six other men want me dead. He indicated you might be one of them. That right?"

Drury's left eye glared intently at Nate. Sweat ran down his face and dripped from the ends of his mustache.

"Wolcott is a pompous liar."

Nate returned Drury's stare. "What about Canton?"

"Canton's a low-life back-shooter."

"Do you know anythin' about a *dead list* bein' made up by six cattlemen?"

Drury moved his gaze from Nate toward Hap. "I've heard some about it." He looked back at Nate. "But I haven't had any part in such cowardly schemes. I don't make any 'scuses 'bout not wantin' nesters in Wyomin'. They'll ruin this country. It's fellas like me an' Moreton Frewen an' Rubin Steed that's pioneered cattle ranchin' in Wyomin'. I came here when the Induns claimed all this country. I've fought for my ranch. Ever'thing I own is right here, but I ain't never murdered for it and I ain't about t'start now."

Dick Drury was easy to believe. "Well, can you explain to me why Wolcott gave me your name?"

"Wolcott is a swelled-headed conniver. I figger he's tryin' t'cause me some trouble and throw you off at the same time."

"Why would he want to cause you trouble?"

"I chopped his legs out from under him after Sturgis resigned as WSGA secretary. When I found out Wolcott was about to get the secretary job, I got enough votes together to give it to Tom Adams—that answer your question?"

Nate looked at Dick Drury's sons and four cowhands sitting next to the spring. Each wore braces of cartridge belts across their chests and walnut pistol grips protruded from paired holsters on their hips. "From the looks of your men, I'd say Wolcott was settin' me up."

"Most likely, he's nothing but a foul turkey buzzard. He wants somebody else to do his killin' for him. That's how that slimy bird thinks."

Nate was beginning to like this one-eyed old rancher. His answers were straight. The penetrating stare from his left eye revealed the man's intense character. Nate admired those traits. Drury's opinion of Wolcott matched his own. "Well, I agree— that's what he is, but don't you agree that a turkey buzzard seldom ever roosts or eats alone? They're usually bunched together."

Dick Drury gave out a hearty laugh and slapped Nate on the shoulder. "You've got that right. They surely do that and Canton along with his six connivers is in Wolcott's flock of buzzards."

"Speakin' of Canton's six, do you have any idea who they are?"

"I sure do," Drury said, still laughing at Nate's remarks. "The biggest buzzard of all is Albert J. Bothwell. The five others are Tom Sun, R. B. Conner, John Durbin, R. M. Galbraith, and Ernest McLain. Before it's all over, those six are goin' to ruin the Wyomin' Stock Growers Association."

Nate rubbed sweat from his eyes. "I doubt their bein' the only buzzards in the WSGA."

"You're right about that, but the others are just chicks compared to those six."

"Where is Bothwell's place?"

"Down on the Sweetwater. Jim Averell has a store on the stage road between Rawlins and Lander. He can tell you how to get to Bothwell's."

Nate stood up and rubbed his crippled right arm while trying to flex his right hand's contracted fingers. "This hot spring sure takes the ache out. I'm really appreciatin' your help, Mister Drury."

"Well, sir, I just hope you can do somethin' about Wolcott and his bunch. You need any help with 'em, just let me know. Me and my boys would be proud to ride with you anytime, Marshal Hamby."

\* \* \* \* \*

Three miles east of Independence Rock, known as *the register of the desert* where emigrants carved names and messages, the Rawlins to Lander stage road crossed the rutted remnant of the Oregon Trail. It was there that Jim Averell built his road-ranch store and established a frontier post office. He had served ten years as an infantryman in the Army, some of the time at Fort McKinney. In 1881, he was discharged and worked as a surveyor for a few years. He then filed for a homestead on the Sweetwater on February 24, 1886 and built a store to accommodate mostly those who traveled the Rawlins to Lander road. However, a number of cowboys working the area ranches began to frequent his store to buy beer and booze and utilize his postal services. He was a natural agitator with a gift of gab that he often used to tweak the noses of lesser-educated men. His acrid comments alienated the Sweetwater range barons by frequently referring to them as tyrants, usurpers, liars and other more profane descriptions.

Shortly, thereafter, he recruited Ella Watson, who the WSGA later claimed was plying her trade in a Rawlins whorehouse, to file for her homestead about a mile and a half west of his store on Horse Creek. They also claimed she was soon busy servicing the baser needs of many Sweetwater cowboys as well as Averell. She was a twenty-eight-year-old, buxom farm girl who had migrated to the West from Lebanon, Kansas. Her manners were no better than those of her mentor, Jim Averell. She was alleged to be a harlot whose sordid vocabulary spilled across her tongue with the fury of an unrequited vixen. Despite her course behavior, she developed her hog ranch into a prospering house of ill repute, reportedly accumulating a sizable herd of mavericks that philandering cowboys had traded for her sexual favors.

Both of their homesteads were on land already claimed by Albert J. Bothwell who had failed to acquire legal possession by either purchasing or homesteading a single acre of his claimed range. However, he and most of the other cattle barons claimed that possession was tantamount to ownership and any and all who violated that illegal assumption would be harshly dealt with.

Jim Averell touched his tongue with a stubby pencil and made an "X" near the Sweetwater River on a surveyor's map. "That's where Bothwell lives; follow the river and you can't miss his place."

"Do you know Albert Bothwell?" Nate asked.

"Do I know Albert Bothwell? Do I know that arrogant son of perdition? What do you want to know about him?"

"Doesn't sound like you hold Bothwell in very high regard," Hap replied.

"Not hardly, he has absolutely no respect for the law or anyone's rights except his own. He thinks he owns all of the Sweetwater valley and everythin' in it."

"Y'don't think he does?" Nate asked.

"No, he doesn't. He hasn't filed homestead or purchasin' affidavits with the land office. He's put up signs declarin' his boundaries and anybody trespassin' is liable to get Winchester justice."

"He ever come at you?" Hap inquired.

"Oh, yeah, after I filed a claim for the land to build my store on, he rode in here with several of his hands. I recall that I was workin' on the roof at the time. He called for me to get my butt down 'cause he wanted to tell me somethin'. When I stepped off the ladder, Bothwell pulled out his .45 and began wavin' it around. 'You dumb squatter,' he yelled into my face. 'This land belongs to me. You ain't goin' to live long if you finish this store. I want you off my ranch.'"

"Well, I see you're still here," Nate said.

"Yeah, I am, but not because Bothwell didn't mean what he said."

"What do you mean?"

"One of his hands is a customer and friend of mine. He's told me Bothwell offered a $500 bonus to any hand that does me in."

"I'd consider buildin' someplace else."

"I've sunk ever' dime of my savin's into this place. I just can't walk away from it."

Bothwell's ranch house was less than an hour's ride. They followed the river most of the way. The Sweetwater is an unusual river, probably best described by an anonymous cowboy wag during Wyoming's early history: *She starts out a yard wide an' faster'n a cowboy with the sage brush trots. After rollin' down-country, she's a mile wide an' a inch deep. There, she's too thick fer makin' coffee an' too thin to plow. If'n it weren't for beaver dams she'd just turn t'mud, dry up an' disappear.*

The headwaters of the Sweetwater River have their origins east of the Continental Divide on a high plateau known as South Pass. The southernmost range of the Wind River Mountains shaded by forests of conifers and aspen lies to the north. Antelope Hills south of the pass affords a panorama of the vast badlands of the Red Desert Basin. The river courses its way eastward, north of the Green Mountains until joining itself with the North Platte River.

Bothwell's ranch headquarters was near the river between Garfield Peak to the north and Ferris Mountain rising over ten thousand feet to the south.

"Watch tyin' yer horses next t'the wife's flower garden," Bothwell yelled from the corral where his men were breaking horses. A solitary rose bush with yellowed leaves and no blooms clung to the hitching rail in front of the house. "Ain't much of a flower garden," Hap said as they led their horses toward the corral.

"Mister Bothwell?" Nate called to the hulk of a man sitting astride the high corral fence. He was tall, lanky, nearing fifty and his shirt was stained with salt mosaics left from sweat evaporated by dry Wyoming winds. Bothwell had a reputation of being not only mean, but also intensely single-minded in whatever he was doing.

"Snug 'im down tight, Jake," Bothwell yelled at a skinny cowboy trying to tether a wild bronc' to a post in the center of the corral.

"I'm United States Marshal Nate Hamby, Mister Bothwell."

Bothwell ignored him, yelling a steady stream of directions laced with profanity at the man trying to saddle the bronc'.

"You big lizard," Hap roared, "get your self down here so's we can talk atcha."

"You'd better get off my ranch," Bothwell yelled back, his gaze fastened on the drama going on in the corral. "If y'don't, you're goin' t'be buzzard crap."

"You know Frank Canton?" Nate called up to Bothwell. His matter of fact tone caused Hap to stop as he reached up to dislodge Bothwell from his perch.

"Yeah, what's it t'you?"

"You know Dick Drury?"

Bothwell stepped down from the fence. "Ever'body knows that old rascal."

"Drury says you, Canton, and five others have made up a 'dead-list.' Is Drury right about that?"

Albert Bothwell's stare bored into Nate's badge. "Who appointed you U.S. Marshal?"

"Judge Saufley, President Cleveland and the U.S. Senate. Is Dick Drury right about you and Canton?"

Bothwell spat on the ground and rolled his chaw of tobacco with his tongue. "Old Dick is three-quarters loco. He's been saltin' your mine, I'd say."

"Maybe, but I happen to believe him. Canton has admitted to the list's existence."

"Well, Mister Marshal, I ain't admittin' nothin' about no list," Bothwell said, his voice more menacing with each word. "If I was you, I'd watch my step real close."

"Anybody takes a shot at me or my deputy, I'm comin' after you. I just hope you resist arrest."

"Get off my ranch."

Bothwell's behavior convinced Nate that Dick Drury had been correct. It would take another year of trying to gather any substantial evidence that could be used to determine who the vigilante's were going to target. Tom Sun, R. B. Conner, John Durbin, R. M. Galbraith and Earnest McClain, the other members of the vigilante committee, were just as obstinate as Bothwell had been. Everyone else claimed ignorance of any conspiracy.

Would the summer of 1889 open the doors for Nate that had heretofore been locked in secrecy? He decided to attack the vigilantes by confronting their head, the WSGA power brokers at the Cheyenne Club.

# Chapter Nine

Four polo ponies with "Postage Stamp" saddles on their backs were tied to the hitching rail in front of the Cheyenne Club. Nate had never met any of the eastern cattle barons known locally as "Club Dandies," nor had he ever been inside the Club. He knocked on the front door and waited for a response. A black man with steel-gray hair, dressed in a black cutaway coat, opened the door. "Yes, sir, welcome to the Cheyenne Club."

The Cheyenne Club was unique on the western frontier. Wyoming's cattle barons from London, Boston, New York and Philadelphia had built themselves a social oasis where they could enjoy all of the amenities to which they were accustomed. They took refuge daily within the walls of the Club to enjoy imported vintage wines, champagne, all kinds of spirits, games of chance and women. All of the girls were beautiful and available to member and visitor alike. Members often came to their festive evening gatherings wearing "Herefords," their name for white ties and tails.

"Thank you," Nate said, walking into the foyer. It was the most opulent establishment he had seen west of the Mississippi River. A massive stairway spiraled upward to the second floor landing. The walls were paneled with walnut and oak. Tapestry inlays lined the hallway. Portraits of handsome young men attired in polo and harness racing habits hung over them. The sweet pungency of Cuban cigar smoke hung in the air. "I'm U.S. Marshal Hamby. Are any of the Club members here?"

The butler nodded. "Yes, sir, they're in the lounge. Won't you have a chair while I tell 'em you're here?"

Nate sat in an elaborately upholstered brown leather chair and waited for the butler's return. He heard faint sounds of female laughter and masculine voices coming from the second floor. He noticed a copy of the Wednesday, July 10, 1889 *Cheyenne Leader* lying folded on a table next to his chair. He found nothing of interest in it until reaching the editorial.

*The appointment of Judge Micah C. Saufley to the Supreme Court of Wyoming Territory last year by President Cleveland has to be one of Cleveland's biggest blunders. Judge Saufley, learned as he is, continues to act like a Confederate "guerrilla." He even wears a Colt forty-five while sitting at the bench. The sentences Judge Saufley has handed down in the courthouses of the Second District reflect an inadequate understanding of the need for harsh punishment of rustlers. He is tying the hands of Tom Albert, chief of the WSGA detectives, as he tries to cope with the rustlers that seem to be multiplying faster than West Texas jackrabbits. Frederic de Billier's call for Judge Saufley's replacement by President Harrison is sound and must be accomplished before the rustlers destroy Wyoming's cattle industry.*

"Ah, Marshal Hamby, Tom Albert has spoken highly of you many times.  I'm Hubert Teschemacher.  Welcome to the Cheyenne Club."

Teschemacher was a young Bostonian who had graduated from Harvard University in 1878.  While visiting his parents in Paris, France, he read about the wonders of the great American West in a newspaper.  He felt compelled to follow Horace Greeley's advice and go see for himself all of the West's touted wonders and opportunities.  After returning to Boston, he convinced his close friend, Frederic. O. de Billier to accompany him on a trip to hunt big-game in the wild West.  The hunting trip ended by their launching a ranching enterprise called the Duck Bar Ranch on the North Platte River in southeastern Wyoming.

Nate laid the *Cheyenne Leader* aside and stood to shake hands.  Hubert Teschemacher was a handsomely bearded man in his early thirties, dressed in shining, black English riding boots and a bright blue satin shirt.  Hubert Teschemacher's greeting, colored by his Bostonian accent, along with his riding habit and the opulence of the Cheyenne Club seemed to come from another time, another place.

"I'm pleased to make your acquaintance," Nate said.  "This

is quite a place you fellas have here."

"We are quite proud of our facilities. There are three other members in the lounge I'd like for you to meet."

The lounge's interior was furnished with mahogany game-tables, large chairs upholstered with brown steer hide and was carpeted with Persian rugs. The faint remnants of stale cigar smoke, French perfume and spilled whiskey reminded Nate of the Richmond brothels he had visited during the war. Three men attired in riding habits similar to Teschemacher's sat at a table under a chandelier of burning candles.

"I'd like for you gentlemen to meet Marshal Hamby," Teschemacher said as they all stood up to greet Nate.

Frederic de Billier, Fred Hesse and W. C. Irvine introduced themselves to Nate and invited him to have a drink. Hesse was the manager of the 76 Ranch, now only a remnant of the spread started by Frewen in 1876. He also owned the 28 Ranch located on Crazy Woman Creek southeast of Buffalo. Irvine, a Pennsylvanian by birth, organized and managed the Converse Cattle Company and the Ogalalla Land and Cattle Company. Both were quite large ranching enterprises east of the Powder River covering much of the Antelope Creek and Cheyenne River country.

"Tell me Marshal, are you from the South?" Teschemacher asked as they sat down. "Your accent is distinctly Virginian."

"Yes, I grew up in Lexington. You sound like a Yankee."

"Yes! Yes, I am, also, my grandfather was the master of a Dutch sailing ship. No doubt, he helped provide your ancestors with some of their slaves."

"That may very well have happened. Not to change the subject, but would Frank Canton happen to be around?"

Teschemacher shook his head. "Oh, no, Canton doesn't belong to the Club. He never comes here."

"What brings you to Cheyenne, Marshal Hamby?" Irvine asked.

The steward of the lounge, a gaunt cadaverous man, served each of them a crystal shot glass filled with Scotch whisky and then offered each a foil-wrapped Havana cigar. "Judge Saufley's advice," Nate replied, peeling the foil from his cigar.

Fred de Billier lifted his glass. "Here's to your good health, sir."

"Hear, hear," the others said in unison, lifting their glasses toward Nate.

Toast after toast was proposed by each of the cattle barons until Nate's head began to spin. "Hey, fellas," he said, "you'll have to excuse me, I need to get on down to see the judge."

Fred de Billier motioned for the steward to bring another round. "Nonsense—we've just begun."

"Yes. Yes, Marshal," Fred Hesse said, "we'd like for you to have dinner with us. Our chef serves the best steaks this side of New York City."

The steak was very good as was the wine and the after-dinner cigar topped off with a snifter of brandy. Fred de Billier held his snifter beneath his nose. "Ah, a delightful bouquet," he said, sipped a small quantity and held the brandy in his mouth, savoring its unique flavor for a moment before swallowing. "Excellent! Excellent choice, Hubert."

"Yes, it is," Hubert Teschemacher said. "How do you like the brandy, Marshal?"

"It's very good. You fellas sure know how to live."

They all laughed, then Teschemacher turned serious. He placed his brandy goblet on the table, leaned back in his chair, sucked smoke from his cigar and puffed a perfect smoke ring toward the ceiling. "Marshal, I'd consider it an honor to sponsor you for membership in the Cheyenne Club.

Nate could not hide his surprise at Teschemacher's offer. "Why would you do that?"

"I like you. You're a rancher. Where else in this miserable town can you find equal accommodations?"

"That's an excellent idea," Fred de Billier said. "We'll make you an honorary member of the WSGA as well. That means no dues and no charges for staying at the Club."

"I'm also the U.S. Marshal for Wyomin' Territory. What you're offerin' sounds like a bribe."

"Nonsense," Irvine said. "We simply want to be friends with you. We'll make life easier for you, if you want, you can do the same for us."

"You want me to be friends with Albert Bothwell?" Nate abruptly asked Irvine.

Irvine appeared puzzled by Nate's question. "I don't understand."

"Bothwell has called for my murder."

"Your murder?" Teschemacher gasped and sucked on his cigar. "How could that be?"

"You mean to tell me that you fellas don't know about Bothwell and his five vigilantes and their *dead list*?"

The four dandies sat silently staring at Nate. He waited for their answer.

Finally, Teschemacher spoke. "We haven't heard anything about a *dead list*."

The others readily agreed.

"What is this *dead list* all about?" Hesse asked Nate.

"Albert Bothwell, Tom Sun, R. B. Connor, Ernest McLain, John Durbin, and R. M. Galbraith, along with Frank Canton, have made up a list of eight men that are to be eliminated. My name heads the list."

"Do you have proof of your accusation?" Irvine asked.

"I've got enough to indict Canton," Nate said, hoping the brag would deceive them. "He's Bothwell's hired gun, you know. I figure that Canton will talk to save his butt."

"Canton's alleged attempt to murder you is well known here in Cheyenne, Marshal Hamby," Fred de Billier said. "But, we know nothing about anyone conspiring with him."

Nate nodded, stood up, and looked directly at DeBillier. "I hope what you say is true. Suborning the conspiracy to do murder is equal to committing the crime under the law. I hope you gentlemen are aware of that fact."

Without waiting for an answer, Nate turned around and walked toward the door. The butler handed him his hat. "Will the marshal be stayin' in the club tonight?"

Nate donned his hat, hesitated a moment and glanced back at the *Club Dandies* as they laughed and raised their glasses feigning a toast. "No, sir," he said to the butler, and then spoke to the dandies in a loud voice. "If you gentlemen change your minds, I will be at Judge Saufley's office."

* * * * *

Nate met with Judge Saufley to update him on his investigation of the *dead list* conspirators. Saufley listened without comment until Nate had finished. He picked up his pearl handled .45 and laid it on the large Blackstone law book that he frequently consulted for enlightenment. With that gesture, he related to Nate how armed disobedience and rebellion had required unusual and oft times unconstitutional actions to become necessary. Lincoln's ignoring the right of habeas corpus and a speedy trial for the Copperheads arrested during the war was one example. Vigilantism was no different from rebellion against a lawfully established territorial government. It couldn't be tolerated. His candid advice was for Nate to get Wolcott's notebook, no matter what. Just get it. Hard evidence was needed for an indictment and successful prosecution of the conspirators.

After his sorrel had been loaded into a stock car, Nate boarded the train heading for Casper. The journey would be long, even by a railroad whose locomotives averaged almost twenty miles per hour. He settled down in a Pullman chair and tried to collect his thoughts. He needed evidence, not just words spoken by a witness. Witnesses in Wyoming had a habit of not appearing for trial for various reasons. The most frequent being intimidating threats, which were often carried out by the intimidators.

As he watched sandy hills covered with sagebrush roll by the coach window, Nate pondered Judge Saufley's remarks. He doubted Wolcott's book would reveal anything more than what he already knew since the names of the conspirators had been revealed to him by Dick Drury.

During most of the trip, Nate tried to sleep but sleep would not come. The notebook in Wolcott's pocket kept dominating his thoughts until he finally reached a decision. Whether or not he could trust Wolcott wasn't important, he had to get the notebook.

The clacking of the train's wheels began to slow as it approached a cluster of dwellings along the North Platte River. The conductor walked down the isle calling the next stop.

"Glenrock! Glenrock! Last stop before Casper."

Nate raised his hand to catch the conductor's attention. "I'm gettin' off here instead of goin' on into Casper?"

"Yes, sir, Marshal, I'll have your horse unloaded."

"Do you happen to know where Frank Wolcott's ranch is located?"

The conductor wagged his head. "No, but the station agent will know."

The day was pleasant and filled with the sweetness of new-mown alfalfa. The sky was clean as polished brass without a cloud in sight. Uncharacteristic of central Wyoming, a gentle breeze was creeping through the box elders and cottonwoods along the river. As Nate reined his sorrel along the road toward the VR compound, he listened to the cicadas in the trees emitting their high-pitched trills.

Wolcott lived on and managed the VR Ranch several miles out of Glenrock. The Tolland Cattle Company owned the ranch, a nonresident concern based overseas. In spite of Wolcott's abhorrence of fences and farming, the VR maintained significant acreage of alfalfa along Deer Creek, a tributary of the North Platte River. Often, Wolcott was away from the ranch, carrying on his various endeavors for the WSGA, but today he was at home.

About a quarter of a mile from the VR compound, Nate saw a man riding toward him astride a sleek black horse. The rider was stocky, wide shouldered, and carried his head slightly askew as if he had a wryneck. It was Frank Wolcott, probably headed for Glenrock to catch the next train to Cheyenne. Nate reined back his sorrel and waited.

"Well, if it isn't my good friend, Marshal Hamby," Wolcott said, reining down his skittish gelding.

"Howdy," Nate said, "I'm glad I caught you at home."

"Just about didn't, I'm catching a train."

"I'll try not to delay you."

"What's on your mind?"

"The notebook."

"I figured as much."

Nate pulled out his wallet. "What's your askin' price?"

"I told you that money couldn't buy it."

"I recall. What then?"

"Leave the WSGA, Tom and myself out of this."

Nate hated giving in to the WSGA, but he had decided to follow Judge Saufley's advice. "You have it with you?"

Wolcott patted his vest pocket. "Right here."

"All right, I'll accept your terms."

"A wise decision," Wolcott said, pulled the notebook from his pocket and handed it to Nate.

Nate took the book but ignored Wolcott's handshake. "Now," Nate said with firmness splinting his voice. "I'll not hold you, Tom, or the WSGA to account for anything in this book, but that is as far as it goes. Is that understood?"

"Understood," Wolcott said, spurring the gelding.

Nate watched Wolcott slapping his reins across the withers of the gelding until the frenzied horse and rider were out of sight. Then he opened the notebook to read the vigilance committee's minutes that were written and signed by Frank Canton.

* * * * *

One could easily mistake the headquarters of the Drury Ranch for a town. The main house resided within a square at the compound's center. The house was massive, painted white with three stories topped by a hip-styled roof containing clusters of dormer windows. A continuous porch surrounded three sides of the house. A wide street ran around the square and on the opposite sides were rows of buildings devoted to various needs. There were barns for storage of hay and grain, a blacksmith shop, a harness and saddle-repair shop, several tack sheds and four bunk houses. A cookhouse completed the conglomerate of buildings. Beyond the headquarters square were horse corrals and holding pens for range bulls. *Don't know why ol' Dick doesn't call this 'Druryville,* Nate thought as he hitched his sorrel to the hitching post and walked up the porch steps.

Dick met Nate on the porch. "Howdy, Marshal," Dick said, reaching to shake Nate's hand. "You look like you've had a hard ride."

"I had to get over to see you quick as I could."

"Y'come up with somethin'?"

Nate handed Canton's notebook to him. "I'd appreciate your lookin' at Canton's record of the vigilante meetin' at Bothwell's ranch."

Drury opened the book. "I'm glad Ramsay didn't go along with those dirty sons of perdition."

*On April 21, 1887, the Vigilance Committee met at Bothwell's ranch with the following members present: Albert Bothwell; John Durbin; George Henderson; Tom Sun; Ernest McLain; R. Galbraith; R. Connor and Ramsay Drury. Bothwell called meeting to order. McLain made motion to activate Article Four of the bylaws. Sun seconded. Carried with Drury and Henderson voting no. Both Drury and Henderson refused to remain in the meeting and left. In compliance with A.#4, a priority list was compiled following long discussion. The final list approved by the comm. is as follows:*

1. *Nate Hamby*
2. *Hap Dugger*
3. *Red Angus*
4. *Nate Champion*
5. *John A. Tisdale*
6. *Orley "Ranger" Jones*
7. *James Averell*
8. *Tom Waggoner*

*The comm. certified these to be known cattle rustlers or thieves and voted for the sentence of death. The comm. issued activation orders to me. I certify this to be true minutes of said meeting of the Vigilance Committee.*

*Frank Canton, Inspector*

"Last Spring, Canton and Bothwell sent a rider up here with a message," Dick said, handing the book back to Nate. "I remember his exact words. He said, 'Dick, we're organizin' a vigilance committee on April 21st. We'd like for ya t'meet with us at Al's place if you're interested.'"

Ramsay's brothers, Jack and Luke, were aggressive and hot tempered. Ramsay was not so turned. He had apparently inherited a calmer and more steadfast nature from his mother. "I knowed Ramsay would make the right decisions. That's why I decided on sendin' him t'their meetin'."

"Has Ramsay been to any more of their meetin's?"

"Not after he told me what those connivers done. I told my boys we wasn't goin' t'have anything more t'do with Bothwell."

"I'd like to talk with Ramsay about that meetin' last April. Is he around?"

"No, he ain't. I sent him over t'Buffalo day before yesterday. He ought to be back in a couple of days. You're welcome t'stay till he does."

"He'll come back through Powder River Pass won't he?

"Yep, he sure will."

"I'll try to meet him. Do you believe Ramsay would agree to testify about that meetin'?"

"Yes, sir, that boy's got plenty of guts," Dick said, patting Nate on the shoulder. "He'll testify; all ya need t'do is ast him."

Nate rode up the western slopes of the Bighorns. He neared the summit of Powder River Pass at half-past noon. The hot July winds blowing across the Bighorn Basin had grown cool, tossing the pines to and fro along the high pass. Nate caught the scent of pine burning before seeing smoke from a campfire rising above a grove of aspen on the summit.

"Howdy, Marshal Hamby," Ramsay called as Nate rode into the aspen grove. "I got a pot of coffee just ready for drinkin'."

"Howdy, Ramsay, hot coffee sounds good."

"Sheriff Angus said you'd gone over to the ranch lookin' for me," Ramsay said, filling Nate's tin cup. "He said you had the minutes of the meetin' down at Bothwell's place."

Nate pulled the notebook from his vest-pocket. "I want you to understand that I'm not accusin' you of conspiracy. The minutes clearly indicate your objections to the *dead list*."

Ramsay accepted the notebook and read Canton's minutes. "This is an accurate record," he said, returning it to Nate. "That's how the meetin' went all right. Reckon Henderson an' me left too soon."

"Will you testify in court?"

"Yep, sure, when'll that be?"

"Not long now, I hope."

Ramsay tossed the dregs from his cup into the fire and

hunkered down on his boot heels.  He grasped a yellow string hanging from his vest-pocket, pulled out a sack of Bull Durham and rolled a cigarette.  "Wanta smoke?" he asked, holding out the bag of tobacco.

"No thanks, I'll just fire up my stogie."

Ramsay pulled a brand from the fire and lit his cigarette and Nate's cigar.  "Marshal," he said, tossing the brand back into the fire.  "Have y'heard about Jim Averell along with a woman that's been whorin' near his place down on the Sweetwater gettin' hanged yesterday?"

"They hanged Jim and a woman?  That's got to be some of Bothwell's doin's."

"Yeah, I reckon so," Ramsay said, blowing smoke around the cigarette dangling from his mouth.  "Red Angus said they hanged 'em in broad daylight."

"That's gettin' about as bold or dumb as they come."

"Yeah, I didn't think those scoundrels had the guts to do their own killin'."

Nate stood up.  "I don't think Bothwell would blink twice at killin'.  I'll let you know when we'll be needin' your testimony."

Ramsay tossed his cigarette into the fire.  "You do that, Marshal.  I'll help anyway I can."

Nate rode across Powder River Pass and down to Buffalo where he checked into the Occidental Hotel.  The following morning, he walked up to the courthouse to see Red Angus.

Jack Flagg, owner of the Hat Ranch and a prolific columnist for the *Buffalo Bulletin* joined Nate as he walked up the hill. Having once been employed by WSGA member T. W. Peters on his Bar C Ranch, Flagg was now blacklisted by the WSGA. During the spring roundup of 1886 he had participated in the strike by Wyoming cowboys for a minimum wage of $40 a month.  After Peters fired him, he homesteaded on the Red Fork of Powder River and bought the Hat brand and a small herd of cattle.  In 1888, he took in four partners: Al Allison, Billy Hill, L. A. Webb, and Tom Gardner.  All of them were experienced cowmen, blacklisted by the WSGA and good with a Colt .45.

"Howdy, Marshal Hamby."

"Howdy, Jack, any news worth talkin' about?"

"Just the same bunch of lies bein' spread by the WSGA. All the Cheyenne papers are callin' Jim Averell and Ella Watson rustlers."

"Maybe they were."

"I doubt it. They also claim that Ella was a whore runnin' a hog ranch all by herself. I know for a fact that she and Jim were married and all the cattle in her pasture belonged to them."

Hog ranches were scattered across the west. They were establishments that pretended to be a ranch, but actually supplied whiskey and whores to their clientele. Most of them were located near military forts and large ranches. Cowboys and soldiers often enjoyed brawling as well as booze and sexual favors in these houses of ill repute.

"What about Averell?"

"I met him while he was soldierin' out at Fort McKinney. You know Jim, he was a lot of things but he wasn't a thief."

"Probably not, let me know if you get anythin' new on that situation."

"I'll do that," Jack said, climbing the courthouse stairs to the clerks office.

Red Angus was hunched over his desk reading the *Cheyenne Leader* when Nate walked in. He opened his desk drawer and pulled out a telegram. It was from Hap.

U S MARSHAL NATE HAMBY (STOP) JOHNSON COUNTY COURT HOUSE (STOP) BUFFALO (STOP) WYOMING TERRITORY (STOP) CASPER JUSTICE OF THE PEACE WILL HOLD CORONERS INQUEST TODAY INTO SWEETWATER HANGINGS (STOP) FOUR WITNESSES WILL TESTIFY (STOP) HAP DUGGER DEPUTY U S MARSHAL (STOP)

Nate stuffed the telegram into his pocket. "Flagg said all the Cheyenne papers claim the woman they hung with Jim Averell was a whore by the name of Ella Watson."

"That's right, she had a homestead about a mile from Averell's store. The *Cheyenne Leader* says she had around fifty head of yearlin's in her pasture."

"They allege all of them to be rustled?"

"Yeah, sure do," Red replied. "The article in the *Leader* dubbed her 'Cattle Kate,' the rustler-queen of the Sweetwater."

"If you'll wire Judge Saufley about this, I'll head for Casper right now."

# Chapter Ten

Nate and Hap entered a maze of intrigue, stonewalling, perjury, cover-up and murder of witnesses as they embarked upon bringing Jim Averell and Ella Watson's murderers to justice. A tangled web of deceit woven on the looms of conspiracy weavers who were sympathetic toward Bothwell's vigilantes soon appeared.

Within hours, following Jim and Ella dying at the end of twin lariats, typesetters for Cheyenne newspapers invented new characters for the dead pair. Ella became "Cattle Kate Maxwell," a notorious dance-hall frail that was quick with a gun. Jim Averell was a malicious killer with several notches on his .45. Both were dubbed thieves that rustled cattle up and down the Sweetwater River. It was a case of: *Good riddance; these rustlers have got to be stopped.*

The spurious news hummed across telegraph wires, spreading grist for sensational journalism. In Chicago, New York and most other eastern cities, the fabrications were printed, reprinted, and quoted within twenty-four hours of their publication in Cheyenne. Wyoming Territory was living up to its reputation of being raw, wild, obscene and governed only by vigilante justice.

Upon learning about the Sweetwater hangings from Red Angus, Hap went to Casper. He arrived on Monday afternoon, July twenty-second. The town was rife with rumors. The telegraph receiver at the depot seldom ceased to clatter out messages. Himey Callaway, editor of the *Casper Weekly Mail*, had not left the newspaper offices since Tex Healy's horse galloped into town Sunday morning. Tex told Sheriff Rice about Frank Buchanan witnessing seven men hang Jim Averell and Ella Watson. Sheriff Rice quickly assembled a posse and rode out of town toward the hanging site near Sweetwater River.

Himey was setting type for a special edition of the *Casper Weekly Mail* when Hap walked into the newspaper office.

"Howdy," Hap said as he looked over Himey's shoulder at the boxes of lead type. "What's the latest on the hangin's?"

Himey continued to set type. "Justice of the Peace Ted Morrison has called for an inquest soon as Sheriff Rice gets back with the witnesses."

"Justice o' the Peace, ain't y'got no coroner in Casper?"

"He's down at Cheyenne and won't be back for several days."

The following morning, Sheriff Rice and his posse rode into town with four witnesses. They were Frank Buchanan, Ralph Cole, John DeCorey and a teenaged boy by the name of Gene Crowder. The Justice of the Peace called to six men loitering on the sidewalk in front of Demorest's Restaurant. "You fellas, come with me. You're on my inquest jury."

Morrison called the hearing to order and swore in his jurors. Sheriff Rice testified that Jim Averell and Ella Watson had been hanged from a scrub pine on Spring Creek. John DeCorey, Ralph Cole, and Gene Crowder described how six men abducted Ella from her home and forced her into a buckboard. The abductors then drove to Averell's place and forced him at gunpoint to join Ella on the buckboard. Frank Buchanan told how he was drinking beer at Averell's store when DeCorey and the kid came running in yelling that six men had captured Ella and Jim. He jumped on his horse and set out to follow the buckboard. He was almost in tears when his testimony ended. "I tried best I could t'stop 'em. I emptied my .45s at 'em, and then had t'ride for my life while they was firin' their Winchesters at me."

Each of the witnesses, with the exception of Frank Buchanan, named the same men as the abductors and killers of Jim and Ella. Frank testified that a seventh man he did not know joined the hanging party just before he opened fire on them. The jury was ready to render their verdict for the hearing when Nate walked in and sat down next to Hap. Morrison read the verdict. "It is the unanimous decision of the jury that the deceased, Jim Averell and Ella Watson came to their deaths by hanging at the hands of the following men: Albert Bothwell, Tom Sun, John

Durbin, R. B. Connor, Ernest McLain, R. M. Galbraith and an unknown man."

Following the inquest, Nate talked with Sheriff Rice who had determined that the hangings hadn't taken place in Natrona County. He was reasonably certain that Jim and Ella had been strangled at the end of vigilante lariats just across the line in Carbon County. If that were the case, any trial would be in Rawlins, the county seat of Carbon County and the inquest verdict rendered by a Natrona County jury would fall by the wayside.

Frank Buchanan was well into a bottle of courage when Nate and Hap found him at Sheppley's Saloon about an hour after the inquest. "I'm a dead man," he said and gulped from his bottle. "I'm just as dead as old Jim an' Ella. Bothwell's bunch ain't goin' ta rest till I'm buzzard bait."

Nate agreed that the chances of Frank's living to testify against the killers in court were slim. The entire state was astir with those who had quickly taken a position either for or against the Sweetwater hangings. The cattle barons and their minions were determined to let the hangings stand as a stark warning to anyone daring to settle on their claimed grazing lands. On the other side were the homesteaders and owners of small ranches and farms that were determined to see the Sweetwater gang of vigilantes brought to justice. The WSGA cattle barons wielded great power throughout the entire state mainly because they were organized and committed to their growing policy of vigilantism. Every gun that they controlled would be ready to erase all living witnesses to the hangings.

"Would you be willing to write a statement about everything you saw," Nate asked.

Frank pulled a folded paper from his shirt pocket. "I already have. I wrote it all down and signed it yesterday."

Nate unfolded the paper, read it and slipped it into his vest-pocket. "Do you have any idea where DeCorey, Cole, and the kid might be?"

"Bothwell's bunch has got the kid. I saw Tom Sun's foreman walkin' the kid to his buckboard after the inquest. I figger DeCorey an' Cole is headed for Denver by now. I ain't goin' t'be far behind 'em neither."

Their tardiness in talking to Cole and DeCorey immediately following the inquest haunted Nate and Hap as they spent nearly a month searching for them. Also, Frank Buchanan had vanished. All three witnesses had disappeared without a trace, lending credence to the possibility of their having been killed and buried in a remote ravine on one of the vigilante's ranches. They finally discovered that the kid, Gene Crowder, was being held by Al Bothwell in one of his line shacks near Ferris Mountain. It was isolated and guarded by a dozen armed men. There just wasn't any way to rescue the kid alive.

The first week in September, Nate and Hap were riding past the grave in which Ella and Jim were buried. Two cowboys were digging another grave and a buckboard with a sheet-shrouded corpse on it was parked nearby. "Who you fellas buryin'?" Nate called, spun out of his saddle and stepped to the ground.

They stopped digging and one removed his hat and wiped sweat from his brow with his sleeve. "It's the Crowder kid," he said, replacing his hat.

"What kilt 'im?" Hap asked.

"Doc Smith said some kind o' kidney trouble."

Nate walked toward the buckboard. "Mind if I take a look at him?"

"Reckon that's your right since you're a U.S. marshal."

Nate pulled back the sheet. The corpse was a slightly built boy of no more than fourteen years. "He have any family?" Nate asked and replaced the sheet.

"Reckon not. He stayed at Ella's afore the hangin'."

"What about after the hangin'?"

"Al felt sorry for 'im. He kept 'im and even had Doc Smith come out from Rawlins t'take care of 'im."

Outside the Rawlins Hotel, chilly October winds buffeted a faded and frayed star-spangled banner. Inside, Judge McDermott had sworn in thirteen men for a grand jury hearing in the lobby. The prosecuting attorney, Hiram Cantrell, paced back and forth in front of the grand jury while nearing the end of his examination of Nate. He paused in front of Nate to ask another question. "Marshal Hamby, is it your sworn testimony that you believe this statement signed by one Frank Buchanan was written in his own hand?"

"Yes, it is."

"Marshal Hamby, I'd like for you to look at this statement that you allege to be that of Frank Buchanan."

"All right. You want me to read it?"

"Yes, but not out loud. Just read it silently."

After Nate had scanned the written statement for several minutes, Cantrell said, "Marshal, have you read that statement before today?"

"Sure, I read it after Frank Buchanan had written and signed it."

"I'd like to ask you to read the second paragraph for the jury. Would you do that, please?"

"All right. It says, 'I follered the six men afore mentioned as they drove the buckboard with Jim and Ella tied together in back. When they got to the ford, they drove straight up the dry riverbed for a couple of miles. There were a lot of arguin' goin' on among the six abductors, but couldn't make out what was bein' said. They turned south out of the riverbed up Spring Creek Canyon. When they reached some pine trees standin' on a cliff, they stopped the buckboard. I spied a man sittin' on a bay up on the ridge above Spring Creek at about this time. He started to ride down to meet the buckboard. After a lot more arguin', the six men made Jim and Ella get off the buckboard. I was certain they were goin' to hang both of them after they put ropes around their necks. I started shootin' at them with both my .45s till I run out of ammunition. All of them including the rider afore mentioned began firin' rifles at me. That's when I hightailed it out of there.'" Nate hesitated. "That's all of that paragraph, Mister Cantrell."

"Thank you, Marshal Hamby. At no place in this alleged statement does Frank Buchanan say that he actually saw anyone hang Jim Averell or Ella Watson. Is that correct?"

"Well, no, not exactly. He had to run or get killed himself."

"Do you not agree that Buchanan opened fire on the men with Averell and Watson?"

"That's what he claims."

"Yes and they responded by shooting back at Buchanan. Isn't that a logical response?"

"Yes."

"Don't you agree that during all that gunplay Averell and Watson could have easily escaped from their alleged abductors?"

"They might have, but I don't know that, Mister Cantrell."

"Since they did not make that effort, isn't it logical to conclude that they did not fear for their lives?"

"I wouldn't say that, they had nooses around their necks, accordin' to Buchanan."

"Yes, according to this alleged statement. But, they made no effort to get away. Why do you believe that was the case?"

"Don't rightly know."

I'd like to direct your attention now, Marshal, to the sixth sentence in the alleged statement of Frank Buchanan."

"All right."

"The author alleges that he saw another man on a horse. Is that correct?"

"That is correct."

"Why doesn't the author identify that man?"

"I don't know the answer. Maybe he didn't know who he was."

"Do you suppose it's possible that the author determined not to identify that man in this statement?"

"I suppose that is possible."

"Yes, that is possible and is it not possible that the six men named in this statement only intended to scare Averell and Watson into leaving the country?"

"Yes, but they still hanged them."

"Now, Marshal Hamby, that's where the rub comes in. There are no witnesses to that event, not even your author of this statement. Is it not within the realm of possibility, even probability, that the unknown rider could have forced the hanging to take place?"

"I'd doubt that ever happened. One man against six?"

"But it is possible is it not?"

"Yes, it's possible."

"If this statement was written and signed by Frank Buchanan as you have testified, why wasn't his signature witnessed by a notary?"

"Well, Buchanan gave that to me after Marshal Dugger and I talked with him about what he'd seen."

"Then, it would seem that you don't know for certain this statement was written and signed by Frank Buchanan. Is that a fair assumption?"

"Well, I never saw him write it or sign it either, if that's what you're drivin' at. He'd done that before we talked."

Cantrell grinned and winked at the jurymen. "You weren't concerned about verifying this document before a grand jury?"

"No, not at that time. I believed Mister Buchanan would be testifyin' about that himself."

"Mister Buchanan isn't here to do that is he? Why haven't you brought Frank Buchanan here to testify?"

"He's most likely dead."

Cantrell stepped up to the witness chair, leaned over, and glared at Nate. "What evidence do you have that caused you to arrive at that conclusion?"

"Him, Ralph Cole and John DeCorey have vanished. My deputy and I have spent over a month tryin' to find them. They are nowhere to be found. Nobody has seen Cole and DeCorey since the day of the inquest in Casper. We finally discovered that Buchanan had taken a muleskinner's job with the Niobrara Transportation Company, but he disappeared on the 13th of September and hasn't been seen since then either. I'm certain that all of them have been murdered."

Cantrell walked toward the jury and continued to question Nate while pacing in front of them. "I see. You seem to be exercising conjecture."

"Maybe, but I believe all three are in graves dug on one of the accused's ranches."

"Now, Marshal Hamby, since you are guessing their fate, don't you agree that they may have just left and got out of Wyoming?"

"No, a man just doesn't travel across Wyoming without being seen by someone, no matter whether he's on a horse, a stage or a train."

Cantrell clucked his tongue and raised his eyebrows. "Marshal Hamby, I am impressed. Are you saying that you and your deputy are infallible? Since you haven't located these men, they are surely dead, their corpses hidden by the men that you have accused? I find that appalling. I have no further questions for this witness."

Judge McDermott acknowledged Cantrell with a nod. "Does this complete all of the evidence for this jury to consider?"

"Excuse me, Judge," Nate said, rising from the witness chair. "I would like to answer Mister Cantrell's questions."

Judge McDermott peered at Nate over his spectacles. "Of course, please do."

Nate spoke directly to the jurymen while standing. "I would be the first to admit we are not infallible. But our investigation has been extensive. There is no record of Cole and DeCory traveling by stage or train. They have not been seen by anyone in all of the towns surrounding Casper. My deputy or I have contacted every sheriff in Wyoming. None of them have been able to find anyone that has seen these men. In my opinion, Cole and DeCorey never left Natrona County."

Nate walked back to the witness chair and sat down. "That's all I have to say."

"Thank you, Marshal Hamby," Judge McDermott said. "Thank you for your testimony, sir. You are excused."

"You're surely welcome, Judge," Nate said as he left the witness box.

Judge McDermott looked at Cantrell as he spoke. "Do you wish to call any additional witnesses, Mister Cantrell?"

"No, your Honor." Cantrell stood up, and removed his reading spectacles. "Gentlemen of the jury, I shall be brief." It only took Cantrell about thirty seconds to get the jury laughing. Within five minutes, they were nodding in agreement to his observations: The absence of any witnesses to the hangings. His accusation of Nate's giving self-serving testimony. The absence of any confirmation of the authenticity of the statement alleged to be authored by Frank Buchanan. Finally, he threw in several suppositions that had questionable logic. "In conclusion gentlemen of the jury," Cantrell said as he paced in front of the all-male, all-WSGA-member grand jury, "the marshal has presented no witnesses of the alleged crime. He has presented no evidence of substance that could incriminate the accused. Gentlemen, I ask that you issue no true bills of indictment severally or jointly against the accused."

Fifteen minutes later, Prosecutor Hiram Cantrell and the men accused of hanging Jim Averell and Ella Watson were laughing and shaking hands. It was over. Al Bothwell, Tom Sun, R. B. Connor, John Durbin, R. M. Galbraith and Ernest McLain walked from the Rawlins Hotel. Al Bothwell strutted and sneered at Nate and Hap as he led his vigilantes out of the hotel. "You bastards stay off my ranch," Al said. "That includes both Averell's and Watson's places. They belong to me."

Nate stepped up to Bothwell and shook his finger squarely in front of Bothwell's nose. "Bothwell, you and your bunch are nothin' more than snivelin' cowards. That includes your legal lackey, Prosecutor Cantrell. You saints of Lucifer hung a defenseless woman. It took six, or was it seven, of you lizards to kill Ella Watson and Jim Averell. I hope you burn in hell."

"Reckon I'll be seein' you there, too," Bothwell said as he led his fellow hangmen to their horses.

* * * * *

Who was the seventh man? This question lingered in Nate's mind as he and Hap rode into Buffalo a week after the grand jury hearing. Red Angus added to their dilemma with more bad news. The bullet-pierced hat allegedly belonging to Frank Canton had been pilfered from his safe after one of his deputies had failed to lock it before leaving the office unattended. Soon thereafter, Canton reappeared on the streets of Buffalo.

Nate and Hap spent the winter trying to determine the identity of the seventh man at the Sweetwater hangings, but none of the vigilantes or the cowhands working for them would talk.

After spring thaw, when Powder River Pass opened, they rode over to the Drury Ranch on the Bighorn River. Dick and Ramsay Drury were Nate's best hope for the solution of the unknown vigilante.

Dick Drury opened the front door to greet them. "Howdy there, fellers. Come on in."

"Millie," Dick called as they all sat down in the den, a large room with a stone fireplace near the rear of the house. "Millie," Dick called a second time.

With hardly a sound, Millie appeared on the mezzanine balcony surrounding the den. *Dick's Millie is really a beautiful woman*, Nate thought, as she descended the stairway. She did not appear to be a full-blood Indian. Ebony hair framed her pleasantly balanced features, which were highlighted by high cheekbones and a well-shaped Shoshone nose, but her eyes were blue. She wore her hair swept back from her face and braided into a bun on the back of her head.

"Yes, Dick," she said, gliding toward them. "Who are these gentlemen?"

"Millie, these are Marshals Nate Hamby and Hap Dugger. Fellers, I want ya t'meet Mrs. Drury."

Millie brought cigars and a decanter of bourbon with three glasses. After exchanging the usual pleasantries, she disappeared as quietly as when she had appeared on the balcony.

"What you fellers needin' today?" Dick asked.

"We're hopin' you can help us on the Sweetwater hangin's," Nate replied.

"Well, now, don't know if I can, but I'll surely try."

"We appreciate that. One of the witnesses, Frank Buchanan, who has disappeared, told us there was a seventh man unknown to him that joined Bothwell's six vigilantes at the hangin's. I was wonderin' if you or Ramsay might know who that man was?"

Dick sipped bourbon while pondering Nate's question. "Yeah, reckon I do. I think y'know who it was, too. Don't ya?"

"I'm not sure—that's why we're here."

Dick chewed on his cigar while staring at Nate. "Tom Albert!"

Hap slammed his whiskey glass into the fireplace. "Damn!"

"Don't think I'm doubtin' your word," Nate said, "but how do y'know Tom was the seventh man?"

"Just rode in from Cheyenne yesterday. Adams told me straight out while we were drinkin' at the Club. They're all laughin' at you boys. Got you beat, they say."

Nate drained his whiskey glass. "That'll be their downfall"

"How's that?"

"Judge Saufley tells me that statehood is only a few months away."

"How will that change anything?"

"The vote," Nate said, holding up a finger. "The WSGA can't win an honest election."

"That's right," Hap said. "Reckon ol' Canton found that out when Sheriff Angus whupped 'im."

Drury guffawed and emptied his glass with one swallow. "I hate t'bust your bubble, fellas, but there ain't an honest card in their deck. You'll find that out come statehood."

T A Ranch house where the invaders took refuge
Photo credit: Wyoming Division of Cultural Resources

Mobile breastwork used by posse against the invaders
Photo credit: Wyoming Division of Cultural Resources

T A Ranch barn used as a fort by the invaders
Photo credit: Wyoming Division of Cultural Resources

6th U. S. Cavalry from Fort McKinney during the Johnson County War
Photo credit: Wyoming Division of Cultural Resources

The invaders (cattle barons & hired gunmen) following their surrender
Photo credit: Wyoming Division of Cultural Resources

# PART TWO

## WAR AT CRAZY WOMAN CREEK

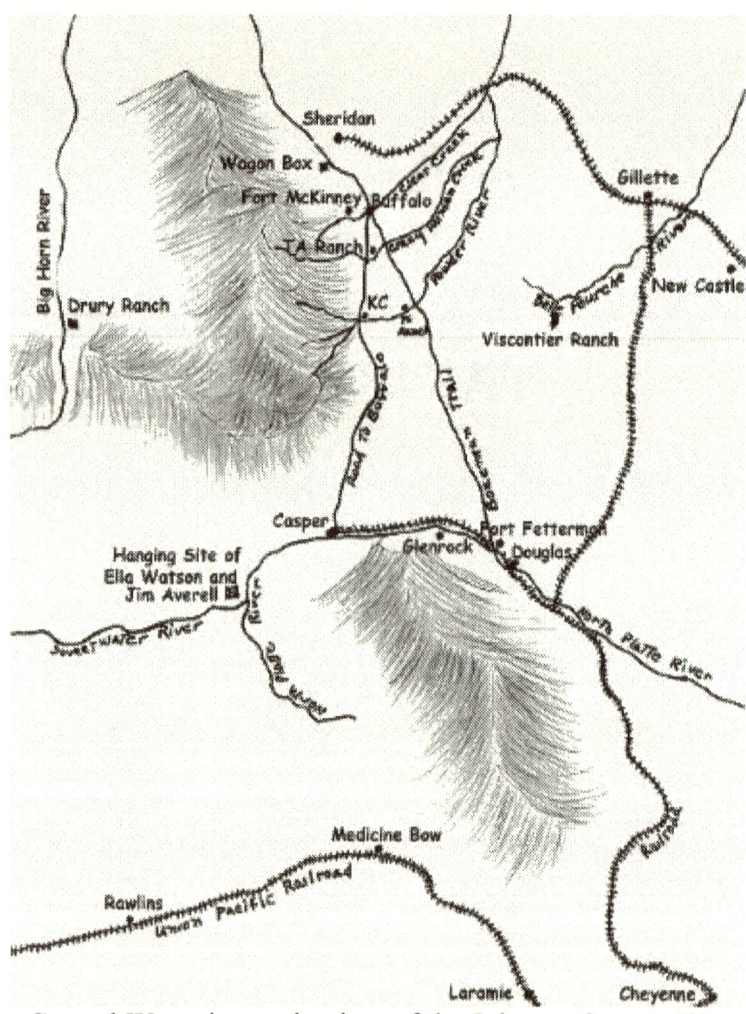

Central Wyoming at the time of the Johnson County War

# Chapter Eleven

During the last week in July of 1891, Carter Viscontier, who had homesteaded his sheep ranch along the Belle Fourche River, sat astride his aged gray gelding watching several thousand of his sheep. Black and white border collies circled around and among the mute flock. An occasional nip or urgent bark kept the woollies in line. Viscontier had lost two of his prized Australian collies and fourteen of their charges the previous night. He patted the old Henry rifle lying cradled across his lap. "Damned wolves," he muttered under his breath, "I'll not have y'killin' my laddies."

A flashing light from atop a low sage-covered hill on the southeastern horizon distracted Viscontier from his stalk. A rider's hat and torso were silhouetted against the sky. Greasy sage tall enough to hide antelope and deer obscured his cantering horse. Viscontier puffed on his pipe while watching the approaching rider whose silver badge glinted intermittently. "Well, if it isn't my old friend, Marshal Hamby," Viscontier called as Nate rode up.

"Howdy, Mister Viscontier, it's sure a hot day to be sittin' still on a horse."

"Aye, mate, it is hot, what brings you to the Belle Fourche?"

"I've been down to Newcastle helpin' the sheriff on a vigilante hangin'."

"Who got hung?"

"Tom Waggoner."

"He's a horse thief, I hear."

"Yeah, he had nearly a thousand horses on his place the day they hung him."

"Who hung him?"

"Tom Albert, Joe Elliott, and Fred Coates were seen together in Newcastle the day before the hangin'. I'm certain they did it."

"Albert's a range detective for the WSGA ain't he?"

"Yeah, so's Elliott and Coates."

"Jack Shetland down at the Sailin' C says the WSGA's gettin' ready to make war."

"He ought to know," Nate said. "He's one of their directors."

Nate left Carter Viscontier scanning the hills for wolves and rode northwest toward the hazy, blue Bighorns and the Wagon Box. The sorrel gelding Nate was riding had become an old friend. He would cock his ears around as if trying to catch every word when Nate talked to him. Those times were when they were alone.

This was such a time: "Killin' somebody hasn't ever given me a good feelin', not that savin' my own skin by doin' it wasn't important. I do get pleasure thinkin' about Tom standin' there ready to draw on me. He's always claimed he could beat my sidesaddle left-handed draw. A pity he hasn't been told that on any given day somebody can get the edge and put you down no matter how fast you may be."

"Somethin' else gives me pleasure. Tom has hurt a lot of folks. I hate him mostly for what he's doin' to Beth. I hate him for what he's become, and what my hatin' him has done to me. When my bullet tears into his chest and its impact jolts his conscience, I'll be smilin'. That's when Tom will see himself through my eyes. That's goin' to give me a good feelin'."

Jess Bass and his two cubs rode into Nate's life that night at the Powder River Crossing east of Buffalo. After he and Hap buried the three rustlers on the bank of Lodgepole Creek, Nate was determined to see Tom Albert and the two Franks, Canton and Wolcott, brought to justice.

* * * * *

The summer of 1891, short in Wyoming, slipped into autumn as frost nipped the green from aspen, cottonwood, willow and box elder trees. The WSGA had accelerated its assault on their perceived enemies. Their range detectives were seizing all cattle shipped by suspected rustlers, which were almost all of the owners of small ranches and farms. Their victim's recourse for compensation, though legally established by law, was an ex parte board whose decisions were always in favor of the WSGA. Wyoming had not changed following statehood. Justice had not awakened, not even stirred.

The elimination of every enemy of the WSGA was now official policy of their leaders. Frank Canton, now their chief enforcer, rode north toward the M-W Ranch and a nefarious meeting with Tom Albert. Winter was making its entry with the season's first snowfall.

"Yes, Tom is expecting you, won't you come in, Mr. Canton?"

"Thanks, Mrs. Albert," Canton said and handed Beth his Stetson, splotched from melting snowflakes.

"Tom is in the study."

"No need to bother, ma'am, I know the way."

Tom remained seated behind his desk stacked with open law books as Frank walked through the doorway. The odor from smoldering alder sweetened the air as the burning logs upon a great stone hearth chased away the evening chill. Above the hearth, a wide map of the M-W Ranch covered the fireplace's stone facade. A safe, which was imbedded in the stone façade below the map, was concealed behind an enlarged M-W brand that was welded to the door. "Howdy, Frank pull up a chair."

"Thanks, how are your legs doin'?"

Tom's feet seemed to be made of cork with no feeling within his cowhide boots. Syphilis, acquired at the Cheyenne Club after his estrangement from Beth, was feeding upon his nervous system, turning his legs into clumsy wooden appendages. A gold-handled walking stick provided the necessary support for each step he struggled to take. "I've got two fence posts to walk on," Tom replied, massaging each thigh.

After Frank Canton had gone into Tom's study, Beth walked down the hallway to her art studio. She sat in front of her latest effort, a portrait of Nate Hamby. All it needed were some finishing strokes with her camel's-hair brush accenting highlights and shadows of Nate's handsome features. She was pleased with his sandy red hair, but a few more streaks of gray were needed at the temples. Beth had captured sadness in his blue eyes left there by Chancellorsville, Gettysburg, the Wilderness and the terrible year in the trenches defending Petersburg and Richmond.

She tried to ignore Frank and Tom's muffled voices coming through the ventilation duct Tom had installed to carry heat from the massive fireplace in his study to several other rooms in the house, including Beth's studio. When Tom's voice grew more intense, Beth stopped highlighting the U.S. marshal's badge pinned on the left lapel of Nate's black leather vest and listened more intently. Frank was talking, but his words were garbled. "I met with the new WSGA secretary, Hiram Ijams, like you told me," Frank said. "He agreed that the rustlin' is so bad that we've got to go ahead with Bothwell's plan."

"I see, how many names are on the vigilante list, now?" Tom asked.

"There's thirty-four, but there's goin' to be a lot more soon as the committee meets next week. I figure every man that helped organize the rustlers into the Northern Wyomin' Farmers' and Stock Growers' Association last month will be added."

A meeting of farmers and owners of small ranches in Johnson County had met in Buffalo to organize themselves into an entity capable of dealing with their problems. The most important issue at the time was the recent stock-seizure move by the WSGA. Other issues were the grievances they held against the open range ranchers moving their herds wherever they pleased, the destruction of their fences and gardens and the loss of their cattle that mysteriously joined the big herds. The name they chose for their organization was intended to be provocative to the older WSGA. It was called the *Northern Wyoming Farmers' and Stock Growers' Association.*

"Who do you plan on takin' down?" Tom asked.

*What does Tom mean by that?* Beth thought as she strained to listen.

"Well, we missed gettin' Nate Champion about three weeks ago up at the Hall cabin. He's the biggest rustler of the lot. I've got one of our detectives, Joe Elliott, workin' on gettin' Champion set up. We'll get him next time."

Nate Champion, a known rustler and a friend by the name of Ross Gilbertson had holed up to spend the coming winter season in the Hall cabin. They were awakened early one morning by three WSGA range detectives kicking open the door. A shoot out took place with Colt .45's blazing away. A lot of near misses took place, but no bullets found their mark. The attack ended as the three detectives abandoned the cabin's close quarters to seek safety in the woods.

"Elliott's a good man, who's next on the list?"

"That's what I came up to talk about, Ranger Jones has been threatenin' Fred Hesse. Says he's goin' to kill Fred first chance he gets. Jones is in Buffalo partyin' it up afore gettin' married. Then, there's John Tisdale. He's rustled nearly his entire herd off the Bar C. It just so happens that Tisdale is doin' a little free time in Buffalo, too."

Orley "Ranger" Jones and his brother, Johnny, had come to Wyoming from Nebraska in 1887. They were both cowboys, rode for the EK Ranch in 1888 and quickly earned the reputation of being rustlers. Ranger later homesteaded on the Red Fork River and quickly acquired a herd of questionable origins.

John A. Tisdale migrated from Texas with his brother, Al Allison. He homesteaded at the head of the Red Fork northeast of Flagg's Hat Ranch. He had been a drover, bossing three herds from Texas to the northern territories. He worked for Theodore Roosevelt on his North Dakota ranch before moving west to Johnson County. His brother Al bought a fifth interest in the Hat Ranch from Flagg. Both John and Al were quickly labeled rustlers by the WSGA.

"You want to take Jones and Tisdale down? Is that what you're tellin' me, Frank?"

*Oh, dear lord, they are talking about murder. I wish they would speak louder. Did Tom say, Johns, or was it Jones?*

"We may not get this good a chance, again," Frank replied. "I figure we can kill both of 'em when they're returnin' home. Both of 'em are drivin' wagons that'll be loaded down with supplies. I've already got two good spots picked out where we can ambush 'em. What do y'say, Tom?"

"How many men do you have lined up to pull this off?"

"I've got four, all respected citizens of Buffalo and they're on our side."

Frank's words were followed by squeaking sounds. Beth recognized them to be the caster wheels on Tom's swivel chair.

Then the distinct *thump, thump* of Tom's walking stick grew louder as he walked toward the fireplace.    The thumping stopped. "I see. That's good," Tom said. "Where are those two spots you've picked out?"

"I figure to get Tisdale nine miles south of Buffalo when he drives down into Haywood's Gulch.  He'll be out of sight and there's a good place to hide just a few feet from the crossin'. Another seven miles down at the Muddy Creek crossin' is where we'll get Jones."

*The name isn't Johns, it's Jones, and the other man's name sounded like Dale.  He said something about a Gulch and a creek.  Oh, dear, speak louder.... please.*

"I know the places; those are good choices," Tom said and then a loud metallic clanging sound erupted through the duct.

*Tom must have taken something out of the safe.*

"Is the full thousand in this envelope?" Frank asked.

"Yeah, but you'd better count it," Tom replied.  A period of silence ensued, then Tom asked, "Are you leavin' their gettin' to those spots up to chance?"

"No chance, Tisdale visits one of Sally Shaw's girls up on Laurel Street ever' time he gets to drinkin' at Zindel's Saloon. I'm payin' Sally fifty dollars to keep Tisdale in town until we're ready for him to leave."

*He said 'Tisdale.'  Yes, I'm certain.  What did he say about Laurel Street?  Oh, darn, Frank Canton, quit your mumbling.*

"After killin' Jones, then you'll wait for Tisdale?"

"Simple as that."

*They are going to kill two men named Jones and Tisdale. Oh, dear, those poor men must be warned; somehow, I must tell Nate.*

The fragmented conversation Beth had struggled to hear between Tom and Frank Canton haunted her as she tried to put it all together.  The voices had waxed and waned.  The only things she was certain of were the men's last names and they both would be killed. Nate stared at Beth from the canvas perched on her easel. "Oh, Nate," she said to the portrait, "I wish you were really here."

Beth sobbed as she cleaned paint from her fingers with a

turpentine rag.    After several minutes, her weeping was interrupted when Tom called, "Beth! Oh, Beth! Frank is stayin' with us tonight."

Beth dried her eyes and smoothed her hair. Tom and Frank met her in the hallway. She prayed her eyes would not reveal the raw panic she was struggling to restrain. "The guest bedroom is next to Tom's, Mister Canton."

"Thanks, Mrs. Albert."

"Why don't you help me climb the stairs," Tom said to Frank. "I'll show you where it is."

Beth spent a sleepless night. She and Tom had ceased to live as husband and wife, being estranged since he had opted to take up residence at the Cheyenne Club. He came home to the M-W Ranch only when summoned by Beth to attend to pressing business matters. They slept in separate bedrooms—she in the ground floor master bedroom and he in one of the upstairs guestrooms.    Within three years' time, Tom had gone from robust health to being nearly an invalid.    He suffered from memory lapses and periods of severe depression.    Booze had subtly become his mistress as he relied more and more upon it to get him through the day and to sleep at night. "Dear, God, show me what to do," Beth prayed, "please, bring Tom to his senses." The shadow of fear swept over her as she listened to Tom's cane thumping back and forth across the floor of his room.

* * * * *

After Frank left the following morning, Beth said to Tom, "I've finished Nate's portrait and this is a good day for me to take it to him."

Tom poured himself a double shot of bourbon, glared at Beth, and then sat down behind his desk. "That's a good day's ride down to the Wagon Box."

"Yes, I know."

Tom emptied his glass with one swallow.   "Do y'want one of the hands to hitch up the surrey?"

"Yes and have him put my saddle in the surrey."

A jealous delusion swept through Tom's diseased brain.    *Of course*, he thought, *she wants her saddle so she and Nate can get off some place far away from prying eyes.* "Your saddle?" Tom yelled. His hand convulsed into a violent shaking tremor as he continued. "You plannin' on shackin' up with Nate in some cow camp?" Whiskey splashed over documents from the decanter as he tried to refill his empty glass. He threw the decanter across the room, smashing it against the fireplace. "I know why y'painted that damned picture. Y'got that bastard in your brain ain't ya? Now, you're wantin' to go traipsin' down there to give him that picture. Hell, y'ain't foolin' me none, Mrs. Albert. I know what you're up to."

The spirochete bacterium of syphilis multiplying within Tom's central nervous system spawned frequent fits of suspicion and outright delusions. Syphilis, alcohol and the lust for power and wealth had unhinged his once-brilliant mind. He was but a shell, often bereft of reason, an easy pawn in the hands of evil men. Tom yelled in a frenzy, "Why don't you admit it, you're runnin' down there to bed down with Nate, ain't ya?"

Beth picked up shards of glass and threw them into the hearth. "You are evil, Tom Albert. I hate what you have become. I will not live one minute more with a murderer."

Tom glared at her, rage filling his eyes. "What do you mean? I'm no murderer."

Beth walked toward the door. "Maybe not, but you will be soon enough."

"Come back here. Who's been fillin' your head full of crap?"

"No one." Beth spun around to confront Tom with the truth. "I overheard you and Canton plotting to murder two men last night."

"You eavesdropping wench."

Tom grabbed his cane and pushed himself up from his chair. He staggered around his desk, flailing the air with the gold-headed walking stick. He became a raving lunatic, spewing demented profanity as he lunged toward her.

Fear cemented her feet to the floor as Tom swung the cane high above his head. "Aaaaaahhrr," rushed from his throat as the gold knob descended toward soft brown curls. He lurched to one side as his legs collapsed causing him to fall like a tree separated from its roots by a woodsman's ax.

A hung-over cowboy awakened to Beth's fists pounding on the bunkhouse door. He rolled from the bunk and stumbled toward the door while trying to pull on his britches. "What's wrong, Mizz Beth?" he asked, opening the door.

"It's Mr. Albert. Please, come help me."

Tom was addled, but had escaped serious injuries. A purple lump swelled beneath his left brow and blood trickled into his mustache from his left nostril. "What happened, Mister Albert?" the cowboy asked, helping Tom into a chair.

"It's these damned sticks I got for legs. Pour me a drink."

\* \* \* \* \*

Beth's pony trotted along with his tail swishing in the wind. The surrey's rubber-tired wheels hissed as they cut through a thin layer of snow covering the driveway to the Wagon Box. The afternoon sun was hanging just above the Bighorns when the little horse slowed to a halt in front of the ranch house.

Nate hadn't seen Beth since she and Tom had moved to the M-W Ranch. As he walked toward her buggy, he wondered why she had come alone to the Wagon Box.

"Oh, Nate, I fear Tom has lost his senses," she said, stepping down from her buggy. "He tried to kill me this morning."

"Tom tried to kill you?"

"It's true. He's sick and drinks day and night. I overheard him and Frank Canton last night plotting to murder two men. He attacked me with his cane this morning when I confronted him."

"Did he hurt you?"

"No, he fell before he could hit me."

"Who are the two men?"

"One is Jones and the other is Tisdale."

"Orley Jones and John A. Tisdale are on the vigilantes' dead list."

"Tom and Frank talked about a vigilante list. Is that what you call a dead list?

"Yes, let's go into the house and I'll explain it durin' supper."

Beth held up the portrait. "This is for you. Let me unwrap it."

Nate stared at his likeness Beth had captured on canvas. "I don't know what to say."

Beth smiled at his shy response.

"Well, thanks," Nate said, leaned down and kissed her cheek. "We'll hang it right after supper."

# Chapter Twelve

Nate made the ride to Buffalo the next morning in just over two hours. The sorrel's withers were smeared with froth as Nate tied him in front of the Johnson County courthouse. He was aware of Red Angus's dislike for both Orley Jones and John A. Tisdale, but neither of them deserved the fate Canton and Tom were planning for them. They were troublemakers that liked to "tweak the noses" of WSGA members, especially those of Fred Hesse and Bill Irvine. It was common knowledge that Orley and John were building spreads with rustled mavericks, many of them gathered from Hesse and Irvine herds. Jones had walked into Zindel's saloon one evening intending to pick a fight with Hesse who wisely ignored Jones's taunts, knowing his draw was not equal to Jones's.

"I can't say those two haven't asked for it," Red said after Nate told him about Canton and Tom's plot. "When did you find that out?"

"Tom's wife told me yesterday."

"She know when?"

"No!"

"Any idea where?"

"Some gulch or crossin'—she didn't catch the name."

"Jones left town headin' south in his wagon yesterday afternoon. If Canton managed to be waitin' for him, Orley Jones is dead."

"Well, I expect you're right. Is Tisdale still in town?"

"Most likely, he's been boozin' more than usual."

"I'll see if I can find him."

"All right, let me know what you find out."

Nate went to every saloon in town searching for Tisdale. He walked up to Laurel Street where Sally Shaw ran 'Sally's Bed and Breakfast Club' in the former residence of Carlisle Packwood. Packwood had founded the C bar J Ranch in 1879 and enjoyed the reputation of being extremely rich. He lived up to that reputation by living like a grand duke. Packwood, a bachelor by choice and his old maid sister, Jasmine, threw dances and parties in the third floor ballroom that rivaled any flings held in the Cheyenne Club. After losing over 90 percent of his herd during the blizzard of '86, Packwood ended those happenings when he went into the ballroom, stuck the barrel of his .45 into his mouth and pulled the trigger.

The facade of the Packwood house was Victorian, but there wasn't anything Victorian about what went on inside. It was a bawdy house *where anything goes* and usually did. Nate pulled the door-chimes cable. The chimes duplicated the clock atop Westminster Abbey, an ironic tune for a house of ill repute.

Sally liked the sophistication passed on from Carlisle and Jasmine, so she kept the chimes. When the last reverberating note decayed into silence, Sally Shaw opened the door. "Well, hello there, Marshal Hamby," she said. "This is a pleasant surprise.... I'm used to entertaining your deputy." She stepped aside, held the door ajar, smiled shyly and then seductively intoned, "Please, won't you come in, Nate. It is Nate isn't it?"

"Yes, ma'am, my name is Nathaniel, but everyone calls me Nate."

"Oh, I love Nathaniel, I'm going to call you Nathaniel." Then, she hesitated, sighed and coyly looked away. "I'm just plain Sally."

Nate smiled at her pretended innocence. "I like Sally. It's a nice name."

Sally Shaw had wheat colored hair, was a bit plump, close to forty and was popular with the local cowboys and the troopers out at Fort McKinney.

"Well, Nathaniel, you are sweet. I hope this isn't an official call."

"I'm sorry, but it's sort of official. I'm tryin' to find John A. Tisdale; thought he might be here."

Sally's back stiffened, her seductive demeanor fading. "I haven't seen him. You won't find him here."

"If Tisdale happens by, I'd appreciate your tellin' him I want to talk with him."

After searching all over Buffalo for Tisdale, Nate walked

back to Red Angus' office.

"Did you have any luck?"

"Well, some; mostly bad," Nate replied. "Sally Shaw denied having seen Tisdale. Katie said he'd been there a couple of days ago; was mean drunk and had slapped one of her girls. Mike tossed him out and she hasn't seen him since. George Munkres admitted to sellin' Tisdale a new shotgun over at his new hardware store day before yesterday."

"Munkres? He's one of Canton's cronies."

"I know, but Tisdale was probably too drunk to be careful who he talked to. The worst is that he left town yesterday afternoon after old Tobias helped load his wagon with supplies."

"Whatever he told Munkres, Canton knew before Tisdale left town."

Loud voices coming from a crowd gathered in front of the courthouse interrupted Nate's reply. He looked out the window, saw the crowd part as Elmer Freeman, foreman at the Cross H Ranch south of Buffalo, ran from the hitching rail toward the courthouse door. "I think John Tisdale just got kilt this mornin'," Elmer said, bolting into Red's office.

"Where—what makes you think so?"

"John stayed all night at the Cross H last night. He was scared out o' his wits; slept all night with his shotgun."

"Did he say who he was scared of?" Nate asked.

"No, just said he expected to have trouble before he got home because someone was out to kill him."

Red leaned back in his chair and motioned for Elmer to have a seat. "Did he ask you to help him?"

"Nope, he didn't."

"Why do you think he may be dead now?"

"Well, I decided to ride in this morning and tell you what John said. I overtook Charlie Basch and rode into town with him. It was what Charlie told me that really got me excited."

"What did Charlie tell you?"

"He said he saw a man on horseback down at Haywood's Gulch leading a wagon and team off the road and out of sight down the gully. Then he heard two shots, followed by the man riding his horse hell bent for leather toward Buffalo."

"Charlie recognize the man," Nate asked, "or maybe his horse?"

"Yeah, he said it looked like Canton's big sorrel, Old Fred."

"Was the man Canton?"

"He wouldn't say, just that he thought the man was probably Frank Canton."

Red Angus and Nate had to appear in court during the afternoon to testify in the trial of a horse thief. Caleb Hoggerman had been caught trying to sell two horses, whose Wagon Box brands had been altered, to Major Fechet at Fort McKinney. Red made a decision he would later regret by sending his two under-sheriffs, Howard Roles and Jack Donahue, with Elmer out to investigate whatever happened that morning in Haywood's Gulch.

They found John A. Tisdale dead in his wagon and his two horses lying dead in their traces. All had been shot, Tisdale in the back and the horses each with headshots. They discovered unshod tracks made by the killer's horse and the killer's own boot tracks, about a size eight, which just happened to be the boot size of Frank Canton. They followed the trail made by the killer's unshod horse back to Buffalo. Now, they had to find out whose horse made those tracks. Old Fred became an immediate suspect, but when they examined his hooves, he had a new set of steel shoes that P. C. Slack had nailed on him that same day.

The next evening, Johnny Jones rode into Buffalo, having just heard about Tisdale getting killed. His brother, Orley Jones, had not returned home from Buffalo. Johnny walked into Red's office—fear was etched into his weathered face. "Come in, Johnny," Red said, then seeing the worry in Johnny's eyes, asked, "how's Orley doin'?"

"I don't know. I just heard about Tisdale gettin' back shot this mornin'. That's when I started lookin' for Orley—ain't been able to find him."

"Me and my deputies are tied up with Tisdale's murder and the coroner's hearing right now. I'll get Marshal Hamby to help you look for Orley?"

"I appreciate that. When can we start?"

"I reckon in the mornin' at first light. It'll be dark soon."

The following morning on the third of December, Nate, Hap and Johnny Jones rode out to the Muddy Creek crossing searching for Orley and his wagon. Muddy Creek is one of several dry streams joining together to form the North Fork of Crazy Woman Creek southeast of Buffalo. The brown hills along Muddy Creek's meandering course are covered with rocks, sage, clumps of bluestem and during winter, snowdrifts carved by howling north winds. The drifts formed during the latter part of November had melted from a Chinook, except those sheltered by sage, outcroppings of stone and bridges.

A Chinook, sunny days and frigid nights had partially thawed and refrozen the drifted snow beneath the bridge. Its surface had become crusted, capturing the tracks of a wolf, several deer and men who had spent some time beneath the bridge. "This must be where somebody waited, most likely for Orley's wagon," Nate said to Johnny.

"Yeah, don't look too good."

Hap ran his fingers over several of the boot prints, pointed at a large track he judged to be a size 12, then a smaller one. "Looks like there was two of 'em."

Nate knelt down beside Hap to study the evidence. "There's a lot more of the smaller tracks, about a size eight," Nate said. "Chances are the big-foot was a lookout."

"I reckon so."

Nate walked to the bridge's far abutment and examined tracks going up the creek bank to the road. "Big-foot was in a hurry when he made these. See how the boot's toe has dug into the bank."

"Yeah," Johnny said, "I can see that."

They climbed up the bank to the road. South of the bridge, the road cut through a low ridge just wide enough for a wagon to pass through. "I'll bet whoever made the big tracks hid on the other side of that cut," Nate said.

"Yeah," Hap said, glancing at Johnny. "He could've grabbed the bridle o' one of the horses when Orley got there."

Johnny grimaced at the thought of his brother's fate. He spat and kicked the ground. "Yeah, Orley's dead, I reckon."

Hap gave Johnny a consoling pat on the shoulder. "Most

likely, but we cain't be for certain till we find him."

They found tracks made by wagon wheels where a wagon had left the road beyond the cut. The tracks crossed over a rocky hill. Out of sight from the road, a buckboard stood, still loaded with pine flooring. On the ground, harness laid stripped from the horses that had been turned loose by Orley's murderers. Jone's bride-to-be would never walk across the floor he intended to lay with those pine boards in the cabin he had nearly completed. A sheet of frozen blood covered the buckboard's spring seat around the corpse of Johnny's brother. The sanguine crystals melted beneath the touch of Nate's finger as he pondered the sticky remnant of life that had drained from two bullet wounds in Orley Jones' back. He had little doubt as to who shot Jones. It could only be Frank Canton, but proving that would not be easy.

The search for witnesses that might have seen Frank Canton and his big-footed accomplice led Nate and Hap down many roads. They talked with every homesteader, rancher and cowboy along the road from Buffalo, across Muddy Creek and up-country to the spread of Orley Jones.

Everyone was in a state of terror. Travelers, whether riding a saddle horse, driving a wagon, surrey or buggy, carried a shotgun, a rifle and at least one six-gun. They stuck to high ground and avoided roadways coursing through gulches and ravines. All men were to be feared, especially those wearing WSGA badges. Chief among those was Frank Canton.

Maude Stringer, widowed, living in near-poverty on a homestead with her teenaged son about five miles from Orley Jones spread was Nate's best hope. Nobody else had admitted seeing Orley Jones and his wagon on the Muddy Creek road the day he was murdered.

"Hold it right there," Maude yelled from her porch while pointing an old .44-caliber Henry rifle at Nate and Hap as they rode into Maude's yard.

"I'm Marshal Hamby, ma'am. My deputy and I would like to talk with you."

"What about?"

"Orley Jones."

"He's dead."

"Yeah, we know that, ma'am," Hap said. "We're tryin' t'figger out who done him in."

"Ha, don't need no figgerin'," Maude sneered. "Ever'body knows Canton done it."

"Yes, ma'am," Nate said, "but we've got to prove that in court."

"Stay on them horses. You can ast your questions where you're sittin'."

"All right, you didn't happen to be on the road to Buffalo the day Orley got shot?"

"Yeah, I was. Me an' Beau drove into town that day."

"Did you meet or see anybody?"

A tall gangly boy with acne covering his face walked out and stood beside Maude. Without looking away, she said, "This here's, Beau. Tell 'em howdy, son."

"Howdy," the boy said, barely above a whisper.

After Nate and Hap said howdy to the boy, Maude continued. "First off, we seen that sheep man from over on the Belle Fourche. He reined up beside our wagon and talked a ways with us."

"You mean Carter Viscontier?" Nate asked.

"That sounds right." Maude glanced at the boy. "Beau, is that what he said his name was?"

"Yeah, Momma."

"Did he say where he was headed?"

"He said he was ridin' over to the fort."

While Nate was quizzing Maude, Hap pulled a pouch of chewing tobacco from his saddlebag and stuffed a wad into his mouth. The boy eyed Hap's pouch the way an owl studies a mouse. "Want a chaw, Beau?" Hap asked, folding up the bag of Kentucky leaf.

The boy's gaze dropped when Maude said, "He don't use it...Then we met Frank Canton astride that big sorrel o' his. He was ridin' fast. Didn't slow down a bit when he went around us headin' back the way we'd come. Then it wasn't long before we met Orley drivin' his wagon towards home."

"Do you remember about what time that would have been?" Nate asked.

"No, I don't carry no watch. Where the sun was at, I'd say around three or four."

"Did y'see anyone else?" Hap asked.

"Not a soul."

"Did you notice anythin' out of the way while returnin' home?" Nate asked.

"No, we sure didn't, ever'thing was like always."

"Would you be willin' to testify to this in court?"

Maude glanced down at Beau and mussed his hair with her hand. Beau looked up at his ma but said nothing. She seemed to be hesitant to commit herself, which wasn't unusual in this land where nightriders often burned out so-called rustlers homes and barns. She knew all too well that if she did testify, the vigilantes would add her to their list of rustlers. "Reckon I can't," she said, gazing directly at Nate. "This place is all Beau and I got left. Reckon we want t'keep it."

Hoping to get some answers from Carter Visconteir, Nate and Hap rode towards Pumpkin Buttes where they planned to camp for the night. The high plains, browned out by the season, were covered by patches of snow that turned the rolling grassland into a patchwork of brown and white. The winds blowing down the snow-packed mountain slopes were cold, as cold as the wind puffing through Nate as he pondered the lawlessness of the times. It seemed that Wyoming was destined to be another outlaw haven just like Indian Territory had been. There was a narrow line between lawmen and outlaws. Men on either side of that line often switched sides just as Frank Canton had done. One day he was an ardent officer of the law that brought order and justice to Johnson County and then, he changed, giving his allegiance to the WSGA and their self-serving vigilantism. "I wonder what makes a lawman turn bad," Nate said, pulling the collar of his parka high about his neck.

"Got t'be money. Ain't much pay for what we do."

Nate nodded. "I suppose that's true, but y'know that when you pin on a badge."

Hap spat and tongued his chaw to the other cheek. They rode on in silence as the frigid winds bit their ears and noses. Both of them knew the temptations that stalked frontier lawmen.

A fast gun and an equally fast horse could turn a lot of men into highwaymen or enforcers for hire. If a marshal or sheriff hoped to survive, he had to have a fast hand and a quick wit. Both of these talents served one equally well on the other side of the law. So, it all depended upon the man, his character, his sense of duty and the ability to refuse to compromise any of these.

"On the other hand," Hap said, "what makes an outlaw shuck his ways and pin on a tin badge?"

Nate glanced at Hap and saw a sly grin lifting the corner of his mustache. "Not money. Maybe gettin' tired of runnin' and hidin'."

"How 'bout religion?"

"Not likely."

* * * * *

They were back in the saddle early the following morning. The day was bleak with a low, gray overcast that reflected both Nate and Hap's mood. The cold winds of the evening before continued to blow from the northwest, stinging their faces with a dusting of snowflakes. Nate settled into his saddle and pondered whether any good would result from their efforts. Maude's refusal to testify as to what she saw the day Orley Jones was drygulched was hard to take. He had almost offered to guarantee that she, Beau and their ranch would be protected from any reprisals if she would agree to testify. Of course, he couldn't make any such guarantee.

After riding in silence for several miles, Hap reined his buckskin closer to Nate's sorrel so he could be heard over the howling wind. "Maybe Viscontier saw what Maude did."

"Maybe."

"Reckon he'd testify?"

"Don't know—he's a persona non grata here in Wyoming, y'know."

Hap wagged his head in disgust with Nate's educated lingo. He never could figure out why Nate just didn't say what he meant in plain English. He usually did, but once in a while, he'd come out with some highfallutin jargon that didn't make any sense at all. "What the hell does this persona crap mean?"

"He's a sheep man. The cattle barons aren't fond of sheep,

y'know.  So, they wished he'd take his sheep and go back to Australia."

Carter Viscontier walked from a lambing shed as Nate and Hap reined their horses up to his hitching rail.

"Howdy, Mister Viscontier," Nate said, swinging out of his saddle.

Viscontier held out his hand.  "G'day, mates, what brings you to the Belle Fourche this fine December day?"

"Murder," Nate replied.  "We're tryin' to find out who killed Orley Jones on the twenty-eighth of November over at the Muddy Creek crossin'."

"Aye, I've heard about that."

Hap tied his gelding to the hitching rail.  "Do y'remember talkin' with a woman and her boy drivin' a wagon toward Buffalo that day?"

"Aye, of course I do.  Her name is Maude Stringer and she called her boy, Beau."

"Did you see anyone else out there that day?" Nate asked.

Viscontier removed his hat and scratched his nearly baldpate while pondering Nate's question.  "Aye, I rode across Muddy Creek close to sundown.  That's when I saw a man with a rifle over by the bridge."

"What was he doin'?"

"Just walkin' up the dry creek bed like he was looking for something."

"Did y'see anybody else?" Hap asked.

"Aye, there was another man sittin' a big sorrel on a hill about two-hundred yards west of the bridge."

"Do you remember whether that sorrel had any markin's?" Nate asked.

"Well, let me think.  I believe he had a white blaze."

"Did his hind legs have white stockings?

"Can't say.  He was standing on a sage-covered knoll."

"Did you see or hear anythin' else?"

"It was getting late, so I kept riding. I made camp that night where the old Bozeman Road crosses Crazy Woman Creek."

The sorrel with a white blaze fitted the size, color and markings of Old Fred, but was the man that sat astride him,

Frank Canton. Nate unbuckled his saddlebags and pulled out a flyer. Canton had nailed hundreds of them onto telegraph poles, barns, porch posts, and just about any other place that he could. It was his campaign flyer for re-election as Johnson County sheriff that Red Angus had found in the sheriff's desk when he assumed office. Nate handed the flyer to Viscontier. "Might the picture on this be the same man and horse that you saw on the hill?"

Viscontier scanned the flyer and handed it back to Nate. "Aye, the sorrel's blaze is the same and he's about the same height, but I can't be certain about the man. He was too far away."

Nate stuffed the flyer back into his saddlebags. "Would you be willin' to testify as to what you saw?"

"Do you know what you're askin' of me?" Viscontier waved his hand at his sheep and grazing land up and down the Belle Fourche River. "If I even set foot in that court house, they'll burn me out and kill my sheep. That is a certainty."

Hap stepped into his stirrup. "Reckon we understand. Can't say I blame y'none."

Nate kicked the ground, reached for his reins, and threw a leg across his saddle. His sorrel pranced a little, having been spooked by Nate's sudden move. Nate quieted him with a yank on the reins and then spoke evenly to Viscontier. "If the county attorney gets a subpoena and the sheriff serves it on you, will you testify?"

"He'll not serve one on me, sir. My place is in Campbell, not Johnson County."

"So it is. So it is. If you change your mind, let me know."

# Chapter Thirteen

"Hear ye! Hear ye! All rise! This hearing is now in session. The honorable justice of the peace, Carrol H. Parmelee, presiding." Thus bailiff Jock LaRue, a frustrated actor come west at the urging of Horace Greeley, elevated the position of Carrol H. Parmelee's office to one equal with a genuine district court on the morning of December 8, 1891.

Parmelee strutted a bit, no doubt from Jock's lordly introduction, as he walked behind the judge's bench in the district court room of the Johnson County courthouse. "Please, be seated," Jock yelled after Parmelee sat down in the judge's chair.

Carrol H. Parmelee was a poorly educated lawyer, but he had attended every hearing or trial held by the second district judge since before the appointment of Judge Saufley. He pulled a brier pipe with a curved stem from his pocket. He screwed the butt of a cigar into the bowl, and carved off the excess tobacco with his pocketknife. He tapped the bowl of his pipe on the bench several times. "Ever'body quiet down, I'm runnin' this here hearin'. Is ever'body ready? How about you, Sheriff Angus?"

"Yes, I am, Judge Parmelee."

"Mister Smith, you representin' Mister Canton?"

Bertrum K. Smith leaned over and whispered into Frank Canton's ear. Parmelee, puffing on his smoldering pipe, was getting impatient with Smith and Canton. "I ast you, Mister Smith, whether you was representin' Mister Canton. Are you or ain't you?"

"Yes, sir!"

"Get up here on the stand, Sheriff. Bailiff, swear in the sheriff."

"Would you read the coroner's findin' for us, Sheriff?" Parmelee asked after Angus swore to speak the truth.

Angus pulled the coroner's report from his shirt pocket and

began to read it aloud. "It is the decision of the jury that John A. Tisdale met his death from a rifle bullet in his back at Haywood's Gulch at or near ten o'clock on the morning of December 1, 1891. We further find that his death resulted from an ambush devised and executed by Frank Canton and other unknown conspirators."

"Did you investigate Tisdale's murder?"

"My deputies Howard Roles and Jack Donahue did most of the work, but I helped some."

"Can you tell me what you believe happened out at Haywood's Gulch?"

"Yes, I can do that. Whoever shot Tisdale was waitin' for him when he drove his wagon down into Haywood's Gulch around ten o'clock in the morning. The gunman's tracks showed that he'd watched for Tisdale's wagon, then he walked down into the gulch and hid behind a clay bank. When Tisdale's wagon started up out of the gulch, the murderer shot him in the back. His first shot glanced off Tisdale's Colt .45 into the neck of one of his horses. The next shot killed Tisdale on the spot. We found Tisdale's shotgun lyin' in the road. His wagon was down the gulch out of sight from the road with Tisdale lying dead in the back. Both horses had been killed with bullets in their heads. The killer got on his horse and rode back to Buffalo."

"Are you certain Tisdale got kilt around ten o'clock?"

"Yes, Sam Stringer testified at the inquest that he talked to Tisdale at nine o'clock about three miles north of Haywood's Gulch. I figure that Tisdale would've got to the gulch around ten because he only had a two-horse team pulling his loaded-down wagon."

"You got any questions for the Sheriff, Mister Smith?"

Smith glanced at Canton, who winked back at him. "Yes, I do. Tell me, Sheriff Angus, just how do you know the killer rode a horse back to Buffalo?"

"The tracks led my deputy straight to Buffalo."

"How did your deputy know those were the killer's tracks?"

"Well, who else's would they be?"

"I don't know, Sheriff, but they could have been made by

anybody's horse. Don't you agree?"

"It's possible, but not likely."

"Thank you, Sheriff. I don't have any more questions for the Sheriff just now, Judge Parmelee."

"You can go back to your seat, Sheriff," Parmelee said. "Charlie Basch, come up here and let the bailiff swear you in, then I want to ast you some questions."

Charlie sat down in the witness chair after being sworn by Jock LaRue. Parmelee sucked on his pipe and studied Basch while blowing smoke through his nostrils. "Charlie, you testified at the coroner's inquest didn't you?"

"Yes, I did, but I've had some time to think about what I said and I reckon this is a good place to get it all straight."

"You got that right, Charlie. Tell me what you saw out around Haywood's Gulch on December the first."

"I was headin' for Rock Crick that mornin' when I ran into Sam Stringer a ways south of Haywood's Gulch. We talked just for a minute. Sam had to move on; you know how them mailmen is—they ride by the clock. When I got near to the gulch, I seen a feller leadin' a horse up on the hill. The horse was a sorrel with a blazed face and white stockings up to the hocks on his hind legs. I figgered he was Old Fred, Frank Canton's big sorrel, you know. But, now I've gotta change what I said at the inquest about Frank being the man. That just ain't quite right."

Carrol H. Parmelee raised his eyebrows and cast an aggravated glance at Nate as Red Angus made room for Nate to sit next to him. Parmelee tapped his pipe on the bench and invoked a surly order, "Bailiff LaRue, don't let nobody else in here while court's in session. Now, where was we? Oh, yeah, Charlie, what made you change your mind?"

Charlie stared over the heads of the audience, making an effort not to make eye contact with anyone, especially Frank Canton. "Well, I just ain't for certain it was Frank. I sort'a assumed it was him since the horse looked like Old Fred. Another thing, I didn't get very close since the man pulled out his forty-five when he seen me. Then he stuck her back into his holster. That was a clear threat for me to keep ridin'."

"When you seen this man leadin' his horse, how far off was he?"

"Oh, quite a ways," Charlie said, still avoiding the threatening glint in Frank Canton's eyes. "Too far for me to tell who he was. I rode on mindin' my own business. When I crossed the gulch, I seen the same man ridin' his horse leadin' a team of horses pullin' a wagon off the road. I kept a ridin' and after a minute, I heard two shots back in the gulch. The man came ridin' out of the gulch with Old Fred stretched out in a full gallop headin' for Buffalo. I paid him no mind. Didn't figger on gettin' my own self shot. No, sir."

"Did you see anybody else out there?"

"Yeah, Elmer Freeman caught up with me a ways on toward Buffalo. He told me about Tisdale spendin' the night with him at the Cross H. He said old John was real spooked and even slept with his shotgun. I told Elmer what I'd seen. We both figgered that was Tisdale's wagon I seen down in the gulch. We rode on into town and Elmer went down to tell Sheriff Angus what happened. I had to get on up to Rock Crick, so I ate dinner at the Occidental and left town right away."

"That's your story now. Is that right, Charlie?"

"Yes, it is."

"Ain't forgot nothin'?"

"Don't reckon I have."

"Mister Smith, you want to ast Charlie anythin'?"

He nodded that he did. "Mister Basch, am I correct in my understanding that you now, after proper reflection, are unable to identify the horse or the man that you saw out at Haywood's Gulch on the first day of December?"

Charlie Basch glanced at Frank Canton, then dried the palms of his hands on the legs of his britches. "No, Mister Smith, I'm reasonable certain the horse was Old Fred. But, I ain't sayin' the man was Frank. That's what I'm sayin'."

"I don't have any more questions for Mister Basch," Smith said to the judge, then he leaned over to whisper once again into Canton's ear.

Parmelee tapped the ash from his pipe into a tin pie pan. No one spoke while he reamed charred tobacco out of the bowl with his knife, then jammed it full with pieces of frayed cigar tobacco. After lighting his pipe, he blew smoke toward Basch. "Charlie, you can step down now, but stay around. I may need you to do some more testifyin'. Frank, it's your turn. Come on up here and let Bailiff LaRue swear you in."

Frank's lengthy testimony denied everything Charlie Basch had alleged. According to Frank, neither he nor his horse, Fred, had been outside of Buffalo at any time on December 1, 1891. Several other witnesses corroborated his sworn statement. Each of them swore they had seen and talked with Frank during the morning in question. Two of them, Reggus Beck and G. T. Sloan, who just happened to be members of the WSGA, said they talked with Frank between ten and eleven o'clock the morning Tisdale was killed. P. C. Slack testified that he nailed a new set of shoes on Old Fred's hooves around eleven o'clock that morning.

Probably from bias, Parmelee did not pursue times that were more specific from the witnesses. He tapped his pipe on the bench after P. C. Slack finished testifying and then pulled his watch from his vest-pocket and held it up to see what time it was. "It's a quarter to seven, so I'm going to recess this here hearing until eight o'clock so ever'body can go eat supper."

Nate followed Red Angus down the stairway into the sheriff's office. "Well, Nate, we're watchin' a circus up there in the courtroom. Charlie Basch will recant even seeing Old Fred out there that day before this hearing is over."

"Yeah, and all the rest are lyin'. Old Carrol is a WSGA man; has been since before he got elected."

"He ought to buy himself a new pipe with some of that WSGA money, damn, does that thing stink."

Nate decided to walk over to Aunt Deana's house. The hearing had quashed his appetite and he hadn't seen Beth since helping her move into Aunt Deana's boarding house. That was the day after Nate tried unsuccessfully to find John Tisdale. "Howdy, Aunt Deana, is Beth home?" Nate asked when she swung open the door.

"She surely is, come on in and have a chair while I go fetch her."

Nate and Red Angus were determined not to risk having Beth testify at Canton's arraignment. Prejudice was the rule of the day in Carrol H. Parmelee's justice of the peace court. His bias guaranteed the hearing would be weighted in favor of Canton. "Hello, Nate," Beth said as she stepped from the stairway. "How is the hearing going?"

Nate stood to greet her. "It's goin' about like I expected. Charlie Basch changed his testimony from what he gave at the inquest. He's scared out of his britches."

"With good reason. He will be killed, too, if Frank Canton is indicted."

"Yes, I'm certain Charlie has gotten that message."

Beth sat down on the sofa and patted the cushion next to her. "Come sit beside me while we talk."

Nate obeyed. "Aunt Deana's place is nice and a good place for you, except you don't have any protection here. I want you to move out to the Wagon Box where Hap and I can look after you."

"I can't. Aunt Deana has boarders to feed, so she couldn't come with me. I'll be safe enough. Don't worry about me."

"I do worry."

She patted his hand. "I'll be all right."

Nate returned to the courthouse convinced Parmelee was just going through the motions of having a hearing. He found Red Angus eating a sandwich at his desk. "Canton's goin' to walk out of this courthouse," Nate said, "either tonight or in the mornin', free of any charges."

"Yeah, most likely, unless Beth decides to testify."

Nate wagged his head. "She can't. Tom won't hesitate in havin' her killed."

"Then Canton will walk free to back-shoot again."

"We can't risk gettin' Beth killed. Got to find another way to get Canton charged."

Jock LaRue reconvened Canton's hearing with his usual gusto. Justice Parmelee called Red's two under-sheriffs, Howard Roles and Jack Donahue, to the stand. Each of them failed to present any evidence of substance. Their bungled investigation soon became grist for dark humor as local wags ridiculed Angus and his deputies. The most popular joke was: Red and his two couldn't find an elephant with a nosebleed after a snowstorm.

Parmelee called Charlie Basch back to the stand at around nine-thirty. "Now, Charlie, you know you're still under oath?"

"Yes, I do."

"Charlie, I need to get something clear in my mind."

"What's that?"

"During supper, I read the inquest testimony given by Elmer Freeman." Parmelee flipped through several pages of the coroner's record book searching for Freeman's statement. "Yeah, here it is. Now we ain't going to accept no hearsay evidence. Guess you know that, Charlie?"

"I reckon I do."

"Elmer plainly said that you told him you had just seen Frank Canton and Old Fred at Haywood's Gulch. Now, what I want to know is did you or didn't you tell Elmer that you recognized Frank and his horse?"

Charlie grew restless. He stared at the pine floor in front of the witness chair and cleared his throat several times while pondering the question. "I don't recall just what I told Elmer, but he didn't hear me right on that. What I said, was that the sorrel looked like Old Fred. Frank could've loaned his horse to somebody. That's why I'm sayin' I don't know who he was."

"Then you're saying Elmer was mistaken in what he said?"

"I reckon so."

"Mister Smith, you got any more questions for Charlie?"

Smith stood up and walked toward the witness stand while keeping his eyes fixed on Charlie with each step taken. He paused in front of the witness chair. "Well, Charlie, like the judge, I'm confused. I'm so confused by your testimony I really don't know why you think the horse you saw was Old Fred. Can you clear that up for me?"

"Well, he was definitely a big sorrel, maybe sixteen hands. He had them white-stocking hindlegs like Old Fred."

"Have you ever seen or heard of another horse with those markings?"

Charlie scratched his head. "I reckon I have, but not around these parts."

"Then you agree that there are other sorrels with similar markings. Is that correct?"

"I reckon so. But, then this here sorrel had a white blaze down his face, too."

Smith chuckled and wagged his head. "Charlie—Charlie—if you don't beat all. Are you saying that Old Fred is the only sorrel standing sixteen hands with white stocking hindlegs *and* with a white blaze in existence? Is that what you're saying, Charles Basch?"

"Well, no, I ain't saying that."

"Thank you, Charlie. I have no more questions."

Justice Parmelee picked up his watch from the bench, looked at it and tapped the bench with his pipe. "It's ten o'clock. This hearing is recessed until nine o'clock in the morning. Let's go home."

After Jock opened the hearing the following morning, Parmelee again tapped the bench with his pipe. "I reckon we've heard all the witnesses needed in this matter, so I'm rendering my decision. Sheriff Angus, you and your principal witnesses have failed to present any persuasive evidence substantiating a charge against Frank Canton in the murder of John A. Tisdale. Ten outstanding citizens of Buffalo have testified that Mister Canton and his horse, Old Fred, were within this town the entire day of December 1, 1891. It is my finding that no charges against Frank Canton will be forthcoming. This hearing is adjourned."

# Chapter Fourteen

John A. Tisdale's brother, Martin "Al" Allison Tisdale, wasn't about to let Joe Horner, alias Frank Canton, escape justice. John, Al, and Frank had a great deal in common. They had grown up in Texas, living in the same county where Al and Frank led lives outside the law. Canton's bent toward robbing banks, rustling cattle and brawling in saloons came to an end as Texas Rangers watched him swim his horse across the Red River. John and Al weren't long in following Canton to the North Country and they all wound up in Johnson County. Frank Canton, whose real name was Joe Horner, seems never to run out of badges, but his murderous bent remained unchanged. Martin "Al" Allison Tisdale, now known as Al Allison, was a partner in the Hat Ranch, but his penchant toward thievery also remained unaltered.

The Texas experience lived by Joe Horner and the Tisdale brothers was one that spawned hatred between them. Joe made the mistake of killing two of John's friends, which caused bad blood to flow between them from that time on until Joe, now known as Frank, ended it with his Winchester.

Al Allison was certain Charlie Basch lied his way through the coroner's inquest and Canton's arraignment before Justice Carrol H. Parmelee. Al rode into the yard of Charlie Basch's spread on the morning of December tenth, determined to get the truth. Their short conversation began on Basch's front porch when Al said, "Now, Charlie, either you're the biggest liar or the biggest coward in Johnson County. I'd like to know which one it is."

"I hope you don't think I'm either one."

"Y'may be both. What happened at Haywood's Gulch?"

"Canton will see me dead if I talk."

"I'll kill ya myself if y'don't."

The anger boring from Al's eyes ignited raw fear inside Charlie Basch. He was convinced of Al's sincerity. "It was

Frank Canton," Charlie said, stepping backward. "Ain't no question. I was maybe fifty feet from him and Old Fred. I recognized him in spite of a red bandana coverin' all his face below his eyes. It was Frank."

"Get your hat, you're goin' t'make a sworn statement."

Nate and Hap walked into the sheriff's office as Charlie was swearing to tell the truth for the third time since John A. Tisdale's murder. Charlie spilled out the details of his riding up on Frank Canton within minutes following Tisdale's killing. After he signed his statement, which had been written down by the court clerk, Nate asked Charlie a question. "Why didn't you testify to these facts at the inquest and Canton's arraignment?"

"Canton said I wouldn't live to repeat this story in court."

"I find it hard to understand why he didn't kill you out at Haywood's Gulch?"

"That's been puzzlin' me, too. Maybe he didn't 'cause I saved his wife and kids in that buggy runaway a few months back."

The runaway had occurred just prior to the WSGA attack on Nate Champion at the Hall cabin. Mrs. Canton was returning to their ranch twelve miles south of Buffalo. While she was closing the gate, her horses were spooked by one of her two daughters. She tried to climb into the buggy, caught her skirts on the wheel's axle, and was dragged quite some distance before her skirt was torn away. Charlie Basch saw the runaway, jumped on his horse, and caught the runaway team before the children were injured. Mrs. Canton was not seriously hurt and she fully recovered.

"Maybe so," Nate said. "Y'still scared of him?"

"You bet I am."

"You don't need t'worry none, Charlie," Al Allison said, patting his .45. "I'm goin' t'look after y'real good."

Alvin Bennett, Johnson County's prosecuting attorney, was in Cheyenne pleading a case before the Wyoming Supreme Court. He did not return until after dark on December the sixteenth, at which time Red Angus handed him Charlie Basch's sworn statement. Bennett pulled off his reading spectacles after scanning Charlie's new story. "Arrest Canton right away. We'll convict him now."

"Me and my deputies will ride out to his place at first light. I don't reckon he'll come in without a fight."

"You'd better have Marshals Hamby and Dugger ride along with you."

"I'll do that."

There were no secrets in Buffalo, not even Alvin Bennett's order for Canton's arrest. The eastern sky was growing lighter as the whirring wheels of Sally Shaw's buggy raced toward Frank Canton's ranch house. Her stinging buggy whip urged Sally's sweating mare to stretch for longer strides. Time was running out for Frank Canton.

Sally rapped on the door. There was no response. She rapped louder. "Frank! Frank! It's me.... Sally Shaw."

Frank appeared in the doorway holding a flickering lantern in his outstretched hand. "Sally! What are you doin' out here?"

"Sheriff Angus and Marshal Hamby will be here right away to arrest you."

Frank lowered the lantern. The cold wind whipped his nightshirt around his bare legs as he stared at Sally. "How do you know?"

"Deputy Roles spent most of the night with one of my girls. She woke me up after Roles left this morning to tell me that you would be under arrest by sunup."

"Thanks for drivin' out to tell me."

Old Fred, with Frank spurring him to run faster, galloped toward Gillette as the sun climbed above the eastern horizon. Old Fred was too fast and much too resilient to be caught by any other horse in Johnson County. He beat the pursuing lawmen to Gillette by over an hour. From Gillette, a circuitous rail journey carried Canton away from the arrest warrant issued by Justice Carrol H. Parmelee tucked inside Red Angus' saddlebags.

Twelve hours later, Nate and Angus boarded the next train to Cheyenne after loading their horses into the train's stock car. Hap and Angus's deputies rode back to Buffalo, leading Old Fred after confiscating him at the Gillette livery stable.

Bart Mitchum, the Laramie County sheriff in Cheyenne, tossed a dime to the delivery boy and tore open the envelope he had just received.  The telegram bore disturbing news about the man sitting across from his desk.

SHERIFF     BART     MITCHUM     (STOP)     LARAMIE COUNTY COURTHOUSE (STOP) CHEYENNE WYOMING (STOP) REQUEST YOU ARREST AND HOLD FRANK CANTON (STOP)  A WARRANT FOR HIS ARREST HAS BEEN ISSUED BY JUSTICE CARROL H PARMELEE CHARGING CANTON WITH THE MURDERS OF JOHN A. TISDALE AND ORLEY JONES (STOP)  WE WILL ARRIVE ON MIDNIGHT TRAIN FROM GILLETTE (STOP) NATE HAMBY  U  S  MARSHAL  FOR  STATE  OF  WYOMING (STOP)

Mitchum tossed the telegram into his desk and closed the drawer.  "Frank, you'd better hightail it out o' here.  That telegram's from Marshal Hamby.  Him and Sheriff Angus will be on the midnight train coming in from Gillette."

Mitchum was a WSGA man who enjoyed all of the amenities of the Cheyenne Club.  He knew the club dandies on a first name basis.  They in turn never hesitated to ask favors of him.

Frank stood up, put on his black Stetson and squared it over his eyes.  "Thanks, I reckon that'll give me time to catch the eastbound for Omaha."

"Yeah, I'll meet Hamby's train and tell him and Angus I just missed catchin' ya.  Where do y'plan on goin'?"

"Illinois.  The wife's already up there visitin' her parents."

"You'd better stay out of Wyoming till the *Association* takes care of the situation up in Johnson County."

Canton's train was rolling east through Pine Bluffs, Wyoming, only a few miles from the Nebraska border, when Nate and Angus arrived in Cheyenne.  "Howdy there fellas," Bart Mitchum said as Nate and Angus stepped from the rail coach.  "I hate to tell ya but Canton left town before I could arrest him."

"Any idea where he's headed?" Nate asked.

Canton had prepared Mitchum for Nate's question by having the bartender at the Cheyenne Club buy a ticket to Omaha for him. In turn, Canton purchased a ticket on the westbound train, which he had no intention of using. He knew the ruse would only buy a few hours of time, but it was time he desperately needed to avoid capture. "I just found out that he bought a ticket to Evanston at the Union Pacific depot," Mitchum truthfully replied. Then he deceitfully added, "His train left a couple of hours ago."

"Did you send a telegram to the Uinta County sheriff?" Angus asked.

"Yeah, I just sent it."

A telegram from the Uinta County sheriff the following morning exposed Canton's trick.

SHERIFF    BART    MITCHUM    (STOP)    LARAMIE COUNTY    COURTHOUSE    (STOP)    CHEYENNE    (STOP) WYOMING (STOP) FRANK CANTON WAS NOT ON THE WESTBOUND TRAIN IN QUESTION (STOP) SHERIFF JACK CRAIG (STOP)

Four days later, Nate and Red arrived back in Buffalo. At the same hour, Frank Canton was watching a comedic drama entitled, *Who Killed The Butler?* with his wife in a Chicago theatre.

Tom Albert, Secretary Ijams, William C. Irvine, and Frank Wolcott met in Ijams's WSGA office in the Cheyenne Club at ten P.M. on New Year's Eve to make final plans for an armed invasion of Johnson County. Sheriff Angus, Nate Hamby, and Hap Dugger along with a number of other men in Johnson County had to be eliminated. "The only way to beat them is to invade that rustlers stronghold with an irresistible force of guns and men," Tom said, tossing the vigilante's "dead list" on Ijams's desk.

Ijams scanned the list of seventy-one names, most of whom lived in Johnson and Sheridan counties. He spread a map across his desk and jabbed a finger at Buffalo. "There is the rustler's heart. That's where we've got to end this once and for all."

Irvine, Albert, and Wolcott leaned over the map while discussing the how and when of vigilante action against Johnson County. "You're a military man," Ijams said to Wolcott. "How many men do you think we need?"

"At least fifty.... more would be better."

"Fifty!" Ervine snarled. "We haven't got fifty members that's got the guts to do this job."

"You're right," Tom said, "but I can name twenty-five. We can hire another twenty-five."

"Where at?"

"Texas.... there's always been a lot of gunmen for hire south of the Red River."

"How do we go about hiring them?" Ijams inquired.

"You can leave that to me," Tom answered. "I've got a friend down in Paris, Texas, that I used to marshal with. He'll get all the men we want."

"All right, Tom, you get the men. Frank, let's take a look at the plans on how to carry out this expedition."

Wolcott pulled a bulging envelope from his coat pocket and handed it to Ijams. "Here they are, Hiram. You'll find everything in there, including organization and execution of our operations. Tom and I have covered the logistics, including procurement of men, horses, munitions and supplies. Transportation of our invasion force will be by railroad to Casper, then we'll head straight to Buffalo. After we eliminate Angus, Hamby, Dugger and the county commissioners, the rest will be easy. Fred Hesse has agreed to organize Johnson County men sympathetic to our cause. We should have around twenty men join us when we reach Hesse's 28 Ranch."

Ijams scanned the written plans while Wolcott continued to cover every minute detail of his and Tom's invasion plans. They seemed well thought out and complete. Governor Barber, Senators Carey and Warren addressed everything, from pre-arranging cooperation, down to tactics.

Secretary of State Amos W. Barber became acting governor when Governor F. E. Warren vacated the position to become one of Wyoming's first senators in 1890. J. M. Carey became the other senator. Warren and Carey were leading cattlemen who supported the WSGA and their planned expedition.

Governor Barber, having been foretold of the WSGA plans, agreed to cooperate with the cattlemen. If anything should go wrong, which none of the conspirators expected would happen, Barber promised to immediately request federal assistance by a telegram to President Harrison. Carey and Warren also agreed that they would back up that request by diligently pressing the secretary of war for his assistance. With the affirmation of these backup arrangements by the governor and senators of Wyoming, the conspirators were confident of their being able to persuade Harrison to send troops from Fort McKinney to assist them if their proposed invasion went awry.

The conspirators had also neutralized the Wyoming National Guard commanded by General Frank Stitzer. Tom persuaded Governor Barber to have Stitzer issue an order for the Guard to respond to no requests for assistance by any civil authorities, unless it came through the office of General Stitzer. Of course, Governor Barber would make certain no such order would be forthcoming unless it were sanctioned by the WSGA.

"Well, Frank," Ijams said, "I hope you are willing to lead this operation."

Irvine voiced his agreement. "Yes, Major Wolcott, you're the man for this job."

Tom also approved their choice. "Frank's military experience will serve us well."

Wolcott walked to Ijams's private liquor cabinet, pulled out a decanter of bourbon and filled four glasses. He handed one to each man. "Tom, we need to get one more thing straight."

"What's that?"

"Are you prepared to see Hamby and Dugger killed?"

Tom lifted his glass. "Here's to success. May Wyoming be ours."

"Hear! Hear!" chorused the others, clinking their glasses together.

A Chinook had softened the heavy cap of snow on the Wagon Box Ranch-house roof. The thick layer of snow crept over the eaves, curling downward to form mammoth ears of white. A large chunk broke loose and crashed to the ground as

Red Angus tied his horse to the hitching rail.

The avalanche awakened Hap from a wintertime afternoon nap. "What was that?" Hap asked himself, yanking open the front door. Two steps onto the slush-covered porch reminded him that his boots were lying beside the fireplace. "Damnit," he yelled, glaring at Red who was convulsing with laughter at Hap's antics. "What y'haw, hawin' about, y'red headed ol' woodpecker?"

Red climbed the porch steps while pointing at Hap's wet socks. "You savin' your boots for summer are y'Hap?"

"Naw, I ain't, I don't wear boots when I'm nappin'. What brings y'out here anyways?"

"I got some disturbin' news to tell you and Nate."

"That so? Well, come on in. Nate's in his office writin' in that book he calls a jar-nell."

As they sat down to talk in Nate's office, Red handed Nate a letter he had received from Lamar County Sheriff Zack Coleman down at Paris, Texas. Sheriff Coleman wrote that Tom Albert and former Texas Ranger Hank Layton were interviewing men at the Lamar Hotel. The men were responding to an advertisement for 'enforcers' Tom had placed in the *Lamar County Democrat*. Nate knew Layton from his marshaling days in Indian Territory. Tom and Layton had been close friends, riding together on a number of missions, before Layton resigned to join the Texas Rangers. The final paragraph of Coleman's letter was especially disturbing. It said: *According to former Ranger Layton, Tom Albert has hired a total of twenty mercenaries who have been promised large amounts of money to allegedly clean out a nest of rustlers in Johnson County, Wyoming. I thought you ought to know about this. Signed, Zack Coleman.*

Nate handed the letter to Hap. "What do you think of this?"

After reading the final paragraph, Hap replied, "I'd say there's a passel o' slingers headin' our way."

"Yeah," Red said, "we need to get ready for 'em."

Nate walked to the fireplace, picked up a poker and began to punch at the smoldering hearth. Reborn flames leaped high, spewing a fountain of sparks up the chimney. "We need eyes and ears in Cheyenne to let us know what the WSGA is up to."

"Yeah, I reckon ol' Wolcott'll be the one needin' t'be watched," Hap said. "Who could we get t'watch that rooster?"

The three fell silent while pondering Hap's question. Nate chucked two pieces of firewood into the hearth. Hap, seeking wisdom in the whiskey cabinet, pulled the cork from a bottle of bourbon. Red drummed the table with his fingers while he gazed at the elk head mounted over the fireplace.

"Well, Hap," Red said, "I'd say that would have to be another rooster in Wolcott's own barnyard."

Nate turned to face Red. "Ramsay Drury! What about Ramsay?"

"Yeah, he'd be perfect if you could get him to do it."

"I'll ask him. I'll leave at first light in the morning."

"Y'can't get through," Hap said. "All the passes will be snowed in this time o' year."

"That's right," Red said.

"I can make it through the old Bridger Trail."

"I reckon you might. Better take ol' Henry Cardin along; he know's all that country."

"I will and while I'm gone, you fellows need to make plans for our meetin' Tom's gunmen."

The ride to the south around the Bighorns and then north up the old Bridger Trail to Dick Drury's ranch would be nearly two hundred miles of drifted snow and bitter winds. Taking Henry Cardin along proved a wise decision. The old Bridger Trail as it traversed the low mountains east of Wind River Canyon was drifted over along Kirby Creek's south fork. Henry spied a small herd of buffalo numbering less than a hundred head near the pass between Bridger Creek and South Fork. Henry reined his horse close to Nate's sorrel and cupped his hands about his mouth so he could be heard above the howling wind. "See them buffers?"

Nate nodded. Henry continued to describe his plan to break trail out of the mountains. "If we ride up behind them ol' shag heads, we can stampede 'em by poppin' our Winchesters. They's goin' t'run down country inta the basin, breakin' trail for us all the way."

"Good idea. Let's go."

They rode into the square of Drury's headquarters on the

sixth day of their arduous journey. Needle-like icicles were clustered about the nostrils of their horses. A thin layer of ice covering Nate's leather chaps shattered into tiny shards as he dismounted. He and Henry walked up the porch steps as Dick Drury opened the front door.

"You fellers look plumb froze. Come on in here and get thawed out."

A raging fire in Drury's huge fireplace and several shots of whiskey flushed the faces of Nate and Henry like an August sun. Stiffened fingers and knees began to limber. They stomped their boots and paced back and forth in front of Drury's hearth. "I haven't been this cold since the siege of Petersburg," Nate said and gulped down another shot of whiskey.

Henry held out his glass for another refill. "Yeah, it might take a whole bottle t'thaw us out,"

Dick refilled their glasses. "There's plenty in the cellar. What made you fellers ride in here through all this weather and snow?"

"We need your help," Nate said.

Dick nodded, recalling the day he and Nate met in the middle of the pool of hot springs north of Wind River Canyon. His promise to help Nate was a contract, one that was binding, irrevocable. "The Drurys keep their word. Me and my boys'll help."

"Wolcott and Tom Albert have hired twenty gunslingers down in Texas to help them take over Wyoming."

"The hell you say."

"We need someone to go down to Cheyenne so we can watch what those roosters are up to. Ramsay came to mind as bein' the best man to carry that out. Do you think he'd be willin' to do that for me?"

"Reckon he would. We'll go ast him."

They walked over to the tack shed where Ramsay was repairing a broken stirrup on one of his saddles. As Dick pushed open the door, the strong odor of leather and stale horse-sweat greeted them. They walked between two rows of saddles of various styles straddling wooden sawhorses. The walls of the shed were covered with wooden pegs from which bridles, assorted bits, saddlebags, braided lariats and chaps hung. Ramsay was bent over his workbench, intent upon his task of patching a leather Tapaderas stirrup. It had been ripped that morning when the horse Ramsay was breaking lunged into the corral fence. As Dick, Nate and Henry walked between the rows of saddles, Dick called, "Marshal Hamby wants to talk with you, Ramsay."

Ramsay's lean torso straightened and a sly grin lifted the cigarette dangling from his lips. "Howdy, Marshal, you know anything about fixin' a busted Tapaderas?"

"Reckon not." He glanced at Cardin. "Maybe Henry does."

For years, Henry had made his own buckskins, leather gloves, rifle and knife scabbards. He knew leather and how to work with it. "Reckon I do."

Ramsay slipped off of his work stool. "Sit down here and see what y'can do with this busted stirrup. What y'got on your mind, Marshal?"

Nate explained the situation and his need for an insider to spy on the WSGA's activities in Cheyenne. Ramsay remained silent, staring at the floor until Nate finished with the question, "How about you? Would you be willin' to do this for me?"

Ramsay straightened and spoke around his cigarette. "When do you want t'ride?"

"How about dawn in the mornin'?"

"I'll be ready."

At first light, Nate, Henry and Ramsay rode through the corral gate and headed down the Bridger Trail. New drifts of snow had blown across the trail during the night. "Them buffers has saved my goslin' more'n once't," Henry said to Nate as their horses slipped and lunged through drifts along Bridger Creek. "But, there ain't none around to get us through this here mess."

Frigid north winds were sweeping powdery snow across steep mountain slopes. The bright clear morning changed into an opaque whiteout. The rising sun faded. Billowing clouds of fine crystals swirled like dust into the crisp Wyoming sky. A ground blizzard was in the making. "You've got that right," Nate yelled through the bandana tied about his face. "We need to keep Ramsay in sight or this wind will cover up his trail."

"You can bet your last swaller o' sour mash on that fact, my friend."

Ramsay's gray stallion barreled his way through powdery drifts like a bull moose breaking trail for his harem of cows. Henry reined his horse in behind Nate's sorrel as they slugged their way toward the alkali plateau south of the mountain range.

The rough terrain and having to breathe air filled with dust-sized particles of snow began to extract a price from the horses. Nate's sorrel seemed to weaken, his chest heaved and head wagged as he tried to get more air. A reddish mist spewed from his nostrils. Unsure of his footing, he slipped and stumbled. Nate swung himself from the saddle and wiped bloody spicules of ice from the big gelding's muzzle. "Whatsa matter with your hoss?" Henry yelled above the raging wind.

"He's bleedin' from his lungs. I'll have to lead him."

Henry reined his horse around Nate's sorrel. "I'll catch Ramsay and slow 'im down."

Nate removed his bandanna and tied it over the sorrel's muzzle. He pulled his hat down, wrapped the reins around his wrist, shielded his face behind the bend of his elbow and trudged along the trail broken by Ramsay's stud.

Henry and Ramsay rode back to meet Nate. "Do you think your horse can walk out of this blizzard?" Ramsay said.

"I think so if I don't push him too hard."

"If he can't, then what?"

"I'll have to put him down. Sure don't want to do that."

"You want to double up on my stud? He's young and stout as a grizzly."

"I'm doin' fine. Y'all ride on and I'll follow your trail."

"I'll slow down some so you can keep up. Shoot your forty-five in the air if you need me."

The wind became more intense as the morning began to crowd noon. The sun grew dim, fading behind a rising chalky tide carried on the wind high over the foothills of the Bighorns. It was impossible for Ramsay to determine direction. He tried to guide his stud to follow Bridger Creek, but everything disappeared inside an opaque world. His stud became skittish, twice bumping headlong into boulders hidden beneath drifted snow. Ramsay dismounted and waited for Henry and Nate.

The rumbling percussion of a forty-five far to the north signaled trouble. Ramsay pulled at the big gray's reins and led him back along the trail. "Nate! Nate!" Ramsay called, stopped and listened, but could hear no answer. "Nate...Henry!"

The answer, "Ra-m-s-a-y," buffeted by the wind, caused Ramsay to hurry on, pulling at the reluctant stallion's reins. Finally, he saw something, too small to be a horse, moving down along the creek bank. For a moment his vision cleared, it was Henry and Nate on foot without their horses. Henry waved at Ramsay. "Nate busted his bad arm."

"What happened?"

"My horse fell and yanked me down," Nate said. "We slid down the slope about fifty yards. He managed to get up and disappeared in the white-out before I could catch him."

"My hoss run off, too, while I was tryin' t'help Nate," Henry said.

"We've got to get out of here," Ramsay said. "Henry, help Nate on my horse. I'll lead him while you bring up the rear."

After an hour, the wind began to slacken. The sky began to clear and the bright evening sun broke through. The ground blizzard had ended as quickly as it had begun. The wide-open sage-covered plateau blanketed in white was spread before them. It was a good place to make camp, but Henry and Nate had no gear. Everything was tied behind the saddles of their horses somewhere up in the foothills.

Henry and Ramsay gathered dead wood along the creek, built a fire and brewed a pot of coffee. Henry splinted Nate's arm with some sticks. Ramsay's bedroll had to serve all three throughout what was going to be a very long, miserable night, but they were alive. "I'll try to find them hosses first thing in the mornin'," Ramsay said, sliding into his bedroll. "Wake me up in an hour an' one of you get your turn."

"I appreciate your agreein' to keep an eye on Wolcott and his cronies," Nate said to Ramsay.

"Yeah," Henry added, "we damn near got y'kilt already."

Ramsay pulled his hat down over his eyes. "Glad t'help. We may get a might cold tonight, but we'll be watchin' the sun come up in the mornin'."

Finding the horses turned out to be easy. Ramsay found them within an hour after sunup. They probably would have walked into camp by themselves if he hadn't met them. Nate looked over his sorrel. He seemed sound, with no evidence of bleeding. After feeding on some oats, the horses were ready to ride.

# Chapter Fifteen

Doc Spoon shook his head. "We could've set this arm straight if you'd busted it in the same place. Since you didn't, it's going to be just as crooked."

"Crooked will do fine. I wouldn't know how to use it straight."

Doc addled Nate with several splashes of chloroform onto a mask covered with gauze, then quickly set the fracture. He had the arm splinted and draped in a sling when Nate focused his eyes on Doc's sweaty forehead. "Settin' arms must be hard work, Doc."

"Naw, pullin' breech babies is hard work." He wiped his face with a towel. "How'd you talk Ramsay Drury into spying for you?"

"The Drurys are decent folks and they'll fight right along with us if the need comes."

"Do you think it's coming?"

"Yeah, Doc, it's comin'. Tom and Wolcott are gettin' ready to try killin' everybody they can't control."

"I never thought Tom would come to that," Doc said, rolling down his shirtsleeves.

"Me neither, but he made a deal with old Lucifer when he put in with Wolcott and the WSGA vigilantes."

"Yes, Tom's turned mean," Doc said, fastening each cuff. "I'm glad Beth is back teachin' in Buffalo again."

Nate stepped out of Doc's treatment chair. He felt a bit dizzy, but after taking a couple of steps the lightheadedness cleared. "Thanks for fixin' my arm. How much do I owe?"

"Two dollars if I get the splint back, three if I don't."

Nate handed him two silver dollars and glibly responded, "You'll get your splint back."

Nate glanced at his watch as he walked across the street. It was only four o'clock, still time to ask Beth if she would have supper with him.

The door flew open as Nate reached for the doorknob. A stream of yelling children cascaded around him.

"Hello, Beth," Nate said, making his way through the noisy melee.

"Nate! What happened to your arm?"

"I slipped and broke it a few days ago."

"I'm sorry, does it hurt much?"

"No, it's swollen and sore, but I can tolerate it. How about havin' supper with me this evenin'?"

"I'd love to."

"Good, how about let's take a ride in your surrey right now?"

Beth smiled. "That would be nice. It is a mild evening and I'd love some fresh air."

They had gone a few miles after driving past Fort McKinney when the evening shadows cast by the Bighorns crept over them. The balmy January afternoon suddenly turned cold. Beth shivered, pulled the lap blanket around her shoulders and leaned against Nate. He glanced at her and smiled as her soft warmth reminded him of his feelings for her. "I should have headed east. We'd better turn around."

"All right, it's not very pleasant when it's so cold."

During the drive back to Buffalo, Nate's preoccupation with the coming showdown with the WSGA was interrupted when Beth asked, "You're awfully quiet. Is anything wrong?"

"I'm thinkin' about resignin'."

"Why?" She leaned away. "Sheriff Angus needs you and Hap to help him."

"Angus is a good sheriff. Oh, he has a lot to learn about detective work, but he's honest and tries real hard."

"That's one reason he needs you. You helped him a lot investigating Tisdale's and Jones's murders."

"Probably, but what did it accomplish? Nothin'. Absolutely nothin'. Canton escaped and I doubt if he ever stands trial. Ella Watson and Jim Averell's murders cry for justice, too, but there isn't goin' to be any. I can go on, Beth, but what I'm sayin' is, I haven't succeeded in even one case."

"That's not your fault. You've gathered enough evidence to

convict the murderers."

"Statehood hasn't changed anything. Dishonest men in positions of power tie my hands. They occupy and possess every branch of Wyomin's government. Some of our lawmen are outright murderers and thieves. Bribed officials riddle the justice system, legislative and executive branches, but the core of evil is within the Wyomin' Stock Growers Association."

"Is your resignation going to solve anything?"

Nate fell silent while pondering Beth's question. Of course, she had struck on the central issue with which he had been struggling. "I suppose not, but is anythin' goin' to be solved if I don't?"

"That's up to you, isn't it?"

"What do you mean?"

"All of those dishonest officials have to deal with truth. Wyoming's citizens are going to demand justice. It's up to honest lawmen like you to keep ferreting out the truth."

Beth's mare pulled the surrey into Aunt Deana's driveway. "You've got a lot of wisdom in that pretty head of yours," Nate said, reining the surrey to a stop.

Beth laughed uneasily. "Thank you...Now...I believe you invited me to supper."

"That I did."

When Nate opened the front door, Aunt Deana overheard Beth tell him she would be ready to have supper at the Occidental at seven o'clock. Aunt Deana pranced across the parlor, voicing her objections. "Dutch Jake don't know how t'cook—and with them rowdies that eats down there, it's nothing good you'll be hearing. Right here, it's a real meal I'll be cookin' and servin' you in my quarters."

"Now, Aunt Deana, I do appreciate that, but I promised to take Beth out for supper."

"Pish-pash! Now, it's a nice quiet meal together you're wantin', isn't it? Tell this thick-headed man, Beth."

"Well, it would be nice right here in Aunt Deana's personal dinning room."

"That settles it," Aunt Deana said. "Supper will be ready at seven. Now git, Nate Hamby, while I get started."

At seven o'clock, Nate climbed the porch steps to Aunt Deana's. The sting of bay rum bit at his freshly shaved face. Anxiety palpitated beneath his new double-breasted frock coat purchased at Foote's store earlier that evening. He hesitated at the door like a youngster picking up his first date. He had walked out on Beth out of jealousy the day she agreed to attend a dance with Tom. The stupidity of his reaction that day had cost him dearly.

He rapped on the door. "Come on in," Aunt Deana said as she swung open the door. "Beth ain't quite ready."

"Thanks, somethin' sure smells good. What's for supper?"

"Never you mind; go get yourself a drink. The whiskey jug's in my private parlor cabinet."

Nate sat in front of the fireplace, sipping from his glass. The dancing flames and whiskey soon warmed his face. A succession of thoughts flowed through his mind. *Though estranged, Beth is still Tom's wife. I wonder how she will react to my renewed attention? She might just be making an attempt to be sociable out of friendship or could there be something more?*

His musings were interrupted when Beth stepped from the stairway. He stood up and saw that her beauty was just as striking as the first time they met at Aunt Deana's breakfast table. With her green eyes sparkling from the glowing fireplace, she walked toward him. Her lithe figure moved gracefully within a tight-waisted, green taffeta gown as she crossed the room. "Hello, I'm sorry for making you wait."

Nate grinned and stood up. "I don't mind waitin' when it's for the company of such a pretty lady."

"Nate Hamby, are you trying to turn my head?"

"Not at all. You are a very pretty lady and I've been waitin' and hopin' for a long time."

Beth's pleasantness faded. "For what?"

"You."

"You haven't acted like you cared."

"I've cared a lot. My bad feelin's toward Tom have poisoned my reason. I'm sorry for the way I've treated you."

Beth's pleasantness returned as she patted his hand. "You're forgiven. Let's go see what Aunt Deana has cooked for supper."

Aunt Deana had outdone any dinner settings known in frontier Buffalo. The dining table in her private quarters was covered with a crocheted cloth of Irish linen. It was one of her treasures, handed down from her Irish grandmother. Two burning tapers of white held by sterling candlesticks stood between two settings of white china at each end of the table. Sterling flatware, lead-crystal water tumblers and linen napkins completed her table. Beth gave a little gasp as she and Nate walked into the dining room. "Oh, Aunt Deana, you've set such a beautiful table."

Nate patted Aunt Deana's shoulder. "My, you sure have."

"Oh, 'taint nothin'. It just gave me a chance to spread out my treasures. Now, you seat Beth and I'll go get the wine."

Beth gave her a knowing nod. It was obvious Aunt Deana was playing cupid and enjoying every moment. The subtle scent of Beth's perfume and the flickering candlelight awakened Nate's innermost fantasies as he slid Beth's chair gently forward. The evening was as it should be. Not only was it a time to enjoy the wine and food, but also he and Beth were together once again—just they and their innermost feelings.

Beth wondered whether Nate was simply trying to comfort her during her estrangement from Tom. He had never expressed any serious feelings to her. She was unaware that those expressions never came easy for Nate. Deep within his being laid the fear of rejection. He tried not to chance that happening.

*The years have been kind to Nate*, Beth thought, as she observed his once sandy hair, now streaked with gray. His temples were almost white; compassionate eyes mirrored his character. The weathered lines on his face added to his handsomeness the way years of rain and sun give texture to an unpainted dwelling.

She did not notice his right arm, limp within the sling tied around his neck. It had become a part of him. He wouldn't be Nate Hamby without that reminder of his war injury. "Come, slide your chair next to mine. I can hardly see you in this dim light."

Aunt Deana nodded her approval and picked up Nate's plate.

"I'll move your utensils while you move your chair."

"Well now, this is more to my likin'," Nate said as he sat down. He reached for Beth's hand and gave it a gentle squeeze. She searched his eyes for the unspoken feelings he was trying to express.

The pleading in her eyes urged Nate to say what was in his heart. "I don't have the right to say what I feel." He hesitated for a moment, and then continued. "Tom won't be comin' home."

"I know."

Nate could see the fear filling her eyes. "Why don't you divorce him?"

Divorce seemed out of the question to her. "Tom's insane. Murder has become his tool for solving every problem."

"I won't let Tom hurt you. Don't worry about him."

Beth nodded but said nothing. Nobody could do what he promised. Tom possessed great power. Men with easy Colt .45s and Winchester rifles would kill anyone for Tom Albert's money. He only needed to give the order.

Aunt Deana handed the bottle of wine and a corkscrew to Nate. He glanced at the label. It was an 1876 vintage cabernet from France. "My, my," he said, peeling the seal from the cork. "Where did you ever come by this?"

She smiled and waved an off-handed gesture. "Been savin' that bottle for quite a spell, just for a special time.... for you and Beth."

Nate smiled, nodded his approval, slipped the cork from the bottle and filled their wine glasses. He swirled the burgundy liquid and sniffed its bouquet. "Ah, very nice. How about you, Aunt Deana, you must try some."

She wagged her head. "No, that's a gift for you two. Enjoy it while I fetch your soup."

"Nate raised his glass. "Here's to you and me."

Beth smiled and nudged his glass with hers. "I like that.... here's to us." She sipped a bit of wine, savoring its heady flavor. "This is very good."

Nate leaned back in his chair and sipped some more wine. He could not take his eyes away from Beth's sparkling beauty.

"It is good to see you smiling again."

"It's easy to smile.... when I'm with you."

Their eyes seemed to be captivated by each other's hunger, a hunger that food or drink could not satisfy. Aunt Deana's grandfather clock measured their silence with slow swings of its pendulum. Their amorous looks were interrupted as Aunt Deana served each one a bowl of Irish potato soup sprinkled with toasted croutons. "You two had better wake up and eat your soup. It isn't any good when it gets cold."

"The soup smells delightful," Beth said. "You are such a good cook."

Nate realized how hungry he was as the soup's aroma and the wine perked up his appetite. Over soup, and then kidney bean with devilled-eggs salad, Nate told Beth about his family. His younger brothers, Howard, George and Carl were 17, 18 and 20 when General Beauregard's artillery fired the opening rounds on Fort Sumter in Charleston harbor. Nate mustered into the Rockbridge artillery under Captain W. N. Pendleton, went off to fight the Yankees and never saw his parents or brothers again. George and Carl were killed at Shiloh, Howard died later of his wounds and his parents died from typhoid fever only two months before Appomattox. "I had nothing to return to after the war. The farm and our home were no more. That's when I decided to go west, find me a wide and high country, raise cattle, and...."

Aunt Deana served the main course; scaloppini of venison with wine sauce, potato dumplings and whole baby beets in sweet and sour wine sauce. Beth's eyes seemed mesmerized by the delightful servings. "What a wonderful meal you have prepared. How did you do all this in such a short time?"

Aunt Deana picked up their empty soup bowls and salad plates and hurried toward the kitchen. "Oh, I've got a full pantry and there's lots more in the smokehouse out back."

Beth glanced at Nate. "What were you saying? You wanted to raise cattle and what else?"

He swallowed and felt a ripple of apprehension. His eyes glanced away, for a moment, then with renewed courage he looked at her. "Have a family."

A smile feathered her lips as she reached for his hand.

"What about now.... is that still what you want?"

A grin brightened his face. "Yes, it is. What about you? Why did you come west?"

"I wanted a new life, to get away from the past, to teach children...."

"Anything else?"

He saw the candlelight reflecting from her eyes, flickering, a flame dancing. She squeezed his hand. "Yes.... but...."

She released his hand and dabbed her lips with a napkin. Tears welled in her eyes as she looked at him. "I'm sorry. I pray that I too will have a family some day."

After they finished their desert of raisin-cream pie, Aunt Deana waved her hand toward the sofa. "Go sit in front of the fire while the table I'm cleanin'."

"Let me help," Beth said.

"No! No! I'll have this done in a minute."

After Aunt Deana finished clearing the table and had busied herself elsewhere, Nate and Beth sat watching the flames. The pungency of smoldering alder logs, good wine and Aunt Deana's cooking perfected their tranquil mood. Beth slipped her hand around Nate's elbow and leaned her head against his shoulder. "Nate Hamby," she whispered, "are you ever going to kiss me?"

He looked into her eyes. All of his desires for her coursed through him, quickening his latent urges. The sweetness of her breath and her hair met him as his lips searched for hers. How soft they were. How eagerly they parted, receiving his kisses, again and again. Her arms embraced him, pulling herself tightly against him. "I do love you," Nate whispered.

"And I love you," Beth said as Aunt Deana closed the kitchen door.

# Chapter Sixteen

Ramsay Drury sipped bourbon while waiting for Secretary Hiram Ijams in the bar at the Cheyenne Club. Ijams had succeeded Thomas Adams who had followed Thomas Sturgis as secretary of the WSGA. The secretary was more than a record keeper. He was a powerful director that often formulated and carried out policies that promoted the WSGA's political goals. The essence of those goals was to dominate and control Wyoming.

Ramsay carried a letter of introduction to Ijams from his father. This was the first time he had been in Cheyenne; consequently, none of the Cheyenne cattle barons, including Ijams, knew him. This, also, was his first move to make himself known to the inside cronies of the WSGA.

The bartender picked up Ramsay's empty glass. "Would you care for another bourbon, Mister Drury."

"Yeah, bring me another'n."

The bar was empty. Ramsay glanced at the tall clock standing against the wall. Its pendulum paced a lazy tick...tock...tick...tock. It was seven minutes past three in the afternoon, that time of day between the noontime crowd and the evening drinkers. After listening to the clock chime the quarter-hour three times, Ramsay grew restless. He didn't want to appear pushy, but Dick Drury was a charter member of the WSGA. His son deserved a little respect.

Another thirty minutes passed and Ramsay had drunk two more bourbons before Ijams walked into the bar. He tried to hide his peeved spirit as Ijams introduced himself. "Good afternoon, Mister Drury, I'm Hiram Ijams. I apologize for keeping you waiting so long."

"Howdy." Ramsay stood up and held out his hand. "I'm Ramsay Drury. I reckon you know my dad."

"Ah, yes and how is Dick?"

"He's doin' right good." Ramsay pulled the letter from his vest-pocket and handed it to Ijams.

Ijams accepted the letter and gestured for Ramsay to be seated. "What are you drinking?" Ijams asked, pulling up a chair.

"Bourbon."

Ijams motioned for the bartender to bring Ramsay and him a drink and then opened Dick Drury's letter. It was short. *Hiram, meet my youngest son, Ramsay. I sent him down to Cheyenne for two reasons. 1. Sell horses to the army. 2. Get Frank Meanea to make him a new saddle. I'd consider it a favor if you would put him up at the club. Dick*

"I'll have Gracie, she's our club manager, put you up in the guest suite while you're in Cheyenne."

"Thanks, I appreciate that."

"Yes, well we do that for all our charter members. How long do you plan on being in Cheyenne?"

"Don't know for certain; a few weeks most likely."

"Well, you feel free to stay long as needed."

Ramsay reached for his drink. "I'll do that."

Ijams quickly finished his drink and excused himself. As promised, Gracie Hart showed Ramsay to his room. It was on the second floor at the head of the stairway. Gracie, a portly middle-aged matron, slipped the key into the lock and opened the door. The suite contained three rooms furnished well enough for royalty, which is how most of the Cheyenne cattle barons viewed themselves.

Gracie winced as Ramsay tossed his bedroll onto the satin bedcover. "I hope you'll be comfortable during your stay, Mister Drury. If you need anything, anything at all, just let me know."

Ramsay went about getting acquainted with Fred de Billier, Hubert Teschemacher, Fred Hesse, W. C. "Bill" Irvine, and Frank Wolcott. Life in the Cheyenne Club was fast and decadent. Plenty of wine, women, gambling and kicking up a ruckus were the order of every day, but most especially on Saturday night. That is when the buffet tables were laden with hors d'oeuvres of smoked salmon, pickled herring, paté de foie gras and caviar. These juicy tidbits were accompanied by magnums of champagne and wine imported from France and Germany. It was during one of these parties, the third week of Ramsay's stay in Cheyenne, that he met Tom Albert for the first time. Tom walked into the dining room with a tall, slender, young woman dressed in blue silks. "That's sure a beautiful woman," Ramsay said to Fred de Billier.

"Ah, yes." DeBillier looked up from smearing goose-liver paté on a square of toast. "She is, isn't she?"

"Who is she?"

"That lady belongs to Tom Albert. See that diamond tiara she's wearing. We call that expensive trinket, *Albert's Brand*." He returned his attention to paté de foie gras. "I believe she's the third la femme Tom has given it to."

Ramsay watched as Tom and his mistress moved along the buffet table, sampling various appetizers. Tom appeared unsteady as he leaned on his gold-headed walking stick. "Just who is Tom Albert?" Ramsay asked, not wanting to reveal his awareness of Tom's identity.

DeBillier washed down a mouthful of paté and toast with several gulps of red wine. "He's chief inspector for the WSGA. Would you like to meet him?"

"Yeah, I would."

"Good. Come with me."

Ramsay was favorably impressed by Tom's friendly manner. After shaking Ramsay's hand, Tom said, "I'd like for you to meet Mademoiselle Marie du Valiet."

Marie's smile was invitingly warm. Ramsay's awe-struck tongue stammered his reply. "I, uh, um, am sure glad t'meet ya, Ma-dem-ozel du Valiet."

Marie's reply conveyed no unpleasantness with Ramsay's awkwardness. "Mister Drury, are you having a good time?"

"Yeah, I sure am, ma'am."

Tom glanced at Debillier. "Fred, why don't you bring Ramsay to our poker game tonight?"

"I will. Do you play poker?"

"Yeah, some."

The poker game ended at five o'clock the following morning. Ramsay piled his chips in several neat stacks. Tom waved for Gracie to bring the cashbox. "You've done right well tonight."

"Yeah, not bad."

Bill Irvine and Fred de Billier had not fared so well. They each stood up to leave. DeBillier gestured with a thumbs-up. "It's been a pleasure. How about giving us a chance to get even next Saturday night?"

"Reckon so.... any time."

\* \* \* \* \*

While Ramsay was ingratiating himself with the Cheyenne crowd, Buffalo was teaming with growing unrest. Rumors were the prime subject for discussion around the potbellied stove in Foote's store. Henry Cardin sauntered into the store and plopped himself down in a chair. "We'll kill them WSGA vigilantes if they ride inta Buffalo," he called to Robert Foote. "Slice me off a chunk o' cheese."

Foote tossed a loaf of cheddar onto his butcher block. "I reckon we'll have to. How much cheese do you want?"

"Gimmy a dime's worth, and whack off a nickel's worth o' bologna, too."

Foote picked up a butcher knife. "I hear Angus, Hamby, and Dugger have got everything ready when the time comes. Do you want some crackers?"

"Yeah, gimme a hand full." He then slid the iron lid of Foote's stove aside, spat his chaw of tobacco into the fire and slammed the lid closed. "We need a general, that's what we need. I hear them vigilantes is goin' t'ride in here with five-hundred gunslingers."

Foote dropped the cheese, bologna and crackers into a paper sack. "Come get your stuff. You're right about that. Maybe the troops out at Fort McKinney will help us out. You want a sarsaparilla?"

"Naw, pop the cork out'n a bottle o' beer. The cavalry might charge down main wavin' sabers after we're all shot or strung up. Now, if'n Induns was fixin' t'lift our scalps, they'd come tootin' bugles right off."

Jack Flagg walked into the store with a bundle of *Buffalo Bulletins* under his arm, handed one to Henry and headed toward the rear of the store. "You can read can't you, Henry?"

"Some, 'bout good as you can write, I'd say."

When Henry looked at the front page, he realized why Flagg was handing out free papers. Above Flagg's byline was a bold headline two columns wide:

*INVASION IMMINENT: FROM HORSE'S MOUTH*
*by Jack Flagg*
*Bulletin Correspondent*

 *Cheyenne is astir with a frenzy of activity. With the exception of Dick Drury, all of the WSGA directors and many members including former Gov. George Baxter have been seen entering and leaving the Cheyenne Club this past week.*

 *Now, for the bombshell. Some alarming information has come to the attention of the Bulletin just this morning. A number of mercenaries from Texas have been hired by the WSGA. Close to a hundred horses arrived at Cheyenne two days ago and are corralled in the railroad stockyard. Three new Studebaker wagons are lashed down on a railroad flatcar parked on the stockyard siding. Major Frank Wolcott and Tom Albert were seen boarding a train bound for Denver this morning. What does all this mean? Are Wolcott and Albert joining their mercenaries in Denver? Will there be a gunslinger astride each one of those horses? Then, there is the matter of three new wagons that are capable of carrying enough ammunition and explosives to depopulate all of Johnson County. Rumor is now fact. The WSGA is dead serious about their "Dead List." It's time for a call to arms, Sheriff Angus. Let's be ready.*

By the time Flagg had handed out all his special editions of the *Buffalo Bulletin*, men were gathering in groups up and down Main Street. Fear and anger fueled words of alarm, accusations of blame, heated arguments and an occasional plea for staying calm.

Flagg headed for the courthouse. He had saved his last copy for Red Angus.

Jack Flagg did not belong to Angus's innermost circle of friends. They often argued differing views about dealing with the divisiveness in Johnson County. The Hat Ranch owned by Flagg, Al Allison, Bill Hill, Tom Gardner and L. A. Webb was populated with cattle descending from two origins, legal and illegal. All of them had been blackballed by the WSGA for many years and had the distinct honor of being included on their "Dead List." A coalition of strange bedfellows had been formed throughout Johnson County. Men with a tainted history like Jack Flagg and full-time rustlers joined together with law-abiding farmers and ranchers who felt justified in occasionally helping themselves to a stray maverick. They all had a common enemy, the Wyoming Stock Growers Association.

Red Angus slammed the *Bulletin* on his desk. "Do you know what you've done?"

"Yeah, as a matter of fact, I do. The people need to know what's coming and you haven't told them."

"You're a stupid dolt. Hamby and I have been plannin' for the WSGA's expedition into Johnson County for weeks. We know exactly what's goin' on. Nate has an inside informant in the WSGA down at Cheyenne. You've got your story right, but there's more you don't know about."

"What's that?"

"I sure ain't goin' to tell you. You'd have another edition out finishin' the panic you've already started."

"Well, I may put another one out quoting what you just told me."

"You try that and I'll lock you up."

"On what grounds?"

"I'll think one up. Keep that press quiet."

\* \* \* \* \*

Hap pulled on his socks, scratched his head and reached for his britches. "It's time t'get up Sally. I got t'meet Nate up at the sheriff's office at ten o'clock."

Sally Shaw rolled over and pulled the covers over her head. "What time is it now?"

"Nine-thirty."

"Oh, lord, I don't ever get up before noon. I work nights, remember?"

He strapped on his gun belt and tied down the holster. "I reckon so. "How much I owe?"

"Ten dollars. You can leave it on the dresser."

"Ten dollars? Do I pay ya fer sleepin' most o' the night?"

"You sleep in my bed all night, it costs ten dollars. Don't slam the door as you're leavin'."

He dropped a ten-dollar gold eagle on the dresser and left. "Ten dollars! Damn, but I'll be happy when Katie gets back from Denver," Hap muttered to himself while walking toward the courthouse.

Hap poured himself a cup of coffee from Angus's pot. Nate handed him the *Buffalo Bulletin*. "Take a look at that."

He scanned Flagg's column, then tossed the paper on Angus's desk. "Well, that'll spook ever'body outa their britches, I reckon."

Nate picked up the *Bulletin* and threw it into Angus's wastebasket. "I'd like to know where Flagg got his information. I sure don't think Ramsay would have told him anything."

The remaining hours of Thursday, March the thirty-first, 1892 were consumed as Angus, Nate, and Hap met with the county commissioners, the mayor and the county attorney. At four o'clock that evening, Angus had Deputy Roles bring Jack Flagg to their meeting. Flagg had caused near panic with his special edition. Now he was going to be asked for a favor. Flagg scowled angrily as he sat down at the conference table. Johnson County Attorney Alvin Bennett spoke first. "We appreciate your coming, Jack. We've decided to take you into confidence about everything we know regarding this situation."

Flagg's scowl slipped into a sardonic grin. "Oh? Well, I'm listenin'."

Bennett acknowledged Flagg's comment with a quick nod. "Yes. First, do you have any questions?"

"No! Not at the moment."

"All right," Bennett said, gesturing toward Nate. "Marshal Hamby, would you explain the situation to Mister Flagg?"

"Just a minute," Angus said. "First, we'd better ask him whether he'd promise to cooperate with us."

"Yes," Bennett said. "Mister Flagg, we have no right to tell you what you can or cannot print; however, we are going to do just that if we confide in you. Will you agree to this stipulation?"

Flagg's scowl returned as he pulled a cigar from his vest, bit off the tip and struck a match across his thigh. He held the flame to his cigar, and then blew smoke toward Bennett. "I tell you what I'll do. I'll not print anything you men reveal to me, but anything and I mean anything I discover on my own, I'm reservin' the right to print. That's the only deal I'll make."

Bennett looked at each man sitting around the conference table; all nodded agreement. "That's a deal," Bennett said. "Please proceed, Marshal Hamby."

Nate ran his fingers through his graying red hair and opened the file folder Angus handed to him. He studied the contents for a moment, and then looked directly at Flagg as he spoke. "We expect the WSGA expedition into Johnson County and subsequently on through Sheridan, Campbell, Converse, and Natrona counties to begin within the week. A letter from our informant in Cheyenne arrived yesterday laying out the following: *'Men in high places have sanctioned the vigilante expedition. It will be made up of an estimated fifty to seventy-five men, half of whom will be hired gunmen from Texas. They will be transporting munitions and supplies in three double-teamed wagons. Wolcott has chartered a train to carry them from Cheyenne to Casper. From Casper they will ride directly to Buffalo where they intend to kill or run out of the state an estimated thirty Buffalo citizens before moving on across most of northern Wyoming. The total number on their list for elimination is seventy-one. I will inform you by telegram when their train departs Cheyenne.'"*

Nate stopped reading and turned the page. "Do you have any questions?"

Flagg was no longer scowling. "Not just yet; go ahead."

Nate leaned back in his chair and rubbed tense muscles in the back of his neck. "We've got a simple plan. When we receive our informant's telegram, two riders will call every man in Buffalo to arms. Ten other riders will cover Johnson, Sheridan, and Campbell counties. Robert Foote has ordered and received enough ammunition and new Winchesters to supply fifty men. Every man that owns a rifle and a horse will be expected to provide his own. Hap and I will provide several more horses from the Wagon Box."

"What about the Wyoming National Guard?" Flagg asked.

"Don't count on 'em," Angus growled. "General Stitzer issued an order about ten days ago prohibiting anyone but himself to call out the local militia. They won't budge. You mark what I say. I'll call on 'em when the time comes, but it won't do any good."

Flagg wagged his head in disgust. "How about the troops at Fort McKinney?"

"They're federal," Angus replied. "They won't intervene unless the governor makes a request to the President. Gov. Barber is up to his eyeballs with the WSGA in this, so you can forget about the Army. It's all up to us."

Flagg struck a match and relit his cigar. "Well, in that case, how are you going to fight them?"

"Simple plans work the best," Nate replied. "We'll pick our own ground to fight them on."

"Where will that be?"

"Opportunity will dictate that. We'll attack them within twenty miles of town. We can't afford to let them get to Buffalo."

"Well, I hope you men know what you're up against. How many men do you believe we'll have?"

"Enough," Angus replied. "Our best estimate is between one and two hundred."

Alvin Bennett turned to face Flagg. "We'd like for you to help us."

"What do you want?"

"Put out another special edition in the morning."

"What for?"

"Tell folks that the vigilantes will be stopped before they get to Buffalo. There aren't going to be any hangings or firing squads in our town."

Flagg said nothing, puffed on his cigar and stared at Bennett. Hap, not being a patient man, startled everyone as he slammed his fist against the conference table. "Jack! Either you promise to do that or we're goin' t'lock your butt up in the jail downstairs."

No one disagreed with Hap. "Well, I don't see any harm in reassuring folks," Flagg said as he stood to leave. "But, they deserve to know how close the invasion is."

"We can't do that," Nate said. "Anythin' you print will be common knowledge within a day in Cheyenne. We can't let the WSGA know that we know. It's just that simple."

Flagg did what he promised, but the effort was a waste of ink and newsprint. The panic had advanced beyond being aborted by written words. There was no reassurance in Buffalo on April Fool's day, 1892. Instead, black Friday dawned overcast with dread.

Spring roundups were due to begin within six weeks. Out on the range, last summer's yet-to-be-counted calves bellowed as their mammas kicked seeking muzzles away from exhausted udders. In town, the ringing of Blacky Tettleton's clanking hammer molding new points on worn-out plowshares echoed through the open door of his smithy. Across the muddy street, Robert Foote stacked one-hundred-pound gunnysacks of wheat and oat seed into wagons as farmers readied for spring planting. Everything seemed as usual on the surface, but fear coursed beneath these benign goings on. All was not well.

* * * * *

Just as the Union Pacific men in Cheyenne had promised, the Pullman car Wolcott chartered had been added to the train bound to Cheyenne from Denver. Twenty men Tom had hired in Paris, Texas, climbed on board carrying their bedrolls. Brothers J. A. and Buck Garrett, M. A. McNally, G. R. Tucker, and D. Brooke who preferred to be called the "Texas Kid," were barely old enough to own a razor. The remaining fifteen were not much older. All of them were handy with a Colt .45 and gullible to the man. Some were sullen while others boasted freely about their prowess with guns and the ladies. The chief boaster was the Texas Kid. He was a skinny, twenty year old with red hair and a quick temper. He sauntered down the isle, tossed his bedroll to the porter and yelled, "Stow that for me, boy."

Buck Garrett, just as fiery as the Kid, grabbed the bedroll out of the porter's hands and threw it back to the Kid. "Y'can ast 'im again after he stows mine."

Tom rapped his walking stick on the floor and yelled as the Kid braced himself to draw down on Buck. "Hold it right there, Kid. Save your bullets for the rustlers up in Johnson County."

"Well, tell Garrett to watch his lip, or I'll make a lisper out of 'im."

Tom ignored the Kid's threat. "We'll get to Cheyenne by one o'clock where more men will join us. Soon as our special train is made up, we'll head on up to Casper."

"When do we get the arrest warrants for your rustlers?" Buck Garrett yelled.

"After we get to Cheyenne."

"Hell, Buck, there ain't goin' t'be no warrants," B. C. Schulze, one of the older gunmen said. "We're all hired killers. Yessir, plain as day, that's what we are."

"Yeah, an' you'd better be ready t'hang if you're caught," another yelled.

The Kid stood up and patted his Colt. "Ain't nobody goin' t'hang this Texas Kid."

Frank Canton walked down the aisle and sat down several chairs behind the grumbling hirelings. He said nothing as Tom registered surprise at Frank's appearing. "Damn, Frank, what are you doin' here?"

"Ijams sent for me."

"Who the hell are you?" Will Armstrong, a former deputy U.S. marshal asked.

"That ain't no concern of yours," Frank snarled.

Armstrong stood up, glaring menacingly at Frank. "The hell it ain't. You ain't welcome 'less we know who you be."

"This is Frank Canton, one of the association's detectives," Tom said, trying to calm Will Armstrong's surliness.

Canton slid down in his chair and pulled back his jacket exposing the butt of a "Peacemaker" slung in a shoulder holster. His hand rested on his chest ready for action. "Mister, you'd better get used to followin' my orders. That's all you need to know."

Armstrong knuckled his scraggly handlebar mustache and glanced at Tom who nodded agreement with Frank. Armstrong sat down. "If he's a detective, I'm Judge Roy Bean, the pride of Vinegaroon."

Tom staggered and grabbed at a chair back as the steam locomotive jerked the train into motion. He steadied himself and continued to speak as the Pullman gathered speed. "Pull all the blinds down before we get to Cheyenne. Nobody gets off this car until we get to Casper."

# Chapter Seventeen

Ramsay awakened. Throbbing pain spawned by booze was coiled around his head like a serpent, making sleep no longer possible. Being a spy was not easy. The decadent life style of the cattle barons at the Cheyenne Club was getting to him. He crawled out of bed and began to splash cool water on his face. A rap sounded on the door. "Ramsay! Are you up? It's me, Sam Clover."

Ramsay had met Clover several days before in the Club Bar. Clover was a reporter for the *Chicago Herald*. Henry A. Blair, a Chicagoan who was the absentee owner of the Hoe Ranch on the Powder River, had sent him west. Blair's motive was simply one of trying to manipulate favorable publicity about the coming invasion. Clover was glib and pushy; two traits Ramsay detested, but he was a good source of information.

"Come on in, Sam," Ramsay said, drying his face, "the door ain't locked."

"Get dressed," Clover said, closing the door. "I've just found out that Albert's Texans will be arriving on the next train from Denver."

"How many are they?"

"Fred de Billier says there's twenty-one. Say, you don't look too good."

"Yeah, it's the whiskey. I've got t'lay off that stuff."

Clover flopped down on the bed and propped his boots up on the footboard while Ramsay was getting dressed. "De Billier said he'd asked you to come along with them. Is that right?"

"Yeah, he did, while we was playin' poker last night."

Clover picked at his teeth with a sharpened matchstick. "Well, are you going?"

"I'm goin'. Are you?"

"Certainly! That's what Mister Blair sent me here for."

Ramsay and Clover watched as the train from Denver pulled into the Cheyenne railroad yard at 1 P.M. They continued to watch as the Pullman was disconnected and moved onto the stockyard siding by a switch engine. The Pullman, plus three stockcars loaded with seventy-eight horses bearing the maverick A brand recently burned into their shoulders, three wagons secured on a flatcar, one baggage car and a steam locomotive were hooked together.

The brand for a maverick, *any stock that was unbranded and its ownership not claimed by anybody*, was a large letter "A". The conspirators reasoned that if all of their horses bore the maverick brand, none of these mounts could be traced directly to them or any member of the WSGA.

"I'm goin' over t'the depot t'take a leak," Ramsay lied to Clover. Instead, he intended to send a telegram to Nate.

"All right. I'll meet you on the train."

Ramsay penciled his message for the telegraph operator. It was couched in a prearranged sentence he had included in his last letter to Nate.

NATE HAMBY, OCCIDENTAL HOTEL, BUFFALO, WYOMING. YOUR SADDLE WILL ARRIVE CASPER TOMORROW MORNING. RAMSAY DRURY

Ramsay handed the message to the operator. "Send that right away."

The operator thumped on his telegraph key several times and waited. There was no reply. He repeated his message. Again, there was no response from the Buffalo operator. "I'm sorry, Mister Drury, the line to Buffalo isn't working. Do you want me to keep trying?"

"Yeah, how much do I owe?"

"Four-bits."

\* \* \* \* \*

Shadows cast by the flickering flame of a conductor's lantern danced across the wall as Frank Wolcott studied the baggage car's inventory. The serial numbers for fifty-three Winchester model seventy-three .44-40 caliber rifles filled one page. Crates of ammunition, dynamite, cans of food, sacks of grain for the horses and every creature comfort to which the

WSGA cattle barons had grown accustomed filled the car. The train wheel's clickety-clack sounds grew louder as the baggage car door opened momentarily, then fainter again as Frank Canton entered. "Who is that," Wolcott yelled, turning around.

"It's me," Canton said, walking between stacks of crates and boxes.

"Get out. You haven't any business in here."

"I got as much right in here as you."

"No you don't. Get out!"

Canton chewed fury between his teeth as he whispered, "You pompous asshole."

Wolcott made no observable sign that he had heard Frank until Canton opened the door to leave. "You're what passes through one," Wolcott said just loud enough to be heard above the clickety-clacking wheels.

Twenty-one cattlemen including Ramsay Drury and the invader's surgeon, Dr. Charles Penrose, who was a close friend of Governor Barber, sat together at one end of the Pullman car. Frank Canton and four other stock detectives occupied seats halfway between the cattlemen and their hired gunmen who were playing poker at the other end of the Pullman car. Ed Towse, a reporter for the *Cheyenne Sun* compared notes with Sam Clover while sitting together behind the Texas contingent. All three teamsters, William Collum, George Helm, and Charles Austin, bedded down in the caboose trailing behind the stockcars. Tom Albert moved from one group to the other like a roving ambassador during their rocking rail ride to Casper.

"Those men Tom hired stink worse than a whorehouse on Saturday night," Fred de Billier said to nobody in particular.

"Yeah," Irvine said. "Where's Wolcott?"

"I hope he's guardin' our booze," another Cheyenne dandy muttered.

The 190-mile trip by rail from Cheyenne to Casper was a journey requiring over ten hours. As the train rolled into Douglas, Ramsay pulled out his pocket watch, flipped open its metal cover and saw that it was nearly two o'clock A.M. Games of chance and all conversations had ceased. All the passengers were asleep. After the train stopped to take on water, Ramsay stepped down from the Pullman, walked into the depot and rapped on the counter to awaken the operator. The man raised his head. "Yes, sir, what can I do for you."

Ramsay began to pencil his message. "Is the line open to Buffalo?"

"I reckon so. Ain't tried it since yesterday."

"Try it," Ramsay said and handed him the message.

The telegraph key clattered its message intended for Buffalo. The operator waited for an answer, but the telegraph apparatus remained silent. He made a second attempt, but it also failed. "The wires are down, I reckon."

"Yeah, I reckon so. Would you do me a favor?"

"Sure, if I can."

"Put that message in an envelope and mail it to Marshal Nate Hamby for me."

Casper's 600 inhabitants slept as the invader's train clattered into the railroad yard at 4:10 A.M. The switching yard wasn't close to any houses, so unloading the train was accomplished without disturbing anyone. Ramsay saddled a big gray gelding and joined the others as they trotted north across the Platte River Bridge around six in the morning. The sky was overcast and low. A crisp north wind bit into each rider. The Texans shivered and cussed, being completely unprepared for Wyoming's fickle weather. The three heavily laden wagons moved slowly as their drivers cussed and whipped their four-horse teams toward the Bighorn foothills. The WSGA vigilante invasion was underway.

* * * * *

Sunday, April the third, 1892 was balmy as a warm bath. The snow-peaked Bighorns glistened beneath wisps of clouds floating high above their whitewashed crowns. As Nate escorted Beth to her surrey, people coming out of the new Methodist church began to mill around them. Reverend Butterworth's sermon calling for calm had fallen on ears that were too preoccupied to hear. "What about our women and children?" one called out to Nate.

"I hear them hired gunmen are whitecap-wearin' Klu Klux Klan members," another said.

"Do you and Angus know what to do?"

Nate held up his hand. "Wait a minute...."

"You and Angus ain't doin' nothin'."

"Yeah, if you don't get started, we'll do it...."

"Hold up there!" came the booming voice of Arapahoe "Rap" Brown. His flour-caked boots slammed against the rutted street as he jumped from his wagon loaded down with sacks of newly milled flour. Brown was huge, unkempt, wreaked of whiskey and stinking armpits. His tangled beard and cactus-like eyebrows were heavily powdered with flour. His appearance was frightening. The crowd fell silent as he continued. "You sniv'lin' Sunday schoolers ain't got the guts of a chipmunk. Instead o' botherin' the marshal here, why don't y'get on t'home an' write out your wills? Then, clean up your guns and help him whip them whitecaps afore they get to Buffalo."

"Listen folks," Nate said. "I know everybody is scared, but we're goin' to stop the WSGA gun fighters long before they get to Buffalo."

"You say that, Marshal Hamby," a crowd member yelled. "So does Flagg in the *Bulletin*, but we hear Tom and Wolcott are coming with several hundred vigilantes bent on wiping us out. How are we going to stop them?"

"Whenever the vigilantes leave Cheyenne, I'll know about it within minutes."

"Is that going to give us enough time to scoot our womenfolk and kids up into the Bighorns?" came the caustic comment of another.

"It may come to that if we can't stop them," Nate said to the skeptic. "What the early warning will do is give Sheriff Angus time to send riders all over Johnson and Sheridan counties callin' every man to arms."

"If you fail to get that warning, then what?"

"We've got sympathetic eyes and ears on the inside of the WSGA. We'll get the word in plenty of time."

"Now, folks," Reverend Butterworth said, making his way through the crowd. "Marshal Hamby and Sheriff Angus are competent lawmen. Let's leave this up to their good judgment and be ready when they call for our help."

Nate reached for the Reverend's hand. "I appreciate your comments."

"I meant every word."

"Me too," Brown said. "You can count on ol' Rap when the time comes to fight them whitecaps."

Nate fell into deep thought as he drove Beth's surrey to Aunt Deana's house. Ramsay had written in his last letter that the cattlemen were assembling in Cheyenne. They were branding horses down at the stockyards and buying rifles, goose-down sleeping bags, and winter parkas.

"A penny for your thoughts," Beth said.

"I'm worried about not hearin' from Ramsay."

"How long has it been?"

"Three days."

"Didn't he promise to send a telegram before the vigilantes leave Cheyenne."

"He will if they haven't cut the wires."

"Cut the wires? Will they do that?"

"Yeah, that's why Hap rode down to Casper two days ago. In case the vigilantes take their train to Gillette, Angus has got a man watchin' the rail yard over there. They won't surprise us, but I can't help worryin' about Ramsay."

* * * * *

"Hard Winter" Davis, one of the WSGA cattlemen squatting next to the breakfast fire, reached for the gurgling coffee pot. His Colt .45 accidentally fell out of its holster. The hammer slammed against a rock, causing the Colt to fire. The bullet hit nothing but Wyoming sky; however, the loud report caused bedlam among the horses. The Texans responsible for wrangling all of the mounts watched most of them galloping away with reins tied to uprooted sagebrush. "Go catch them horses," Wolcott yelled at the Texans.

"Hard Winter" holstered his gun and sipped coffee as if nothing had happened. The expedition finally got started again after three hours, but April was destined to deal the invaders more misery. It was cold and getting colder. Rain began falling during the afternoon and then turned to snow early Thursday morning. The silty prairie soil became gumbo, a sticky mess sticking to the horses' hooves and wagon wheels alike. The wagons began to founder as gumbo fouled the wheels. The Cheyenne dandies grumbled about having to leave all their creature comforts behind in the bogged-down wagons. The riders finally reached Rob Tisdale's ranch on Willow Creek about sixty miles south of Buffalo late Thursday night. The cattlemen bedded down in the ranch house while the hired gunmen filed into the bunkhouse.

"Where did Wolcott go?" Bill Irvine asked Tom after the horses had been corralled.

"He rode back to check on the wagons just before sundown. I expect he'll be along in a while."

It was still snowing Friday morning when Wolcott stomped snow from his boots on the porch. "It's a bitch out there," he said to Tom. "I had to bed down in a haystack last night."

"Yeah, it's bad. Where are the wagons?"

"They're coming pretty slow back about ten miles."

"These men aren't goin' to budge without those wagons."

"I know. If they don't show up by evening, we'll have to go give them a hand."

Tom was right about the cattlemen not going on without their booze, grub, cots and camp gear. They also persisted in refusing to associate with their hired gunmen from Texas. Things were not going well for either group. The weather was frightening. A combination of cold drizzling rain, snow, and mud began to erode patience and wisdom alike. Tempers were short and explosive.

Bill Armstrong left the bunkhouse and sloshed through mud and snow toward the ranch house. His fellow Texans wanted some answers. "Tom!" he called and rapped on the door. "It's me, Bill Armstrong, I want to talk."

Tom joined him on the porch. "Howdy, Bill. How you boys doin'?"

"We're tired of this crap. What are we goin' t'do?"

"We've got to stay here until the wagons catch up."

"Why don't y'send some men back to fetch 'em? We're gettin' real tired o' suckin' hind tit, if ya follow me."

"Those wagons are bein' driven by three of the best

teamsters around. If they don't show up by evenin', we'll go back for them."

Bill doodled in melting snow with the toe of his boot. "I don't see no need waitin', but that's up to them 'dogie kings' crapped out in there. The boys want to know when we'll be gettin' them warrants you promised."

Tom leaned against a porch post and wrote his answer with his walking stick on the snow-covered porch floor: "Don't need any."

Bill stared at the message as Tom scratched it out with his cane. "Y'got to be crazy. We're gunnin' for rustlers an' outlaws, ain't we?"

Ramsay opened the door and walked out on the porch before Tom could reply. "You boys got a deck of cards?"

"Yeah, that's all we've got."

"How 'bout me joinin' you boys for a little poker?"

"Hah.... how 'bout the rest o' you 'dogie kings'? I reckoned all of you think you're too good t'sit under the same roof with us."

Ramsay's jaws rippled as he gritted his teeth. "Bill, I ain't talkin' for nobody but Ramsay Drury. The way I see it, this house, nor the bunkhouse either, is big enough for fifty men."

"Reckon you're right. Go ahead—they've got a game goin' right now."

"Thanks," Ramsay said and walked toward the bunkhouse.

\* \* \* \* \*

Hap watched the vigilantes and three wagons cross the Platte River Bridge heading north toward Buffalo. He made two failed attempts to get a warning message to Nate. The telegraph wires had been cut, leaving Buffalo isolated and ignorant about the riders coming to slam vigilante justice upon them. Hap had no other choice but to ride around the invaders and push ahead of them toward Buffalo. He rode toward Pumpkin Buttes, staying east of the riders and their wagons.

He rode all day Wednesday. It began to drizzle cold rain in the late evening. After traveling sixty miles by three o'clock Thursday morning, Hap rested his horse and boiled a pot of coffee where the Bozeman trail runs west of Pumpkin Buttes.

The damp branches of greasy sage crackled as they burned in his shallow fire pit. He began to nod. Sleep was stalking him.

When his gelding snorted and pawed at the ground, Hap awakened. The coffee pot sat silent and cold amid burned-out ashes. The Pumpkin Buttes were silhouetted against the eastern sky by dawn's first light. "Damn, hoss, it's cold." Hap stood up and stretched stiffened limbs. "I reckon it's time t'ride ol' fella."

After several swallows of cold coffee, Hap urged his gelding down the Bozeman trail toward Buffalo. The wind grew brisk and frigid as it pummeled the high plains. Freezing rain sank into his britches and parka. The gelding was tiring. Hap reined him down at the Powder River crossing where the gelding filled his belly with cold water turned muddy from rain, sleet and snow.

Forty miles of hard riding remained before he could reach Buffalo and warn Nate of the coming invaders. When he reached the Crazy Woman crossing at two-thirty in the afternoon, Hap couldn't remember when he had been as tired or as cold. He struggled to get off the gelding. The muscles of his legs seemed fixed inside frozen britches. His right boot was heavy, so heavy he couldn't slide it over the gelding's rump. Likewise, the gelding had about reached the limit of his endurance. He stood with head sagging downward, too tired to turn his rear into the wind. Hap leaned forward and patted the gelding's shoulder. "Just rest ol' fella. I'm gettin' off ya soon as I kin get my knee t'bend."

Hap found walking a relief after so many hours of pounding saddle leather. He trudged along leading his horse most of the remaining twenty miles to Buffalo. He knocked on the door to Slack's livery stable at seven o'clock. Dobbie Brown, Slack's night man, pushed open the livery door. Water dripped from Hap's hat brim and mustache. Frozen mud clung to his pant legs. "Gawd, y'look plumb froze. Gimme your hoss and get on over to the hotel."

"I'm thankin' ya. Feed 'im and rub 'im down real good, would ya?"

Hap knocked on the door to Nate's room. "Come on in....it's open."

Hap staggered through the doorway, slumped into a chair and sat quietly for a moment. Slowly, his bearded chin sank into his soggy parka. He tossed his hat on the floor and combed his matted hair with fingers blanched white from the cold. "Nate, I'm plumb tuckered."

Nate poured whiskey into a water tumbler and shoved it between Hap's stiffened fingers. "This will thaw you out. You look done in."

Hap chugged down half the whiskey in one long gulp. "I didn't figger t'live long enough t'taste this sweet nectar one more time. The invaders left Casper yesterday mornin' headin' this way."

"Get out of those clothes. I'll have Jake bring up a tub and plenty of hot water. We'll talk after you're thawed out."

# Chapter Eighteen

It was well past dark when Mike Colby, foreman for the Sailing C Ranch in Weston County, reined his horse to a sliding stop. "Hey, Tom!" he yelled, tying his horse to the hitching rail in front of Rob Tisdale's ranch house.

From inside the house came whiskey-bolstered laughter and loud voices doing a little hell raising. The cattlemen were so overjoyed by the arrival of their three tardy wagons that they had broken open a case of whiskey to celebrate. All three wagons were parked in the yard with their teams still in their traces while cattlemen, Texans and teamsters alike drank toasts to their anticipated victory over Johnson County.

Tom opened the door for Colby to enter. "There's a bunch of rustlers holed up at the KC."

"How many?"

"More'n a dozen, I'd say."

"Did you say there's rustlers up at the KC?" Wolcott bellowed.

"I counted fifteen horses in the KC corral."

Wolcott drained the last swallow from his glass. "Let's go get 'em, boys."

Frank Canton was still smarting from his encounter with Wolcott in the baggage car. "Whoa, hold on. We need to hit Buffalo first."

"Canton's right," Fred Hesse yelled at Wolcott. "It could take another day to clean out the KC. The longer we take, the more likely Buffalo will discover where we are."

Tom faced Walcott. "I agree. We can't afford the time needed to attack that ranch house."

"Just one minute," Bill Irvine said. "Wolcott's right. If there are fifteen of the rustlers we're after at the KC, let's go get 'em. We may not get another chance."

Wolcott won over enough of the cattlemen to get a majority vote for attacking the KC. They saddled up and headed into the frigid north wind at midnight. The muddy road had frozen solid. A torrent of snow blasted their faces. Ramsay was determined to take advantage of the storm to separate him from the others and ride for Buffalo. When Wolcott asked Mike Colby to ride ahead to scout out the situation at the KC Ranch, Ramsay spoke up, "I'll ride with ya, Colby."

"Okay, let's go," Colby yelled into the roaring wind.

Snow carried by the wind slammed into Ramsay with such intensity that he tied a bandana over his mouth and nose. He constantly urged his horse to move faster. They had been following the Powder River's south fork when Colby reined north from the riverbank toward the KC. Ramsay urged his horse to follow. The blowing snow grew heavier, obscuring Colby and his horse from view. Ramsay dismounted and led his horse while trying to follow Colby's tracks. Finally, all tracks disappeared, having been completely covered by new snow. His gelding abruptly reared and ripped the reins from Ramsay's grasp. As the spooked gelding disappeared into the stormy night, Ramsay staggered after him. Peering into the blackness, he could see nothing. He walked on, hoping to find some kind of shelter, but he was unfamiliar with the country. It was going to be a long night.

The storm ceased sometime before dawn. The darkness remained but the agonizing winds abated. Ramsay trudged onward, each step a painful burden, his eyes scanning the snow covered high plain. He needed to rest, but dared not lie down lest he should fall asleep and die from the terrible cold.. He wandered about unable to walk in a straight direction until exhaustion finally took its toll. He slumped into the snow and fell asleep.

All of the pain from the cold that had penetrated his bones dissolved into a swirling vortex of nightmares. Time evaporated like a morning fog being swept away by the rising sun. Then came an abrupt awakening by a voice yelling, "Wake up! Wake up." The voice kept repeating its command each time a hand slapped his frostbitten cheeks. When Ramsay opened his eyes, he saw Tom Albert kneeling beside him. "Thank god, he's alive," Tom said, pouring whiskey between Ramsay's lips.

Tom had two of the Texas gunmen lift Ramsay onto one of their horses. The invaders rode on toward the KC, determined to take care of the fifteen rustlers holed up in the ranch house.

The jolting gait of Ramsay's horse gradually awakened him. He ached all over, especially his frostbitten face and hands as they began to thaw.

The sky broke clear with scattered clouds floating beneath winking stars. Ramsay heard Colby's voice telling Tom and Wolcott how he had gotten separated from Ramsay and was relieved that they had found Ramsay alive. He listened as Wolcott quizzed Colby about the KC.

"How far is it to the KC?"

"Less than a mile."

"Let's go see if we can get this taken care of."

The invaders rode on until reaching the bluff overlooking the middle fork of the Powder River. Cottonwoods and willows with leafless limbs sheltered the river's banks. Several log buildings were huddled beside the stream. A ribbon of smoke spiraled from the chimney of the KC's main house.

Ramsay managed to dismount and walked about stamping life back into his feet. He stepped up beside Tom and spoke his gratitude for being rescued. "Thanks for savin' my hide."

"Just glad you were alive when we found you."

"What now?" Colby said to Wolcott.

Wolcott responded in a military manner. "We'll hobble our horses out of sight and deploy our men so as to surround the house."

He directed several men to hide in the stable. The rest were to spread out along the river and in a brushy draw leading down toward the river.

As they deployed, a freighter's wagon and buckboard were found near the house.

Wolcott counted six horses in the corral. "There aren't any fifteen horses."

"Colby's either blind or a liar," Irvine chortled.

Wolcott didn't reply, motioning for all of the invaders to stay down. They waited for the occupants of the ranch house to make an appearance. Ramsay crouched beside Tom, wondering how he was going to get away, ride to Buffalo, and let Nate know what was happening. He watched the ranch house and its dark windows. They waited, shivered from the cold and cursed the rustlers.

As the eastern sky began to pale, the cabin's door opened and a man walked across the porch carrying a bucket. He headed for the river to get some water for breakfast. He walked past the stable and on toward the river until out of sight of the house. Two Texans, Buck Garrett and Bill Little, raised up and aimed their Winchesters at the man. "Stop right there," Buck said. "Who are you?"

The startled man stopped and stared at the two Texans. "Ben Jones."

"Well now, Mister Jones, who else is in the house?"

"My partner, Bill Walker and there's Nick Ray and Nate Champion."

"You fellers all partners?"

"No, just me and Bill. We're trappers."

"What does Ray and Champion do for a livin'?"

"Punch dogies, I reckon."

"You mean they rustle dogies don't you?"

Wolcott walked up to the Texans, laughed, and slapped Buck on the back. "Good work, boys. Who did you bag?"

"He claims he's Ben Jones," Buck replied, "says him and his partner, Bill Walker, are trappers."

Wolcott nodded. "Reckon, he's tellin' the truth. Neither one is on the list. Anybody else in the house, Ben?"

"Like I told them, Nate Champion and Nick Ray."

"Damn," Wolcott squealed, "we want those two."

The two Texans escorted Ben into the brushy draw where he crouched out of site, scared out of his reason. A half-hour passed before the cabin door opened again. A younger man stepped onto the porch, waited, and looked around apparently trying to see what had happened to Ben. "That's my partner, Bill Walker," Ben said to Wolcott.

Walker headed toward the river, meeting the same fate that had befallen Jones. He was taken prisoner without incident and escorted to where Jones was crouching. "What's all this about?"

Walker said to Jones.

"I don't know."

Wolcott leaned toward Walker. "We're cleaning up Wyoming. We're goin' to kill every rustler in Johnson County. That includes Nate Champion and Nick Ray."

"There's one of them," Tom said, pointing at a man walking out onto the porch.

"That's Nick," Jones said.

Wolcott nudged the Texas Kid crouching beside Tom. "Kill him."

The Texas Kid slid into a kneeling position and cradled his Winchester in his left hand. With slow determination, he rested his left elbow on his knee and aimed the rifle at Nick Ray. As Ray stepped off the porch, the Winchester roared. Ray stumbled. Several other rifles fired. Ray fell. He squirmed around on the ground, rose up on his hands and knees, and crawled toward the door. When he reached the porch, Ray staggered to his feet. Another bullet fired by the Kid's Winchester slammed into his back. He fell, his hand reaching for the door. The door flew open. Nate Champion reaching for Ray's arm, grasped him by the wrist, and dragged him into the cabin.

Every Winchester opened fire, pouring round after round through the windows and door of the house. The fusillade continued for over two hours without any significant results.

Inside the cabin, Nate Champion sat at the kitchen table, counting Colt .45 and Winchester .44-40 cartridges. Nick Ray was lying on the bunk with his life ebbing away as blood soaked into the mattress from his bullet pierced chest. Champion stacked his cartridges into separate groups of six Colt and twelve Winchester rounds. He leaned back and counted two stacks of Winchester and four stacks of Colt reloads. He stared at the meager supply and listened to the invaders' bullets slamming into the cabin's log walls. The constant onslaught sounded like the rolling beat of a snare drum as they shredded the exterior walls into splinters.

Champion turned his attention to Nick. He stared at his friend and listened to each shallow, wheezing and gurgling breath that Nick took.  Frequent coughing attacks began, sending the stricken man into convulsing contortions.   Each paroxysm spewed crimson sputum between crusted lips.  *You're a goner*, Champion thought.  *Well, so am I.   There's enough men and guns out there to kill a dozen men.*

Frustrated and angry, Champion grabbed his Winchester, threw open the door and fired off twelve rounds at several invaders crouching beside the stable.  He slammed the door closed, walked to the table and slowly reloaded the rifle.

His thoughts turned to friends and family, especially his brother, Dudley.  Wanting to let them know how he and Nick met their fate, he opened a cabinet drawer, and pulled out a pencil and a little notebook.  He sat at the table and began to write an account of the day.

Like many of the gunmen laying siege to the KC Ranch house, he was a Texan, born on September 29, 1857 in a ranch house near Round Rock, Texas.  Now, thirty-four years later, his luck was running out.  He and his brother, Dudley, came to Wyoming with a trail herd in 1881.  Like many other Texas cowboys, they stayed to work for the prospering cattle spreads.  Their first job had been with the EK Ranch.  By 1884, Nate worked for the Bar C as a wagon boss in the spring roundup.  Two years later, he was back at the EK as a wagon boss.  In 1888, for unknown reasons, he was fired along with EK foreman Curt Spaugh.  He became a wanderer, worked for various spreads and got into trouble.  He acquired the reputation of a rustler by frequently helping himself to mavericks.  According to the WSGA, he carried a running iron with which he changed many brands.  His reputation took on another aspect, which was being fast with a Colt .45 and the willingness to use it whenever provoked.  His left-handed draw was said to be like lightning and deadly accurate.  But all of that talent was of no use on this day.

Champion glanced at Nick Ray lying on his bunk.  His blood soaked shirt laid on the floor beside the bunk where Champion had tossed it.  He touched a pencil to his tongue and began to write in his notebook.  *Me and Nick was getting breakfast when the attack took place.  Two men here with us-Bill Jones and another man.  The old man went after water and did not come back. His friend went out to see what was the matter and he did not come back. Nick started out and I told him to look out, that I thought that there was some one at the stable and would not let them come back. Nick is shot, but not dead yet. He is awful sick. I must go and wait on him.*

Champion leaned over Nick. "How you feelin'? Wished I had some water for ya."

Nick's eyes slowly opened. His lips, dry and sticky, separated as he tried to speak. "Ain't no use. I'm near dead. Save yerself if y'can."

Champion stroked Nick's forehead. "Ain't leavin' y'here."

Nick's eyes closed. Champion walked back to the table, picked up his pencil and began to write again. *It is now about two hours since the first shot. Nick is still alive; they are still shooting and are all around the house. Boys, there is bullets coming in like hail. Them fellows is in such shape I can't get at them. They are shooting from the stable and river and back of the house.*

Nick gasped. Champion jumped up and went to the bunk. Nick lay quiet and made no effort to breathe. Slowly his eyelids parted revealing sightless eyes. Champion closed them and pulled a blanket over his dead friend. Outside, the fusillade of bullets continued to pour into the cabin. Champion slumped into his chair, looked at his watch, and began to write. *Nick is dead, he died about 9 o'clock.*

Standing inside the stable, Wolcott called for a cease-fire. He, Tom, Frank Canton and Bill Irvine began to parley the situation. Ramsay listened as the four discussed what action was needed. They all agreed that time was being consumed and they needed to finish this and get on to Buffalo. "We got to get this over," Tom said to Wolcott.

Canton sneered, being delighted that Wolcott's tactics were failing. "Burn down the damn house. It's the fastest and surest way to get them both."

Tom, leaning on his walking stick, looked at Wolcott and nodded approval. "I agree. We can push a wagon loaded with hay against the house and set it on fire."

"Where can we get some hay? There isn't any here."

"It's only several miles over to George Baxter's ranch," Irvine said. "He ought to have some."

"Good idea," Tom said. "I'll get a couple of men to hitch up the trappers' wagon and go get a load."

The invaders waited for the wagon to return, not firing a shot the next two hours. It was nearly noon when the wagon returned empty. There had been no hay at the Baxter ranch. "What do we do now?" Wolcott said to Tom.

"Find something else that will burn well enough to do the job."

"I'll have some of the men look around the ranch. There ought to be something we can use."

"We ain't got all that much time," Irvine said. "Why don't we charge the cabin? He can't kill us all."

"You want to lead the attack?" Tom said and grinned at Irvine's stuttered reply. "Now, now, ah, Tom, I ain't no military man like Wolcott."

"No, I didn't think you would."

The four leaders continued to argue over the best way to kill Nate Champion. The rest of the invaders settled down into inactivity, most of them lounging about, some snoozing, and others arguing how the job should be done.

Meanwhile, Champion continued his vigil, writing in his notebook and watching the invaders through a window. When the gunfire ceased, it became profoundly quiet like the passing of the eye of a hurricane. Champion crawled to a window, slowly raised his head, and looked outside. Gray smoke was rising from the stable. He was unaware that Fred de Billier had built a fire to make coffee. "Damn," he said, crawling back to the table. He made another entry in his deathwatch notebook. *I see a smoke down at the stable. I think they have fired it. I don't think they intend to let me get away this time. It is now about noon. There is someone at the stable yet; they are throwing a rope out at the door and drawing it back. I guess it is to draw me out. I wish that duck would get out further so I could get a shot at him. Boys, I don't know what they have done with them two fellows that staid last night. Boys, I feel pretty lonesome just now. I wish there was someone here with me so we could watch all sides at once. They may fool around until I get a good shot before they leave.*

Alonzo Taylor, Jack Flagg's seventeen-year-old stepson, driving two horses hitched to a wagon approached the KC Ranch just before three o'clock. In the wagon was Jack Flagg's Winchester rifle and his suitcase. Flagg, astride his sorrel, followed several yards behind. He was on his way to Douglas to attend, as a delegate, the Democratic state convention. Fred Hesse and several of the Texans walked toward the road as the wagon and Flagg approached. "Halt," a Texan yelled.

Flagg was ignorant of what was going on. "Don't shoot me, boys. I'm all right."

Hesse recognized Flagg. "Jack Flagg! It's Jack Flagg!"

Some invader's Winchester bellowed. The bullet swished past Flagg and kicked dust into the air several yards beyond him. Alonzo snapped his whip, yanked hard on the left rein and screamed at the team of horses. "Hah, get up there, git, git, git..."

The wagon spun around and headed back toward Buffalo. Flagg, in Indian style, threw himself on the side of his sorrel and spurred him into a frenzied gallop. When he caught up with the wagon, he yelled for Alonzo to toss him the Winchester. He fired at seven pursuing mounted invaders galloping toward them. The invaders reined to a stop and sat their horses, reluctant to ride into range of Flagg's rifle. Alonzo unhooked one of the horses from the wagon, then he and Flagg galloped away with several of the horsemen pursuing them. Flagg continued to shoot at the invaders as he and Alonzo headed for Buffalo. The invaders finally gave up the chase and returned to the KC and the wrath of Tom and Wolcott.

Champion, alerted by the initial shot fired at Flagg, watched the event through his window. He returned to the table and made another entry in his notebook. *It is about 3 o'clock now. There was a man in a buckboard and one on horseback just passed. They fired on them as they went by. I don't know if they killed them or not. I seen lots of men come out on horses on the other side of the river and take after them.*

He resumed his vigil at the window. As he watched, a man

crouching low ran from the river toward the stable. Champion grabbed his Winchester, leveled it through the shattered window and squeezed the trigger. The rifle fired. The man leaped, disappearing behind the stable. Immediately, Champion dropped to the floor to avoid the invaders' return fire. He lay on the floor and began to write another entry.

*I shot at a man in the stable just now. Don't know if I got him or not. I must go look out again. It don't look as if there is much show of my getting away. I see twelve or fifteen men. One looks like Tom Albert. I don't know whether it is or not. I hope they did not catch them fellows that run over the bridge toward Smith's.*

Wolcott was livid. Tom's patience was frayed. Frank Canton taunted them both. "Now, you've done it. We've dillydallied around here most of the day. When Flagg gets to Buffalo, Angus and Hamby will be leading a posse down here."

"Canton is right," Irvine yelled, his face crimson. "Forget Champion, we'll get him later."

Wolcott jumped around like the rooster Hap had said he was. "No, damn it, no. We'll take care of this fellow first. I want that cabin set on fire right now."

Buck Garrett walked into the stable and pointed toward pine posts in the fence around the corral. Them posts is full of pitch. They'll burn like gunpowder.

"You're right," Tom yelled. "Get some men and chop off those posts and load them on Flagg's wagon. Scrape up what hay is in the corral and pile that on the posts."

Garrett proceeded to carry out Tom's orders. With Flagg's wagon piled high with posts and some hay, everything seemed ready to fire the house. Tom ordered everyone to begin shooting at the house as soon as the wagon began its lethal journey. Five men volunteered to push the wagon to the house and ignite it. On the side of the house facing the river was a window, its glass blown away by the invaders' bullets. They hoped to lodge the wagon against the house below that window. Finally, the wagon began to roll. Every invader's Winchester erupted in the most intense fusillade of the day.

When the shooting began, Champion laid on the floor. With

his Colt and Winchester beside him, he scribbled another entry. *They are shooting at the house now. If I had a pair of glasses, I believe I would know some of those men. They are coming back. I've got to look out. Well, they have just got through shelling the house again like hail. I heard them splitting wood. I guess they are going to fire the house tonight. I think I will make a break when night comes, if alive.*

As they neared the house, the shooting ceased. The five volunteers were relieved. "Our bullets will kill you just as dead as Champion's," one of them said. "Push harder, let's get this under that window quick before he sees us."

Finally, they lodged the wagon against the house beneath the open window. One man struck a match and tossed it into the pile of tinder. Flames leaped upward. A strong wind blowing from the river drove them through the window.

As the men ran for cover, the rifle barrage began again. Champion, sensing the end was near, wrote his final entry. *Shooting again. I think they will fire the house this time. It's not night yet.*

Smoke and flames belched across the room. Champion quickly finished his entry. *The house is all fired. Goodbye boys, if I never see you again. Nathan D. Champion.*

He jumped up, slipped off his boots, grabbed his Colt and Winchester, and opened the door. He ran through the doorway, raced across the porch, and charged across open ground toward a ravine south of the house. As he reached the ravine, several Texans rose up, and aimed their rifles. A bullet slammed into Champion's right arm. His Winchester fell from his paralyzed hand. He reached for his Colt jammed beneath his belt. Lead thumped into his chest. As he began to fall, two more bullets found their mark, the heart of Nathan D. Champion.

Tom, Wolcott, Irvine and Canton headed toward the ravine. Tom quickly fell behind, being unable to keep up on his crippled legs. Canton reached the grisly scene first and began to search Champions pockets. He found the notebook, opened its bloodied cover, and read Champion's record of the day. As Tom reached Champion's corpse, Canton handed him the notebook. Tom opened it and began to read the penciled entries. "Well, Tom,"

Canton said, "I see your name found a place in Champion's diary."

Tom said nothing, continuing to read until reaching his name. Canton held out the pencil he had pulled from Champion's pocket. "You may want to scratch that out before Sam Clover reads it. We don't want you making headlines in the *Chicago Herald.*

Ramsay walked away from the burning house, climbed on the horse Tom had given him and reined him toward the road. Not one of the invaders paid any attention to his departure. All of them were engrossed in the burning house and Nate Champion's bullet riddled corpse. As he crossed the bridge over the river, he feathered his spurs across the horse's flanks. Smoke from the burning house, swept by the wind, rolled across the river as Ramsay's horse galloped toward Buffalo.

Ramsay rode into Buffalo around three o'clock in the morning. It was a town in turmoil. Main Street was seething with angry and frightened men. Horses with Winchesters protruding from saddle scabbards were tied at every hitching rail. In spite of the early hour, Foote's store was filled with men buying supplies of food, blankets, ammunition and rifles. Ramsay tied his horse with the invader's maverick A brand burned into his shoulder to the courthouse hitching rail next to Sheriff Angus's black mare. Nate met him at the courthouse door. "Ramsay! I'm sure glad to see you. Come on in; we've got a fresh pot of coffee on the stove."

"I reckon from what I see you already know about the invaders."

"Yeah, Hap brought that word to us a couple of days ago," Nate said, pouring coffee. "We sent riders out yesterday mornin' callin' for men to help us defend Buffalo."

Ramsay held the hot cup between his hands and slowly sipped. "Anybody ride over to let Dad know?"

"Yeah, we've got over a dozen riders coverin' every ranch and farm within a hundred miles."

"I tried to send you a telegram twice, but the vigilantes had already cut the wires."

"Yeah, we caught one of their wire cutters yesterday and locked him up. No tellin' how many more they've got tearin' up the lines."

"That ain't all that they've been doin'. They killed Nate Champion and Nick Ray."

"They did? Where did that happen?"

"We were at Rob Tisdale's ranch down on Willow Creek last night when Shonsey rode in saying there were rustlers holed up at the KC. Wolcott and Irvine persuaded the others to take care of the KC before riding on to Buffalo."

Angus' spurs jingled as he descended the stairs from the courtroom. His meeting with the new mayor, Charles Hogerson, had just ended. "Well, howdy," Angus said, reaching for Ramsay's hand. "You look like you've been doin' some hard ridin'."

"I was just tellin' Nate that the invaders attacked the KC Ranch and killed Champion and Ray."

"How many vigilantes are there?"

"About fifty. They've enough ammunition and dynamite to wipe out Buffalo."

Ramsay poured more coffee into his cup. "Did Jack Flagg make it back to town?"

"No, we haven't seen him," Nate said. "Why are you askin'?"

Ramsay held his forefinger and thumb an inch apart. "He and another fellow came that close to getting shot when they came by the KC. The last I saw of them, they was ridin' hell for leather toward Buffalo."

Angus pulled a Winchester from his gun cabinet and slipped twelve rounds into the magazine. "No tellin' what Flagg will do, he'll try anything to get a story to write."

"Well, we can't worry about Flagg just now," Nate said. "We've got to find the vigilantes."

Dick Drury walked into Angus's office. "We're here to help, Marshal Hamby."

Ramsay spun around. "Dad! Damn I'm glad t'see ya."

A glint filled Dick Drury's unpatched left eye as he stared at Ramsay. "I'm real glad to see you too, son. Jack, Luke an' ten o' our hands is waterin' our horses over at the livery right now. What ya need us t'do, Marshal?"

"There are fifty gunmen ridin' toward Buffalo right this minute. We need to find them."

Dick slapped his holster and winked at Ramsay. "All right, I'll have a cup o' that coffee, then let's go find them."

# Chapter Nineteen

The eastern horizon began to pale as Nate, Angus and the Drurys reached the ranch of John R. Smith about fifteen miles south of Buffalo. Mrs. Smith informed them that her husband had gone with Flagg and Alonzo. Their intention had been to gather men from the other ranches in the area and return to the KC to assist the men they thought were still besieged.

Nate and the others headed toward the KC, determined to find the invaders. They reined their horses to a halt after riding them hard for several miles. They had not found any sign of the invading vigilantes or Flagg and his bunch of men. They began to wonder whether the invaders had abandoned the road and were approaching Buffalo by a more discrete route. After Jack Flagg had escaped their guns, the invaders had to believe Buffalo would be informed of their whereabouts. Nate turned toward Dick. "You know most of those cattlemen. Now that they've botched surprisin' us, what do you think they'll do?"

"Wolcott thinks he's a smart general. He'll contrive up some plan to take Buffalo. You can bet on that."

"Do you think he will stop somewhere to organize his assault or just barrel on into town?"

"Oh, that's an easy one. He'll stop at one of the WSGA ranches, preach to his 'troops', and make certain he's got everything covered."

"That will give us some more time."

"Reckon so."

"We need to ride back to Buffalo and send out riders to every WSGA ranch within twenty miles of town. While they are scouting for the invaders, we'll have all our men ready."

"Good plan," Angus said. "Soon as the scouts find them, we'll hit 'em."

Dick reined his hors around. "Let's ride."

As they galloped into town, Frank Cobb ran out of his office into the street, waving his arms. Nate reined back his sorrel as

Cobb yelled, "Hap and Flagg headed out to the TA Ranch with over fifty men a couple of hours ago.  Hap said to tell you and Angus that the vigilantes have taken refuge out there."

"Thanks," Nate said, "we'll get fresh horses and head for the TA."

Monday morning had dawned cold and overcast.  Nate led a posse of fifty men into the headquarters of the Covington Ranch less than two miles from the TA.  Over fifty saddled horses filled the corrals and more were tied to fences, trees and wagon wheels.  The yard was packed with armed men listening to Rap Brown.

Nate made his way to the porch where Rap was giving the crowd a 'go get 'em' speech.  "Now, fellers, I see Marshal Hamby finally got hisself out here.  Marshal, these men have elected me captain.  Got any objection t'that?"

Nate was surprised at the crowd's selection.  Rap Brown had an odious reputation, being repulsive in habit and character.  He seldom used soap or tact.  But, his dictatorial attitude seemed to be what the men gathered at the Covington Ranch valued.  "None at all for the time bein'. However, Sheriff Angus is the legal authority here and he will be along later today with more men."

"We can use all the men he can bring out here," Rap said, ignoring Nate's admonition.  "Your deputy and Flagg deployed their men over at the TA durin' the night, so me an' my men are goin' over t'join 'em."

Aunt Deana and Beth walked from the house, carrying a steaming coffee pot, stacks of tin cups, and a platter of pastries.  "Afore you men go traipsin' off to fight," Aunt Deana called to the crowd, "come and get some hot coffee and goodies."

Nate reached for a tin cup.  "Hello, Beth."

She filled Nate's cup.  You must try Aunt Deana's kuchen cakes.  They are delicious."

"Thanks.  I guess this is as good a time as any to tell you some bad news."

Beth's pleasantness grew somber.  "What is it?"

"Ramsay tells me that Tom is so crippled he has to be tied in his saddle. Also, he says Tom is livin' with another woman down at Cheyenne."

Beth looked away for a moment, and then faced Nate. "I'm not surprised at either one. I'm sorry he isn't well."

"Tom and Wolcott are leadin' the invaders."

"I knew that he would. Please, be careful. Tom will try to kill you."

After the crowd of angry men had warmed their bellies, Rap Brown mounted his big buckskin. "All you men ridin' with me get your butts in the saddle. Let's go stomp them whitecaps."

*  *  *  *  *

"Nate, if this ain't crazy," Hap grumbled, "I'm a purple goose." Spittle stained brown by chewing tobacco seeped from the corners of his mouth as Hap peered through brass binoculars. "Look down there in the bend o' Crazy Woman Crick at that lunatic asylum."

Major Wolcott had engineered an impressive fortress for the vigilantes. The TA Ranch house and out buildings were surrounded on three sides by Crazy Woman Creek. The WSGA vigilantes had fortified the house, icehouse and stable with heavy timbers. They also had built a sharpshooters' log fort a dozen feet square atop high ground about fifty yards west of the stable. A network of trenches had been dug connecting defensive breastworks that had been raised around the main house.

By afternoon of Monday, April the 11th, 1892, the Johnson County posse commanded by Sheriff Angus had built breastworks completely surrounding the vigilante's fortress. Over two hundred men who were being reinforced by riders arriving throughout the day manned these fortifications. Continuous rifle fire cracked and rumbled from the vigilantes and their besiegers.

"Yeah, Hap, you're observin' a genuine standoff," Nate commented while sharing Hap's binoculars. "We can't get at them and they can't hit us with their Winchesters as long as we stay behind these breastworks. What I couldn't do with a twelve-pound Napoleon cannon."

Red Angus crawled into the rifle pit from which Nate and Hap were studying the besieged ranch house. Nate handed the binoculars to Red. "We'll never get them out of that fort with rifles. They'll pick us off if we try an assault without artillery support."

"Yeah, even one well-placed cannon shot could end this standoff."

"Reckon we could get one from the fort?" Hap asked Nate.

"No!"

"Why not?"

"The Army doesn't sell or loan cannons."

"Some pickets over at the Covington Ranch captured the vigilantes three wagons about an hour ago," Angus said, gazing at the TA Ranch house. "There's several cases of dynamite in one of them. If there was some way we could get close enough...."

"We could blow 'em clean t'hell," Hap blurted.

"Yep," Angus replied.

"I've got an idea," Nate said.

"What is it?" Angus asked.

"A movable fort."

"What is a movin' fort?"

Nate explained to them how one had been put together during a fight for a bridge in the Shenandoah Valley in 1862. They lashed two caissons together and built a shield out of stacked railroad ties on the front. A squad then pushed it close to the bridge. They fired grenades at the Yanks until they abandoned the bridge.

"The wagons!" Angus exclaimed.

Nate nodded. "That's right." His answer was cut short. Screams from horses down in the vigilante's corral cut through the rumbling fusillade of rifle fire. Rap Brown's men had gotten the range, downing several horses before the vigilantes could herd any into the stable.

The vigilantes finally got the range of the closest rifle pits surrounding them. A torrent of their .44-40 bullets tore relentlessly at each of the earthen breastworks. Choruses of ricocheting bullets added their screams to the discordant mayhem along Crazy Woman Creek.

Angus tapped Nate's shoulder. "Could you put one of those contraptions together?"

Nate took the binoculars from Angus and rose up to determine the distance they would have to cover in moving the mobile fort into place. "Sure! Are those wagons over at the Covington Ranch?"

"Yeah."

"Come with me," Nate yelled at Hap, "let's go make that mobile fort."

* * * * *

Tom peered through a gun port the vigilantes had cut through the wall above a barricaded window of the ranch house. He spun the focusing wheel of his binoculars while scanning the fortified rifle pits of the attacking posse. He saw Nate rise up to look through Hap's binoculars. "There's Hamby—bring me the scoped rifle."

The Texas Kid handed Tom a custom-built buffalo rifle fitted with a long telescopic sighting device. Tom pushed the rifle's barrel, which was double the length of a Winchester model 73, through the gun port. "Is this thing loaded?" Tom asked, fondling the black walnut stock.

"She's carryin' a full load."

Tom pulled back the hammer. "What's the range of this monster?"

"Way past any of them rustlers. That gun has killed at nearly one-thousand yards."

Tom held his breath while holding the sight on Nate's head. Slowly, his finger curled around the trigger. "She's got a four-pound trigger pull," the Kid said, stepping backward to get prepared for the rifle's thunderous report.

Tom gradually squeezed the monster's trigger. The hammer slammed down. The heavy rifle recoiled like a battering ram. His crippled legs were no match for the big gun's mule-like kick. The recoiling gun shoved him backward. He spun around like a diver plummeting from a high board as the room filled with acrid gray smoke. He sprawled toward the floor. The tumbling rifle cracked against the side of his head. "Jeez," the Kid yelled, lunging to break Tom's fall.

Within moments, a purple lump closed Tom's left eye. His addled brain did not turn itself off, but seemed to stop the way a movie projector freezes a single frame. All he could see was Nate's face nearly covered by binoculars facing the big gun's muzzle. Gradually, Nate's face faded until the Kid's face took its place. Tom struggled to sit up. "That gun doesn't mind who it kills, does it?"

"Reckon she don't."

Wolcott leaned over Tom. "What happened?"

"I shot Nate Hamby."

"The hell you say! Are you sure you hit him?"

"I don't see how I could have missed."

"Well, y'did," Frank Canton said, scanning the area with his binoculars. "Ya overshot Hamby by a couple of feet."

Fred Hesse helped Tom to his feet. "Killing Hamby isn't going to help us. We're completely surrounded by god knows how many men and more ridin' in every hour."

The Texas Kid started to reload the buffalo gun. "If we don't get help, we're done for."

"Yeah," Hesse said. "We've got to get a message to Governor Barber."

"You got us into this mess, Wolcott," Canton said. "Why don't you try a breakout tonight?"

Ignoring Canton's sarcasm, Wolcott addressed the Kid. "I'll make one of you boys richer by five-hundred dollars for sending a telegram to the governor."

"How we goin' t'do that? The lines is all cut."

"The lines out of Gillette are open."

"That's near fifty miles as a crow flies," Hesse said.

"You fellers got five-hunderd with ya?"

"Where's de Billier?" Wolcott asked. "He's got five-hundred."

Canton was still gazing through his binoculars. "Freddy's takin' his afternoon nap."

Wolcott's short temper exploded in a bellowing response. "Somebody wake him up and get the money."

"Our best rider is Smiley Tubbs," the Kid said to Wolcott. "You give him the money and I promise he'll head for Gillette after dark."

Smiley was a wiry little man. He hardly topped a hundred-twenty pounds. He hated saddles, having learned to ride bareback when only six years of age.

Any fast horse without the added weight of a saddle and with Smiley's tendency to ride with foolish abandon had a good chance of succeeding in a breakout. After darkness blanketed the high plains, Smiley picked out his mount, a sleek bay stud with rippling muscles and a deep chest promising superior lung capacity. With five-hundred dollars and a written message addressed to the governor in his pocket, Smiley swung himself onto the bay. He leaned low over the galloping horse's withers and raced toward Crazy Woman Creek. Twenty men behind a breastwork east of the creek heard the bay's pounding hooves. Several raised up to peer into the darkness just as Smiley reined the bay in a huge leap over the startled riflemen. Two bullets swished by before Smiley was beyond the range of their rifles.

A gray dawn filtered through a low overcast on the morning of Tuesday, the twelfth. Its blandness seemed to accentuate the vigilante's desperate situation. Tom, with binoculars back at a gun port, peered intently at unusual activity on high ground west of the posse's positions. After studying the object a number of men were working to build, Tom called for Wolcott, "Come here, Frank."

Wolcott climbed up on a chair and looked through Tom's binoculars. "What do you make of that?" Tom asked.

"Well, I'll be damned!"

Tom's curiosity heightened. "Well, what are they buildin'?"

"That's a damned mobile breastwork. Somebody up there is experienced in military engineering."

"Nate Hamby!"

Wolcott handed the glasses back to Tom. "Too bad you aren't a better shot."

\* \* \* \* \*

"She's done," Hap shouted at the twenty men assembling Nate's mobile fort, soon referred to as the "Go-Devil" by its builders. It was an awesome device constructed from one of the vigilante's new Studebaker wagons. The wagon's front running gear had been separated from the rear running gear. They had then been lashed together side by side with all four wheels in front. Seven layers of heavy timbers were then piled and secured behind the wheels, providing a thick shield. Stacking bales of hay as wings off the front shield provided additional protection for the Go-Devil's occupants. It was ready to be moved down the hill toward the vigilantes' fortress.

Nate motioned for them to move forward. "Let's get her rollin'."

The Go-Devil moved slowly toward the ranch buildings as its twenty builders strained to move it over the rough snow-covered ground. Behind the log shield were two cases of dynamite and a coil of fuse. Three sharpshooters fired through gun ports at the vigilantes who were concentrating their fire at the Go-Devil. Breaking the standoff seemed close at hand. Throughout Tuesday night, the Go-Devil inched closer to the besieged in the TA Ranch house.

Wednesday morning dawned with the taste of approaching victory in the mouths of every man attacking the vigilantes. The vigilantes, in turn, were filled with gloom. Wolcott had run out of ideas for coping with the advancing Go-Devil. Their only option left was a desperate attempt to ride through the attackers' lines. Hope was nearly gone.

Angus had ridden over to talk with Rap Brown when a rider came galloping toward them from the Covington Ranch and slid his horse to a stop. "Sheriff, the cavalry is comin'."

"How far away are they?"

"No more than a mile."

"Well, Rap," Angus said, "looks like the President has yanked victory out of our hands. Let's go meet 'em."

Rap reeled his horse around. "Damn it!"

Col. Van Horn, at the head of three troops of the Sixth Cavalry, trotted toward Angus and Rap who were waiting astride their horses out of sight of the TA Ranch house. Cavalry swords clanked against stirrups. A stars and stripes banner fluttered from the staff of a flag bearer who was riding behind a huge officer wearing the gold leaves of a major on his shoulders. At the fore of each troop, bearers carried red and white guidons flapping atop hickory staffs. Col. Van Horn raised his right arm, halting the troopers. He urged his mount, a big black gelding, into a prancing gait toward Angus and Brown. "Howdy, Colonel," Angus called.

"Good morning, Sheriff. I trust you gentlemen know why we're here?"

"I reckon we do."

"Why don't you take your soldier boys back t'your fort?" Rap Brown snarled. "We can take care o' this."

Col. Van Horn wagged his head. "I think you know I can't do that. I've been ordered to intercede, with force if necessary, in this insurrection. I'm asking you gentlemen to declare a truce."

Angus hoped to garner a successful conclusion to the siege. "We will, on one condition."

"Which is?"

"That the vigilantes we've got surrounded be turned over to civil authorities for trial." Rap scowled at the idea, but didn't speak.

"There isn't anything in my orders to prevent that from happening."

"Good! Rap, would you go give the order for our men to cease firing?"

Without replying, Rap angrily wheeled about and galloped toward the sounds of battle.

Col. Van Horn nor Angus were aware of the intrigue and conspiracy involved within the orders Van Horn carried in his pocket. As soon as Governor Barber had received the telegram Wolcott had paid Smiley Tubbs to send him from Gillette, he set the political wheels in motion. He immediately sent a telegram to President Benjamin Harrison, stating that United States troops located at Fort McKinney were required to quell an *insurrection* against the government of Wyoming. Several hours passed with no reply from the President. Barber, fearing that his WSGA friends under siege at the TA Ranch were about to be wiped out, sent several telegrams. One went to Brigadier General John B.

Brooke, commanding the Department of the Platte at Omaha, who was Van Horn's immediate superior. He also wired Colonel Van Horn apprising him of his actions. At the same time, telegrams were sent to Wyoming senators Carey and Warren in Washington, D. C. They immediately went into action by calling on Grant, the acting secretary of war. All of them went to the White House. It was 11:00 P.M. Harrison had retired for the night. They insisted that the President be awakened. Harrison listened to his old friend, Senator Carey and quickly agreed to send troops to the TA Ranch. Within minutes, the President had telegrams sent to General Brooke and Governor Barber. The men under siege at the TA owed their lives to Barber, Carey, Warren, Grant and President Harrison.

Col. Van Horn steadied his prancing mount with a firm pull on his reins. "I'll give your people ten minutes to comply before I order my bugler to sound the advance."

Within minutes, the attacking posse's breastworks fell silent. Only intermittent rifle fire came from the besieged vigilantes. "Won't you join me and Major Fechet?" Colonel Van Horn asked Angus.

"Glad to."

Van Horn called for the bugler, a tow-headed lad hardly old enough to shave, to ride forward. Major Fechet turned around in his saddle. "Guidons to the fore."

Major Fechet, flanked by the flag and three guidon bearers, ordered the troopers to advance at a trot. Van Horn pulled out his watch to check the time as he and Angus fell in with Fechet. They advanced up and over the hill until the ranch house and the posse's breastworks came into view. "Blow your bugle, Private," Van Horn ordered.

All rifle fire ceased as the bugle's clarion notes cascaded in waves over the TA Ranch house at Crazy Woman Creek. The advancing troopers continued down the slope. They trotted past the Go-Devil where Hap lifted his stained Stetson. "You fellers sure are a sight."

One of the vigilantes held up a white banner tied to a rifle barrel before the cavalry troops reached the log fort west of the stable. Col. Van Horn raised his arm, signaling the troopers to halt. Simultaneously, Major Wolcott came out of the house and marched like a martinet toward Colonel Van Horn. "Good morning, sir, I am Major Frank Wolcott."

"I'm Colonel Van Horn. By order of President Harrison, I'm here to bring this situation to a close. Will you and your party agree to surrender?"

"I'll surrender to the United States Army, but we'll die before surrendering to Angus or Hamby."

Where is Marshal Hamby?" Van Horn asked Angus.

"He's back at that mobile fort."

Van Horn turned around and gave an order to one of the guidon bearers. "Ride up to that contraption and bring Marshal Hamby down here."

Everyone waited in silence while the trooper rode up to the Go-Devil. Nate, riding double with the bearer, jumped to the ground. "Good mornin' Colonel Van Horn.

"Marshal, Major Wolcott has asked to surrender only to me. Is that agreeable with you?"

Wolcott glared at Nate who responded without taking his eyes off Wolcott. "What do you say, Sheriff Angus?"

Angus glanced at Nate then looked squarely at Wolcott. "I agreed to a truce provided these vigilantes answer to civil authority."

"I'll agree to that," Nate said to Van Horn.

# Chapter Twenty

The bugler's trumpeting notes of 'assembly' echoed across the quadrangle of Fort McKinney. It was Easter Sunday, four days after Wolcott's surrender of the invaders. Major Fechet walked briskly toward his dapple-gray mare being held by his orderly in front of the assembling troopers. Transfer of the surrendered invaders to Fort Russell at Cheyenne was about to begin.

The men of power in Cheyenne and Washington D. C had dealt the citizens of Johnson County another blow. Although the battle at the TA Ranch had been concluded, the Johnson County War was far from being over. Colonel Van Horn's agreeing for the prisoners to be turned over to civilian authorities for trial had been countermanded. Governor Barber, by executive decree, had prohibited the serving of arrest warrants by Sheriff Angus upon the invaders held captive at Fort McKinney. Instead, through his and Senators Carey and Warren's influence, the military had been ordered to transfer the invaders to Fort D. A. Russell in Cheyenne. The power of the WSGA was alive and well.

Fechet's three companies of troopers quickly surrounded the prisoners standing beside their horses. On Fechet's order, prisoners and troopers swung themselves into their saddles.

It was after ten o'clock in the morning when Major Fechet bellowed the marching command to his troops. They were heading for Fort Fetterman on the Platte River, where the prisoner vigilantes were to be loaded on a train bound for Cheyenne. A cold rain began to fall as the columns of troopers surrounding their prisoners trotted out of Fort McKinney to the strains of *Sweet Betsy From Pike* being played by the garrison band.

Sheriff Angus, Nate, and Hap joined Buffalo's citizens lining Main Street while the hated vigilantes were being escorted through town. The people were furious, angry that this outrageous event was happening. Their fists flailed the air as they taunted the prisoners. The crowd became a mob, furious and unruly. They pressed closer to the escorting troopers. "Get back!" Major Fechet barked. "Everybody get back!"

Captain Stanton, commanding C troop, yelled at his troopers, "Move 'em back, boys. Ride into 'em."

Major Fechet's gauntleted hand grasped the handle of his saber as the complaining citizens pushed toward the prisoners. "Cut 'em out!" Major Fechet bellowed. With his saber drawn, Fechet wheeled his mare around and charged at the growing mob. The people scattered before the charging troopers. Fechet slammed the saber back into his scabbard, reined the mare about and trotted back to the fore of his troops. With sabers clanking, the cavalry escorted their prisoners out of Buffalo and on across the high plains toward Fort Fetterman.

At Fetterman, they were to be turned over to troops from Fort D. A. Russell at Cheyenne. They in turn would escort the prisoners by rail to Cheyenne.

The ensuing days were filled with frustrations as Nate and Hap strove to expedite the invaders' trial. They met WSGA opposition almost daily. They tried to locate the whereabouts of Jones and Walker, the two trappers captured by the invaders. Wolcott had turned them loose after Champion was killed, telling them to "go south and keep going." The two men had obeyed by going to Casper. Sheriff Angus, Nate, Hap and Sheriff Rice of Natrona Country tried to keep these witnesses safe. Their efforts failed as the Wyoming power brokers used both legal and illegal methods to either remove Jones and Walker from Wyoming or silence them with a hired gun. They succeeded when the trappers boarded a train in the company of hired guns. They crossed the border into Nebraska, never to be seen in Wyoming again.

The invaders were incarcerated at Fort Russell, waiting to be charged and tried for their crimes. Even though they were prisoners of the military, they found increasing sympathy from Washington for their predicament. Restrictions relaxed, many being allowed to sleep at home and others were paroled to travel. Wolcott made a trip to Omaha and Chicago garnering political influence to free him and his cohorts.

The cattlemen began to boast their intentions to return to Johnson County as soon as they got out of their trouble and "clean the rascals out." News of the fiasco reached Johnson County, causing fearful anticipation of a second raid upon their homes and property.

Every move to expedite the legal processes for trying the invaders met opposition within the WSGA controlled state government. Also, the WSGA's influence in Washington through their senators misled President Harrison, making him believe that the citizens of Johnson County were plotting insurrection. This resulted in threats of martial law by the federal government. Johnson County had to bear the expenses for keeping the prisoners incarcerated which rapidly depleted the county treasury. Political and legal maneuvering continued throughout the remaining months of 1892.

Finally, on January 21st, 1893, the case of the State of Wyoming vs. the Vigilantes was called in the Laramie County courthouse in Cheyenne. Most of the cattlemen responded, but the Texans, free on bail, did not appear. Many of them had already returned to Texas. The proceedings were short. Alvin Bennett, Johnson County's prosecuting attorney, offered a motion to enter a *nolle prosequi* (no prosecution). After discussion, the court accepted the motion and the prisoners were discharged. Another *nolle prosequi* motion was made concerning the Texans with the same results. Thus, the Johnson County War ended.

"Damn these sticks!" Tom groaned. A number of times, he repeated his contempt for the unruly limbs carrying him out of the courthouse. Paranoid delusions were changing his personality. Fear and suspicion constantly stalked him. Sleep, when it came, brought nightmares. One of them repeated itself almost every night. During the dream, voices out of the past kept calling to one another from behind him. One long-dead outlaw killed by a bullet from Tom's forty-five would yell over and over, "There goes the bastard. Kill 'im." As the hounding voices drew nearer, he would turn to face his dreaded pursuers. The moonlit hills, or dark street, or dimly lit saloon were always empty. "Damn these sticks I got for legs," he said, staggering along like a drunken cowboy on Saturday night.

Wolcott walked down the courthouse steps. "Wait up, Tom. I'll give you a lift over to the Club."

Tom turned around and leaned on his walking stick. "Thanks Frank, these legs ain't workin' too good."

The carriage from the Club drawn by a prancing team turned the corner and stopped in front of the courthouse. Wolcott helped Tom into the carriage. "You'll feel better after you get some Scotch into ya."

"I reckon so."

Wolcott pulled two cigars from his pocket and offered one to Tom. "We showed 'em, didn't we?"

"Yeah, reckon we did."

"Well, Tom, we'll do it right next time."

"Next time; don't be a fool."

"Hey, that doesn't sound like our chief inspector. Where's your grit?"

"I'm goin' home, back to Beth and the M-W."

"What makes you think she'll take you back? I hear she's real cozy with Marshal Hamby."

Anger surged through Tom. "I'm goin' to kill him."

Wolcott smiled and blew smoke out the carriage window. "That may take some doing. Why don't you forget about Beth. Stay with Marie."

"I'm leavin' for Buffalo in the mornin'."

"That's stupid, if I may say so. Most likely you'll be gunned down within a week."

"I'm gettin' Beth and takin' her back to the M-W."

\* \* \* \* \*

Nate was spooning ketchup onto his eggs when Angus walked into the Occidental restaurant. "Aunt Deana's over at the office, cryin' and takin' on. She says Beth is gone. Her bed ain't been slept in."

Nate stopped eating and reached for his hat hanging on the back of an empty chair. "Let's go talk to Aunt Deana."

Aunt Deana was so distraught she could hardly speak. "I told her to keep her door locked," she said, dabbing a handkerchief to her eyes. "I told her—I told her no tellin' what Tom would do if he comes back. That man is insane."

"Now, Aunt Deana," Nate said evenly, trying to sound calm. "I'll find Beth; don't you worry."

"Oh, Nate, I am worried. I just know he's taken Beth. He's crazy."

It only took Angus and Nate a few minutes to determine what had happened. Beth had been abducted. They found buggy tracks in the snow behind the stable in back of Aunt Deana's house. Boot prints led them to the house. The boot prints beneath the window of Beth's upstairs bedroom indicated that the intruder had loitered there for some time. They followed the intruder's trail toward the outhouse. About ten feet from the outhouse, the snow-covered pathway was gouged and marred. "Looks like this is where he grabbed Beth," Angus said.

"Yeah, someone, but I doubt Tom has taken her."

"Who else would grab her?"

"Someone Tom hired—he's too crippled to do it himself."

They mounted their horses and followed the buggy tracks. They headed north, crossed the Clear Creek Bridge and continued up the Bozeman trail. "My guess is that they're headed for the M-W," Nate said. "I'll stop at the Wagon Box and get Hap."

Angus nodded. "You want me to come with you?"

"No need. The M-W is in Sheridan County. Hap and I can handle this."

"You sure?"

He was certain; Tom had a debt to pay. He and Hap were going to collect it. "Yeah, I'm sure."

As Angus rode back toward Buffalo, Nate pulled out his U. S. marshal badge, fastened it on his shirt and spurred his sorrel into a gallop.

* * * * *

Squire, the man Tom had hired, reined his team to a stop so he could read a sign beside the road going from Sheridan toward the Montana border. Beth sat beside him dressed only in a nightgown and a robe. Her wrists and ankles were bound with rope. She shivered and pulled the lap blanket tighter about her shoulders. "Please untie my wrists and ankles. My hands and feet ache and I'm so cold."

"Can't do it."

"I won't run away, I promise."

Squire laughed, sneered and turned to read the sign. "Oh, yes you would."

Beth glanced at Squire, and then she looked back at the sign. It was faded, weathered, and its painted letters were peeling. It said: M-W cattle company boundary. Rustlers beware; bearers of running irons will be hung. Signed, Tom Albert, owner and member of WSGA.

Squire flipped the team's reins. "Hah! Get along hosses. We're almost there."

Squire reined the team into the driveway to the M-W compound on the Tongue River. The road was growing muddy, its snow pack having been thawed by a Chinook during the night. The frigid north wind had swung about, becoming a gentler southern breeze.

About a mile from the ranch compound, there was a bridge that crossed over a dry gully. Just as the buggy's wheels rolled onto the bridge, a man ran from under the bridge. He grabbed the bridle of one of the horses. "You lost?"

Squire glared at the man's menacing features. He was a burly fellow wearing a dirty sheepskin parka and a battered black hat. He gave a toothy grin exposing teeth stained brown from tobacco. "I'm one o' them good smare-tins. You some kind o' drummer?"

"Y'got somethin' agin drummers?"

Beth apparently hoped a half-truth would dissuade the man from whatever he intended. "We live here. This is our ranch."

The man walked toward Beth. "Well, I declare little lady, where you folks been?"

"Sheridan."

The fellow grinned, lifted the lap blanket, and spied the rope tied about her ankles. He dropped the blanket and yanked a derringer out of his pocket. "Well now what we got here? This man tryin' to hurt you, little lady?"

"Ain't none of your concern," Squire said.

"I'm makin' it some of my concern. Y'got any money on ya, Mister Drummer?"

Unable to reach for his Colt, Squire tried to pacify the highwayman. "Some. I'll give it to you—just put that derringer away."

"Can't do that. Sit right still while I get your wallet. Where do you carry it?"

"The right hand pocket of my parka."

The man reached inside the pocket, retrieved the wallet, pulled out all of the money and counted each of the fifty and one-hundred dollar bills. "I swear, Mister Drummer, you must be rich. Maybe you do own this here ranch."

Squire didn't reply. The fellow laughed, his fetid whiskey breath blowing into Beth's face as he looked her over. "Just who are you little lady? This ol' boy takin' a whore home with him?"

Squire's eyes flashed. The fear of Tom Albert's anger, if he allowed Beth to be harmed, made his trigger finger twitch. As the man began to peel away the blanket from Beth's shoulders, Squire eased his hand inside his parka toward the Colt in his shoulder holster. He grasped the grip. Like lightening, the barrel leveled between the highwayman's eyes. Beth cringed and the Colt bellowed. The bullet slammed into the man's head like a battering ram, propelling him backward off the bridge. All of the money flew out of his hand before his corpse landed in the bottom of the gully. Green bank notes, carried by the wind, blew away as Squire yelled, "Get goin' hosses."

* * * * *

Hap and Nate galloped their horses out of the Wagon Box driveway onto the Bozeman trail. They had a thirty-mile ride ahead of them to reach the M-W Ranch compound.

The last week in January had seen new snow. The buggy heading north had left deep tracks that Nate believed to be several hours old. He was worried, more worried than he'd been since the winter of 64 during the Yankees' siege of Petersburg, Virginia. Tom's mental balance had been teetering on the brink of a full-blown psychotic collapse for several months. No telling what Tom would do when one of his delusions surfaced.

As they hurried north, Nate wondered if his renewed

courting of Beth might have triggered Tom's reaction. One month before, at Aunt Deana's Christmas party, he and Beth stepped out onto the porch to spend some time together. It was a clear, crisp night. The sky was alive, effervescent like champagne with millions of twinkling stars. The moon, full and mellow, lingered just above the Bighorn Mountains. Its brilliance accentuated the whiteness of the blanket of snow covering the landscape like a Currier and Ives picture. He put his arm around Beth; she snuggled closer. Neither of them said anything. They just enjoyed the moment. He pulled her tightly against his chest and leaned down as her lips met his. Several kisses quickened his hunger. While holding her tight, he whispered, "I love you Beth Todd."

Beth giggled, light and airy, like a schoolgirl. "Don't you mean Beth Albert?"

"You ceased to be Mrs. Albert a long time ago. No, I mean Beth Todd."

"I wish that were true."

"It can be."

Beth knew what his next question would be. She was very much in love with Nate and longed to be with him as his wife. "All right, I'll ask Mr. Cobb to file my petition with Judge Blake."

Nate laughed. "That is good news." He kissed her, and then looked into her eyes. "Will you marry me and move to the Wagon Box."

"Yes, yes, just as soon as the divorce is final. Oh, I love you so much."

Nate's musing ceased when Hap said, "We've gotta hurry if we're goin' to get there before dark."

Nate slipped out his watch and flipped open its cover. "It's four minutes until one, got a lot of ridin' yet."

Darkness settles over the high country early during the winter. Nate peered into the late twilight and pointed at a buggy standing next to the corral as they rode up the driveway toward the M-W compound. They reined their horses to a halt, pulled out their Colts and spun the chambers. Light was streaming through the ranch house windows, reflecting rectangular orange patterns on the snow-covered grounds. "We got to go at this right," Nate said, holstering his Colt. "Don't want to risk Beth's gettin' hurt."

Hap spat out his cud of tobacco. "Or worse."

Nate glanced at Hap and winced at the thought.   He motioned for Hap to follow him as he reined his sorrel toward cottonwoods growing along the Tongue River.   Once they reached cover, they dismounted, tied their horses to saplings and began creeping toward a tack shed back of the house. With a whisper, Nate said, "We can hide in that shed while we decide how to go about this."

Hap nodded agreement.   One at a time, they crept through the grove of cottonwoods, advancing from tree trunk to tree trunk.   Fortunately, the door to the shed faced away from the house.   Nate eased the door open and Hap closed it behind them. Hap swiped his kerchief over a window facing the house.  As he cleared years of accumulated grime from the glass, Hap peered at the house.  The porch was high.  Its roof, which was supported on tall pillars, pitched upward until meeting the main building just below dormer windows jutting from the third story. "Take a look at this."

Nate removed his Stetson and looked through the window. "What do you see?"

"That porch...them windows.   If we can get on top of the porch, we can get into the house."

"Yeah, most likely we'd be above where Tom and his henchmen are."

"You can't shinny up one o' them pillars with that arm of yours."

"No, I reckon I can't.  Do you think you can?"

"I think so.  Sure goin' t'try."

We need to hurry.  Soon as the moon comes up, it'll be light as day on this snow."

Just as Hap reached for the doorknob, the hoof beats of a galloping horse coming up the driveway stayed his hand.  Nate looked through the window.  The full moon was rimming the eastern horizon, casting a fiery orange glow across the snow-clad landscape.  The approaching rider dressed in black with a cape flapping behind him was astride a palomino. In the rising moonlight, the horse was pale, ghostlike with mane and tail tossing in the wind. The pale horse slowed to a trot as the rider approached the hitching rail in front of the house. A man opened the door and walked across the porch toward the horse and rider. Nate and Hap watched as the man unloosed leather straps from the rider's stirrups. "That's Tom," Hap whispered.

The shed was close enough for Nate and Hap to hear their conversations. The man helped Tom off the pale horse. "Where have you been?"

"My horse broke down. Guess I rode him too hard. I had to borrow this palomino from Fred Hesse's foreman."

"I thought you was the devil hisself ridin' up that driveway."

Tom laughed and glanced at the horse. "Yeah, he is spooky in the moonlight. Where's Beth?"

"Inside, tied up. That woman is madder'n a hornet."

Tom slapped the man on the shoulder. "You've done good, Squire. Untie my walkin' stick from my bedroll."

Nate whispered to Hap. "Now's our chance. We've got to stop them before they get into the house."

"What if there are more of Tom's slingers inside?"

"Got to take that chance. We'll never get to Beth if we don't take on Tom and his hired-gun outside.

Nate eased open the door. "Hold it right there!" He and Hap stepped outside with their Colts drawn as Squire handed Tom his cane.

Tom and Squire froze, their boots cemented in the snow. "Well, hello, Nate...Hap." Tom sounded calm. "What you doin' here?"

"To arrest you," Nate replied, "and your hired-gun and to get Beth."

Tom started to move. Squire held up his hand to stop whatever Tom intended. Squire's face twisted into a sinister grin. "Tuck those guns and I'll take y'both on. I can shuck a hog leg faster than both of you."

Tom began to squirm, being certain that Squire's challenge would get them killed. The fingers of his right hand, afflicted by a palsied tremor, were no longer capable of the once quick-draw that had never been beaten. "Now, Squire," Tom mumbled, his jaw locked by fear, "I didn't hire you for a stand-up shoot-out."

"Shut up," Squire snarled. "I can take 'em both down by myself. Just step aside if you're a mind to. Which one o' you wants to be first?"

"Your butt belongs to me," Hap yelled, slipping his .45 back into its holster.

Squire nodded and glanced at Nate. "You're next after I kill this old codger."

"No, deal. You're both under arrest. Unbuckle that shoulder holster and drop it."

Squire stared at Nate, his eyes dark with rage. "Come take it off yourself."

"If need be, I will, but you'll be dead when I do."

"He can and will," Hap said. "Forget it."

Squire spat in disgust and dropped his holster and .45 in the snow. "Cowards."

"I'll take your Colt," Hap said to Tom.

Tom slid back his cape, unbuttoned his parka and slipped his .45 from its holster. He hesitated, and then handed the gun to Hap.

Nate holstered his Colt and clamped handcuffs onto the wrists of Squire and Tom. Hap shoved Tom's gun behind his own belt.

"Where's Beth?" Nate said to Squire.

"Hold it right there," a scrawny man said, stepping out onto the porch, a double-barreled scattergun in his hands.

"Where've you been, Jake," Squire yelled.

"Upstairs, guardin' that purty filly like y'told me."

"You took your sweet time."

Jake spat and chomped his cud of tobacco between toothless gums. A hollow grin spread across his face as he wagged the scattergun. "You fellers drop your guns and take them cuffs off ol' Squire and Mister Albert."

Nate and Hap tossed their guns into the snow with the exception of Tom's Colt. It remained tucked behind Hap's belt, hidden by his parka. Hap stepped behind Squire and started to insert a key into the cuffs. Instead, he dropped the key and feigned frustration as he searched for it in the snow. He winked at Nate and yanked out Tom's Colt. Nate lunged toward Squire, knocking him off his feet. In an instant, Hap fired. The bullet slammed into Jake's shoulder. The scattergun bellowed as he spun around. Buckshot unintentionally fired by Jake's convulsing finger shredded the front of Tom's vest. Tom staggered backward and collapsed in the snow. The Colt in Hap's hand belched lead again. Jake's head jerked backward as the slug bored through his skull.

For a moment, Nate stared at Tom, and then ran into the house. "Beth! Where are you?"

She didn't answer.

He climbed the stairway, paused on the landing at the second floor and listened but heard nothing. "Beth! It's all right, Hap and I are here."

From the third floor came a voice, muffled and distant. He ran to the third floor landing. "Beth, where are you?"

The muffled voice, louder now, answered, but was garbled. Nate walked down the hallway, cautiously opened a door and found the room empty. He opened the door to the only other room on the third floor. Beth was on the bed. A towel gagged her mouth and her wrists and ankles were tied with rope.

Nate knelt beside the bed, removed the gag and untied her bonds. "Thank god. Are you all right?"

"Oh yes," she whispered, tears welling in her eyes. I'm fine. I'm so happy to see you."

Nate kissed her and wiped away her tears. "And I you."

As they left the house and crossed the porch, Beth gasped at the sight of Tom lying in the snow.

Hap, kneeling beside Tom, looked at Beth. "He's still alive."

"Please," Tom muttered between parched lips. "I'm nearly dead... water... please."

Nate and Beth walked down the porch steps and stood beside Hap. Beth was crying, not from grief for the man dying in the snow, but from relief that Nate was alive and uninjured. As Nate stared at the pathetic shell Tom had become, he felt only pity for this man that had adopted a code bereft of principles; no right, no wrong, just whatever promoted power and riches. But the fiasco in Johnson County had revealed Tom's sins to the world. His web of deceit had entangled everyone. There were no winners, only losers.

Tom looked up at Beth. "Beth, water... please."

Beth went into the house and returned with a glass of water. After they lifted Tom up, he could take only a few swallows. His strength was gone. He began to ramble, pleading for mercy. "Help... God... Nate... Nate." He looked at Hap. "Hap... Hap."

Hap stroked his callused palm across Tom's forehead. "Now, Tom, don't y'fret none. Me an' Nate'll take care of ya."

Nate glared at Hap, unable to believe he could feel any kindness toward Tom. "No, Hap, he's headed for jail."

"Can't put a man this sick in jail."

"I can and I will. That's where he belongs and that's where I'm takin' him."

Hap stared at Nate, angry with the best friend he ever had. "Tom's dyin'. He ain't goin' no place. Can't you understand that?"

Hap's rebuke jarred Nate. He looked down at Tom and began to remember how close all three of them had been. Tom struggled for air. Hap was right. Tom was dying. Nate tried to muster forgiveness, but could only find condemnation.

Tom died as Hap, Nate and Beth knelt beside him.

Squire and the corpses of Tom and Jake were loaded onto a buckboard. During their return to the Wagon Box, both Hap and Nate searched for answers within themselves. They seldom spoke to one another during the trip. Nate was distressed, realizing hatred had sown bitterness that he seemed unable to shake. Hap found peace with his conscience and was comforted by his memories of better days when friendship reigned between him, Nate and Tom.

After turning Squire and the corpse of Jake over to Red Angus, Nate, Hap and Beth buried Tom on the Wagon Box in a plot of ground overlooking Little Goose Creek. It was like an estranged family burying a wayward member. Tom had been a friend, a husband and an unrepentant prodigal. Nevertheless, it seemed fitting to bury him there as if he had finally come home.

While Hap and Bill Maner shoveled chunks of frozen soil into Tom's grave, Nate and Beth walked down the snow-clad incline, back toward the ranch house. Nate reached for Beth's hand. He pulled the silver marshal's badge from his pocket with the gnarled fingers of his right hand. For a moment, he looked at it, and then gazed at the Bighorns glistening under the noonday sun. He tossed the shield into a snowdrift. "I'll not wear a badge again. The struggle to come here after the war, the fight to get our ranch and the battle against Tom and his kind is over."

"Has it been too great a price to pay?"

"Oh, no. You are worth all of the battles. I knew that the first time I saw you on Aunt Deana's stairway."

Hap stopped shoveling, wiped his brow and watched Nate and Beth embracing. "Well, I reckon we'll be movin' Beth's stuff in soon as Preacher Butterworth ties the knot. Then we'll give 'em a first-rate shivaree. Yes sir, that's what we'll do."

www.ingramcontent.com/pod-product-compliance
Lightning Source LLC
Chambersburg PA
CBHW061613100726
47898CB00002B/639